Caroline Roberts

The Cosy Christmas Tea Shop

Harper*Impulse* an imprint of
HarperCollins*Publishers*
The News Building
1 London Bridge Street
London SE1 9GF

www.harpercollins.co.uk

A Paperback Original 2016
2

A catalogue record for this book is available from the British Library

ISBN: 978-0-00-821268-1

This novel is entirely a work of fiction.
The names, characters and incidents portrayed in it are the work of
the author's imagination. Any resemblance to actual persons,
living or dead, events or localities is entirely coincidental.

Typeset in Minion by Palimpsest Book Production Ltd, Falkirk, Stirlingshire

Printed and bound in Great Britain by
Clays Ltd, St Ives plc

MIX
Paper from
responsible sources
FSC® C007454

FSC™ is a non-profit international organisation established to promote the
responsible management of the world's forests. Products carrying the FSC label
are independently certified to assure consumers that they come from forests
that are managed to meet the social, economic and ecological needs of present
and future generations, and other controlled sources.

Find out more about HarperCollins and the environment at
www.harpercollins.co.uk/green

For my home county of Northumberland –
stunning scenery, wonderful people

Five years ago, Ellie Hall arrived at the beautiful, yet slightly crumbling, Claverham Castle, with her ambitions of running her own teashop. Armed with only her hopes and dreams, her love of baking, and her late Nanna's Be-Ro recipe book, she took on the teashop lease, leaving behind her close-knit family and dull insurance job. Starting her rollercoaster adventure, she learnt on her feet, making a whole host of new friends, as well as falling in love with the rather gorgeous estate manager, Joe.

A wedding, a fire, and the revelation of a family secret later, we return. Welcome to Ellie's world. Welcome to the Cosy Teashop in the Castle . . .

1

'There's a coachload of fifty people due in twenty minutes.'

Ellie turned to see Joe smiling at her; he must have slipped quietly into the teashop kitchen.

'You're kidding.' He was often teasing her, it might just be a wind-up. She'd hardly stopped today as it was. It had been a *very* busy August Bank Holiday Monday – the end of the school summer holidays. Good for the till, but tough on her feet. She felt like she'd been juggling all day; keeping up with the lunch orders, whizzing up a couple of extra lemon drizzle cakes in between, when it looked like they might run out, despite having baked lots of extra cakes and cookies all week in the build up to the weekend.

Joe was shaking his head, looking serious. 'Nope . . . Deana's just had a call from the driver. All good for business though.'

'Right then, well I'd better get my skates on and see how we're doing for cakes out in the teashop.' Ellie wasn't quite sure what she could rustle up in twenty minutes, but there might be something stored in the freezer. Cupcakes came to mind, she often kept a spare batch of vanilla ones just in case; she could ice them pretty fast if she needed.

'You better had. But first . . .' He came close, put his arms around her from behind and kissed the nape of her neck, just where the bare skin showed beneath her pony-tail.

It sent a little quiver down her spine. 'I haven't got time, Joe. You can't tell me *that*, and then expect a kissing session.' She turned to face him, trying to look cross.

'Why not?' He smiled cheekily.

The smile that *still* got her. 'Ah, okay then. Just *one* kiss. A short one.'

She pressed a pert kiss on his lips, and went to pull away. He pulled her closer, his arms around her. Kissed her again, warm and tender, and teasingly good.

She stepped back, reminding herself this was *not* the time or the place. 'Doris'll be marching in any moment. It's not right. And, I've got far too much to do. *Go.*' But she was grinning.

'Okay, okay, I know where I'm not wanted. I should have let them all turn up on you without warning.'

He headed for the swing door.

'Thanks,' she finished.

He gave her a wink as he exited.

They'd been married for over three years now, meeting at her first ever interview for the lease on the Claverham Castle teashop. He was the estate manager, tall, with dark, slightly floppy-fringed hair – he had it cut a little shorter nowadays – and she was a rather naïve twenty-six-year-old, coming straight from her uninspiring insurance job in the city of Newcastle-upon-Tyne, armed only with her love of baking, her Nanna's cookbook, and her teashop dream. Nanna's slightly charred Be-Ro Recipe book still held pride of place on a shelf in the teashop's kitchen – that was another story.

Now, five years on, her husband was still as affectionate as ever, probably more so. Love and trust, and tenderness, having grown between them. But at hectic times like this, she really had to focus on running the teashop. They would catch up later, back in their castle apartment, and hopefully they might carry on where they left off.

The afternoon flew by, in a flurry of making vanilla and chocolate frosting for the spare cupcakes (yay – she'd had some in the freezer!). She also found an extra batch of choc-chip shortbread in a tub in the store cupboard, and after rearranging the remaining cakes and biscuits in the counter display of the teashop, it looked a pretty good selection.

Irene (the newest addition to the teashop team and Ellie's wonderful, sixty-something, baking assistant), Doris (waitress, gossip-lover, difficult at times, yet with a heart of gold) and Lauren (a lovely girl from the village who helped on weekends and holidays) were in full swing too.

Serving fifty additional people in a teashop that was nearly full as it was, was a challenge. Luckily, they had some extra tables outside in the courtyard, and as it was a sunny day that worked well, but it meant even more to-ing and fro-ing for the waitresses. The coffee machine was spluttering and frothing, very much on overdrive but still sending out those gorgeous, rich aromas. The cakes and scones were plated up – the lemon drizzle proving to be a hit.

Ellie's feet were sore, her back was aching. It was nearly four-thirty, and they normally closed around now. But there were still several stragglers, sat chatting and sipping their drinks like they hadn't a care in the world. And, that was fine. Let them enjoy their trip out, and their treat at the end of their castle tour, that's what it was all about. But boy, she'd be looking forward to soaking in a deep, bubby bath tonight.

They were wrapping up for the day, it had just gone five-twenty, well past their normal closing time, and one remaining middle-aged couple were still lingering over a pot of tea they'd been sharing for the best part of an hour.

Ellie was behind the counter restacking the crockery and cutlery from the dishwasher tray, ready for the next day. She felt that telling nag of period pain, along with a dull ache of disappointment.

Oh no, not this. Not again.

It was early days, she knew that. She and Joe had been trying for a baby for five months now, but she couldn't help but get excited this time; she'd been four days late, and her hopes had soared. She'd already planned to get a pregnancy test on her next day off, and had pictured herself telling Joe the wonderful news.

Bloody hell.

Doris was clearing up around the couple who *still* remained seated, chattering away, oblivious to the time. The waitress made herself busy wiping down *all* the other tables, encircling theirs, but to no avail. Then, she started with the broom, sweeping loudly in their direction. Tact was not her thing. Ellie couldn't help but give a wry smile.

'Doris, I just need to nip out a minute. Are you okay to stay on a little while?'

'No problem,' she announced noisily. 'We'll not be long now, anyhow.' Doris smiled across at the couple, stirring them from their comfortable reverie. 'Everything all right?' she asked them, the message as clear as if she had come straight out and told them to leave. How did she do it? Ellie had tried her best with training Doris in customer service over the years, but there were some elements of her waitress's nature that just couldn't be curbed. And in a strange way, Ellie had grown fond of them.

Ellie traipsed off to the ladies. Sure enough, the telltale not-pregnant-at-all bloodstain was there. Bloody hell.

It was okay, she reminded herself, as she washed her hands at the sink, all early days stuff. Her face looked pale in the mirror, tired. No wonder, after the hectic day she'd had. Her thick blonde hair was tied back in its work-style ponytail. She sighed at her reflection. It was just one of those things. After all, she'd read only recently that most couples took up to six months to conceive. She'd just *hoped*, hadn't she? She'd been so excited at the thought of telling Joe. They both felt so ready for a family, to move on to this next exciting phase of their lives together, they had talked about it so much of late.

She had extra help at the teashop now with her fabulous assistant Irene, who made the most wonderful cakes and quiches. Deana was also getting on well, helping her with all the wedding bookings they had been taking. It seemed like a good time for her and Joe to plan for their family. She'd keep up her work, of course, the teashop and the castle were so much more than a job, they had a huge place in her heart and life, but she'd take a step back, and allow the team to help some more.

Ellie loved doing the wedding coordinating – making a couple's wedding day as special and unique as she could for them. The weddings were a fairly new venture for the castle that Ellie and Joe had developed in the last few years. The castle was now growing a good reputation as an up-and-coming wedding venue, being one of the most beautiful locations in the area. A stunning old stone castle, surrounded by formal gardens, small lakes, and the most beautiful rolling countryside.

If anything did happen baby-wise, Ellie planned to stay on and carry on working, doing less hours naturally, and with some childcare help she'd still keep her hand in with everything. It wasn't as though she lived far away – just one floor up in the West Wing in Joe's original suite of rooms!

Anyhow, she stopped her daydreaming, it wasn't to be, not this time. Despite the sinking feeling of disappoint-ment, she knew she'd have to just keep her chin up and keep going. They could wait, she told herself. They'd have to wait.

She dried her hands on a paper towel, and headed back to the teashop.

Sure enough, the middle-aged couple had disappeared and Doris was mopping the tearoom floor.

'Thanks Doris, I'll take over here.'

'You sure, pet?'

'Yes, get yourself away. You're running a bit over time as it is.'

'Okay, thanks then, Ellie. See you in the morning.'

'See you, Doris.'

* * *

All was quiet. She looked around the teashop, Ellie's Teashop in the Castle, and felt a sense of pride. She'd really made a go of it. It was looking lovely, with a little late-afternoon glow of sunshine coming in through the leaded windows. She'd kept the vintage-flowered oilcloths, though she was on her second set now. And the tables were set with the posy jars she'd originally bought from Wendy's flower shop, in the nearby town of Kirkton. Today, they were full of pretty lilac and pink sweet peas, that Colin had let her snip from the walled gardens as they were in abundance. They smelt absolutely gorgeous.

She had kept some of the handmade bunting from her own wedding day and swooped it around the old stone walls. The log fire was burning; come summer or winter it was always lit, keeping the chill off. It really was such a cosy, pretty spot. Just the place to while away an hour with a cup of tea and a slice of Victoria Sponge or chocolate cake, or whatever might take your fancy.

The door swung open. 'Nearly done?' Joe's dark hair and smiling face appeared. That smile that still melted her heart.

'Yes, just give me five minutes.'

'Do you fancy a walk out? It's such a lovely evening?' he asked.

'Yeah, okay. Sounds good.' That might be just what she needed. A nice stroll and some fresh air. It had been a tricky day to say the least.

'We could take an evening picnic? It's still warm out there.'

Even better. 'I'll pack up a few of the leftovers. There're some slices of Irene's quiche left – a bacon, leek and mushroom today. It looks scrummy.'

'Any lemon drizzle going spare?'

'Yes, just a couple of slices, I think. You're as bad as Derek and Malcolm. I think you've all got a lemon drizzle fetish.'

'Absolutely.' He gave Ellie his cheeky look that always made her smile. 'You know I'll do *anything* for a slice of your lemon drizzle.' With that, he left the tearooms, turning at the last to give her a cute wink. 'See you upstairs shortly, then.'

Despite the challenges of the day, she felt a little better.

The valley stretched out below them, in late-summer shades of green and gold; rectangular crop fields patterning the landscape, a tractor trundling in the distance, sheep and cattle grazing. The purple-tinged Cheviot Hills of Northumberland rose majestically on the horizon. And looking down below them, they could just make out the stone turrets and crenulations of the rooftops of Claverham Castle, there at the base of the hill they had just climbed, nestled in the valley and sheltered by a host of centuries-old trees.

'You seem a bit quiet, Ellie. All okay?'

'Yeah.'

She nestled in beside him, the pair of them sat with their backs against a limestone rock. Ellie remembered when they had first looked out at that stunning view together, sharing apples, and their first kiss.

'Joe . . . it still hasn't happened.' Her voice was small.

He looked at her quizzically.

'Not this month, anyhow.' Ellie couldn't hide the disappointment in her tone.

'Oh.'

'Sorry,' she whispered.

'Hey.' He tightened his arm, which was already around her. 'No need to be sorry. It's just one of those things . . . It'll happen soon enough, you'll see.'

'Hope so.'

'And . . . I'm quite enjoying practising.' He gave her another of his cheeky looks.

For a second his comment seemed a touch callous, but she realized he was just trying to cheer her up. She was probably being hypersensitive. Her emotions felt like bare wires at the moment.

'Yes, that bit is quite fun.' She tried to join in the lighter tone of the conversation. But already it had changed for her, she knew. Sex, had moved to something more. Something wonderful that might produce a child. A child with Joe. And that yearning had grown in her.

'Come on, don't worry. It's really early days yet. We'll

have a whole tribe of them soon enough. And then you'll be desperate for five minutes peace. And hey . . .' he looked more serious then, reached up to touch her cheek, 'whatever happens, we'll always have us.'

'I know, I know. I'm just being silly.'

He gave her a little squeeze. 'No, you're not. You just *really* want to be a mum. And you'll be a great one, I know it. And, I can't wait to be a dad, too. But maybe we're just going to have to wait a bit longer, by the looks of it.'

Life was good, Ellie realized that. They should just be enjoying the here and now. She had so much to be thankful for. Being married to Joe was just wonderful. She loved him as much as the day she had fallen for him nearly five years ago, probably even more so. And life in the castle was working out great. The teashop kept her busy, as well as all the wedding coordinating. There were the usual ups and downs, of course. A huge part of her dreams had already come true. But a child, Joe's child, would make it all the more special.

Ellie leaned into him, let her head rest against his chest. She felt the rhythm of her heart slow to the strength of his, and closed her eyes for a few seconds.

2

'Hi Ellie, it's Lucy.'

Just four words, but there was something in her tone, seemingly flat at first but then that lilt of panic, that made Ellie's heart freeze. It was the day after Bank Holiday, Ellie was back in the teashop kitchens, preparing salad, ready for the lunch session. She'd just picked up the phone.

'Lucy, is everything okay?' This was not how a bride-to-be, just two weeks from her wedding day, should sound.

'No.'

Oh, no. 'What's happened?'

'It's Daniel . . . We-we're going to have to cancel the wedding.'

But they had seemed so well suited. Ellie had got on really well with both of them during the wedding planning. They had come to feel like friends. Was it just pre-wedding jitters?

'He's had an accident, Ellie. Come off his motorbike . . . he's in a real mess.' A sob echoed down the line.

'Oh, no. Is he going to be all right?'

There was a little hiccuppy noise, 'I think so . . . but it's not good. He's broken that many bones, his left leg in I don't know how many places, his ankle, collarbone, wrist and . . . he's lost the feeling in his legs.'

'Oh Lucy, how awful. I'm so sorry.'

'But the wedding . . . We're going to have to let you and the castle down. There's no way it can happen now. And, there's the florist, and the band booked, and you've probably made the cake already, and all the catering . . .'

'Hey, that's the least of your worries right now. What's important here is Daniel's recovery. We can sort out all that other stuff. Just leave it to me to contact the florist and the band.'

Yes, some food might be wasted, Ellie realized. They had hired caterers for the main wedding meal, but she was catering for the arrival drinks and canapes, and break-fast for the overnight guests. Her special-recipe fruit cake was already made, ready to be iced, but that could be used up somehow.

Dear God, wasn't life precarious. They were such a lovely couple, in their early thirties. They seemed very much in love, what a terrible thing to happen. Ellie felt a little queasy. She so hoped Daniel would be okay. But, if he'd lost the use of his legs, how bloody frightening.

Ellie remembered vividly when they'd first turned up to view the castle as a potential wedding venue, with some friends on a trio of Harley Davidson motorbikes roaring up the driveway. Yes, she should know better than to judge by appearances, but she couldn't help but imagine some kind of Hell's Angels types as they'd rolled up in their black-leather biker jackets. Then they'd taken off their helmets, given her broad smiles, shook hands, and had been so warm and friendly. They had clicked and chatted easily as she'd shown them around, and they had just loved the quirkiness and character of the castle as a wedding venue.

'Honestly, don't worry about us, Lucy,' Ellie took up, 'You just concentrate on getting Daniel better. Then you can make a decision about the wedding at a later date. Let's think of it in terms of a delay, that's all. Just let me know in time, and we can rebook. Okay?'

'Okay . . . thank you. Can you hang on to the deposit then, and I'll keep you posted.'

Bless her, she sounded in shock.

'Of course, if that's what you'd like. And, I'll go ahead and advise the other parties involved, as far as postponing the booking here. Don't worry, I'll sort all that out.'

'Thank you so much.'

'Is there anything else we can do to help at all, Lucy?'

'Not really, I don't think so. Dan's still in the hospital for now. The Royal Victoria in Newcastle.'

'Okay, well send him our best wishes . . . Which ward?'

She'd send a card, maybe some of her homemade fudge – he'd loved it when she'd served it with their coffee as they were chatting through their wedding plans. It wasn't a lot, but it might just help to cheer him up. It was hard to know quite what to do to help, in such circumstances.

'Ward Seven. I'm popping to see him again this afternoon, I'll say you're asking after him . . .' There was a long pause. 'It was a lorry, you know, that did it. Cut across on the wrong side of the road on a bend, just took him right out.'

'Oh God, how awful . . . I'm so, so sorry, Lucy.'

'At least he's still here. He might be all bashed up, but oh God, to think . . .'

It was almost too dreadful to go there, to let your mind take that next step.

'Take care now, both of you. And don't go worrying about anything here. It's just one of those things. It's fine, we can rebook whenever you are ready. Just let us know how things go for you both.'

'Thank you . . . for being so understanding.'

'Hey, it's no problem. He'll get through this, Lucy. I'm sure he will, my lovely. After all, he's got a wedding to get to.'

* * *

Ellie was stood in a bit of a daze after putting the receiver of the landline down. Deana had put the call through to her in the teashop kitchen. Joe came in, found her stood stock-still, staring at the work surface where she'd been slicing tomatoes and cucumber.

'You okay?'

'Oh . . . I've just had a bit of a shock. You know Daniel and Lucy, the next wedding booking?'

'Uh-huh.'

'Well, that was Lucy . . . Oh Joe, it's Dan, he's had a really nasty accident. Came off his motorbike and is in a right mess by the sounds of it.'

'Oh, Jeez. Is he going to be okay?'

'Hopefully, but he's broken loads of bones, and at the moment he's lost the feeling in his legs. That's so worrying.'

'Ah, shit.'

Life could change in a split second. We were all so bloody fragile. Ellie began to feel a bit wobbly, there were tears misting her eyes. 'It's just taken me a bit by surprise. They're such a nice couple. It seems so unfair. They should be getting their lovely wedding day.'

'Come here.' Joe's strong arms were around her, comforting, steady.

She rested her head against his chest and allowed a tear to run down her cheek. She felt so lucky that they had met, that she had taken the chance on coming up here to take on the lease for the teashop, five years ago now. Even three years after their own wedding, she still had to pinch herself that it had worked out so wonderfully. It felt so very precious to have found the right person, having his arms around her at night, and at times like this.

'Right,' she rallied. 'I'd better get on with this cooking and my next batch of baking, or the tearooms will be out of cookies and cake, and that will never do. Oh, and I must ring the catering company, and Wendy at the florist's and the band from Berwick that were booked too, to let them know the wedding's had to be cancelled.'

'I'll see you later, then. I need to go over and check the farmstead next. You sure you're okay now?'

'Yes, of course. I just really feel for them. What a dreadful thing to happen, and what a shock.'

'Yeah, they're a great couple. He was chatting to me about his bike last time they were here. He was going to let me have a go on it, when they were next back up. I fancied blasting it along the castle driveway.'

'I didn't even know you could ride a motorbike?'

'Yeah well, hidden talents of a misspent youth. Right, I'd better crack on.'

Doris bustled into the kitchen soon after; she'd been waiting expectantly for news on the urgent phone call that she had intercepted, and had to fetch Ellie for.

'Everything okay?' she angled.

'No. Not really.' Ellie was still feeling the shock, trying to take it all in.

The middle-aged waitress's eyebrows shot up.

'You know that lovely couple who've been planning their wedding with us, Daniel and Lucy? It's in two weeks' time. The ones who turn up on the motorbike. Well, he's been involved in a terrible road accident.' She felt her voice catch on the words. 'That was Lucy, she's devastated. They're going to have to cancel.'

'Ah, bless. Yes, I remember them, they were nice sorts. Not like those awful ones from down south for the other September wedding, the ones who keep changing their damned minds on everything. She's turning out to be a right Bridezilla, that one.'

Ellie knew *exactly* who Doris meant, and had to agree with her. They were the most difficult couple that they'd had to deal with *by far*, in the last four years of hosting weddings at the castle. To be fair, the groom seemed okay, he had probably learnt to do what he was told, but the bride and her mother . . .

'Yes, I know . . . But there you go, the customer is always right Doris, and they come in all shapes and sizes. We have to do our best to meet all their needs, however demanding.'

'Hah,' Doris spluttered, 'it would help if they knew what those needs were!'

'Agreed.' Ellie gave a small smile and a sigh all at once, and started rolling out another batch of cookie dough for some white chocolate and hazelnut biscuits.

Why did the bad stuff always have to happen to the good guys? Life didn't seem fair sometimes.

3

'She wants a bloody unicorn now!'

Ellie had phoned through to Deana's office, her fifty-something friend and colleague, and Lord Henry's long-term PA. Deana was down-to-earth, warm-hearted and had been Ellie's rock in times of crisis through her early years at the castle. She was also helping Ellie with the wedding coordinating that seemed to be taking up so much of her time these days. Ellie needed to share this latest, crazy request from Bridezilla. The wedding itself was only three weeks away, and the daily phone calls and demands from the bride and her mother were getting more and more extreme. It wouldn't be so bad if they'd choose something and stick to it, but it was an ever-evolving wish list, that pushed Ellie's organisational skills and patience to the limit.

'A *unicorn*, how the hell do we get a twatting unicorn

to a wedding?' Deana gave an exasperated sigh down the line.

'It'd be funny, if it wasn't us had to deal with it,' Ellie commented. 'Are there any white horses around the village?'

Deana laughed, 'It's a starting point, I suppose . . . But how exactly are we going to make it grow a horn from its head?'

'I have no idea. I'm just trying to think creatively.' Ellie was shaking her head at the craziness of the situation.

'Come and see me later, when Irene's in, and you get five minutes. We'll put our heads together over a cup of tea.'

Irene was the latest addition to the teashop staff and what a godsend she had been. Wendy, the florist, had recommended her. She'd been a school cook, was now retired, but found she had too much time on her hands and was desperate to find some local work. She was a happy soul, never made a fuss, and could bake like Mary Berry; her cakes were very traditional but amazing. Her Victoria sponge was to die for, and her fruit cakes, wow, they were proving quite a hit as wedding cakes. Irene would make the fruit-laden cakes, feeding them well with brandy over a month or so, and Ellie would use her creative skills to ice and decorate them – they made fabulous celebration cakes. The lovely Irene was also a dab hand at quiches and scones.

At the interview, she'd reminded Ellie of a younger Nanna, with her neat grey curls, warm smile, and with her love of baking too, that had sealed the deal. Ellie had learnt her baking skills from her Nanna. She remembered vividly standing on a stool as a little girl, stirring the cake mix, in her Nanna's galley kitchen in her brick terraced house in Newcastle-upon-Tyne. She still missed her so much; Ellie would love for her to have seen the success she'd made of the Castle Teashop, and to be able to have a really good catch up with her over a slice of cake and a cup of tea. But yes, having Irene to help, was the next best thing, and it had freed up some valuable time for Ellie to coordinate the wedding events they hosted at the castle, knowing the teashop was in safe hands.

'Well, we can't afford to upset the bridal party. We still need the final payment.' Deana brought her back to the here and now.

'Yes, I know. We really can't scoff at the money they're prepared to pay. But blimey, we'll be working for it. Oh and get this, we need hundreds of white rose petals to line the chapel aisle, the reception tables *and* the honeymoon suite. Wendy's going to love having to peel those off one by one. *And*, they have to be perfectly fresh – done on the day. *Silk ones just won't do.*'

'Oh well, Wendy'll just have to charge an hourly rate for petal picking on top of the flower bill.'

Whatever they did for this wedding, Ellie was sure it

would never be quite enough in the end, but they could only try their best. She usually loved her wedding co-ordinator role at the castle, but this particular wedding was turning into a bit of a nightmare, pushing her to the limits.

'Right, better get on, Deana. I'll catch you later. I'll pop across when I get chance.'

'Yeah, see you soon, pet.'

Ellie couldn't stop thinking about poor Daniel, wondering how he was after his accident. It had kept her awake in the night. She wished it was *their* wedding she was sorting out, not this bloody nightmare couple's. Before the customers started piling in for the day, she'd give Lucy a call, and see how they were getting on.

But first, Ellie quickly looked in on the tearooms. Irene had just arrived and was busy baking; a couple of Victoria sponges by the looks of it. Her fresh strawberries and cream filling was going down a treat with the summer visitors; perfect with a cup of Earl Grey, or Darjeeling. Ellie had extended the tea range with a host of new flavours and some herbal specialty teas. Doris had struggled with this at first, *Who on earth would be wanting peppermint or ginger tea, and camomile and honey, really? What's wrong with a cup of Rington's traditional breakfast?* But they had, and she continued to serve it with a frown.

They were also doing well with their 'afternoon tea' special. Irene's mini-scone selection was a delight, and she'd cut dainty slices of all the teashop favourites for the three tier stands, including Ellie's lemon drizzle and the now famous Choffee Cake (chocolate and coffee in layers), as well as crust-free perfect fingers of smoked salmon and cream cheese, cucumber, and ham and local honey-mustard sandwiches.

'Morning, Irene. You've cracked on well already.'

'No time like the present. And how are you today?'

'Good, thank you. Ready for another busy day. We have a coach booked in for lunch at oneish, so I'll pop some extra jacket potatoes in. Do you think you could make a couple of extra quiches too?' Irene's quiches were amazing – leek and bacon, salmon and asparagus, and her good old Quiche Lorraine with roasted ham and extra-strong cheddar, yum. Her pastry was even crispier than Ellie's.

'Of course, lovey. I take it you've ordered in all the ingredients I need.'

'Yep, all in the store and the fridge. Thanks, Irene.'

Ellie popped through from the kitchen to the teashop itself, where Doris was giving the pretty rose-patterned oilcloth covers a wipe-over ready for the day ahead, and topping up the water in the posy vases. Ellie felt proud as she walked in there; of how the teashop had come on, and how she had grown herself, what she had managed to achieve by following her dream.

The teashop was set in an ancient sandstone-walled castle that dated back to the Thirteenth Century. The tearooms had the same rugged stone walls, and high ceilings, with a minstrel's gallery that looked down over the twelve tables. There was a huge fireplace that was always lit whatever the weather or season, keeping the tearooms cosy. There were two sets of lead-patterned windows on the inner wall that, if you stood on tiptoes on the seating nooks, you could peep out from into the courtyard of the main castle. So much must have happened here over the centuries. So many lives lived out. Kings had stayed en route to and from Scotland – the castle being nestled in the border lands of Northumberland. Servants and masters will have loved and lost, had their children, grown old, died young, here. The dramas, the dreams, the happiness, the sorrows.

Ellie carried through two cakes she had baked that morning to set on the counter; a carrot cake and a rich chocolate sponge with dark cherries layered with whipped cream. Her chocolate-chip cookies were cooling on wire racks and would be ready shortly, and Irene's scone selection would appear next. The counter display looked scrummy, she had to admit. It was nice to have a lovely selection of cakes and goodies on show for the castle visitors, and hopefully it would tempt them to spend out on a homemade treat. Ellie had had to develop a keener business mind as well as her baking skills – there were staff to pay and a living to make for herself. She'd started making up pretty cellophane-wrapped bags of mini brownies, shortbread and meringues that guests could buy to take home too – they were proving very popular.

Once everything was set up, Ellie nipped back to the kitchen. There was one phone call she really wanted to make.

'Hi, Lucy. How's Daniel getting on?'

'Oh Ellie, how lovely of you to call. Well, he's so, so . . . It's going to be a long job. To be honest, he's in a bit of a bad way.'

'Oh no. What a shame. I'm so sorry to hear that.'

'He's just got so many broken bones, his whole body has got to recover. It's tough on him.'

'And you too, I bet. How are you? It must be so hard for all of you, Dan's family too.'

'I'm okay, surviving. I'm trying to stay strong for Dan's sake. I'm at the hospital every day with him. Fitting it around work . . . my firm have been great actually. And, he's chatting a bit now, which is brilliant, but he gets really tired. Even a conversation can whack him out. But hey, we'll get through somehow.'

Bloody hell, there she was, her fiancé in hospital, her wedding day cancelled, trying to make the best of things. And bloody Bridezilla had it all, and couldn't see it. *Really,* what did it matter if it was a unicorn, an Aston Martin or a push-bike taking her to her wedding, as long as she had one and a healthy groom to be with? Just to be able to take those vows, and to mean them, that was the special thing, the important thing. Yes, of course try and make it a wonderful day, but hey, count your blessings, and all that. Ellie felt very lucky to have had her lovely wedding with Joe there at the castle, with all their friends and family around them. But it was more than just that day – it was now, it was forever, a partnership.

'Yeah, you will. The two of you will get through all this. You make a great couple.'

'Thanks, Ellie. It's just so hard seeing him like this, you know. And, he still hasn't got any sensation back in his legs yet.' Lucy's voice broke a bit then, 'What if he can't walk, or ride his motorbike again? That'll be so hard for him.'

'I know, petal. But fingers crossed it's just a short term thing. You'll just have to hope, and trust in the doctors.'

'Yeah, of course. Well hey, thanks so much for phoning.'

'No worries, I just wanted to find out how you both were.'

'Thank you. And sorry to be a bit down . . . it's just hard keeping positive all the time. And I try not to show Daniel if I'm worried, I'm trying my best to cheer him up. But every now and then I wilt a little. It's so frustrating for him at the moment, trapped in that hospital bed.

Even though the staff there are lovely with him. Anyway, it's nice to be able to be honest with someone, and I feel like I can be open with you.'

'Thanks, I'm glad you feel that.' Ellie felt a catch in her throat. It had become so much more than just a job, arranging the wedding for this couple. It had already grown into a friendship. 'And Lucy, it's totally understandable to feel upset. God knows how I'd be if Joe ever got hurt like that.'

'Well, I've got to get off to work, and then I'm straight back to the hospital again. But thanks so much for ringing. It means a lot.'

'You're very welcome. Pass on our best wishes to Dan.'

'Will do.'

'Actually, I was a little worried it might upset you, me calling you, reminding you of the castle, and your wedding and everything.'

'No, absolutely not. That's what's keeping me going for now. It's my dream to get back up there, Ellie. Whatever it takes, whether Dan can walk or not, I can't wait to have our wedding day. It might have to be a bit different to the one we'd planned, but I want it even more now. One day, I'll be Mrs Daniel Clark.'

'Well, whenever you are both ready let us know. We can soon get everything sorted out at this end for you. And if there's anything at all we can do in the meanwhile to help, just shout, yeah?'

'Will do. Thanks Ellie, I appreciate that.'

'Take care, both of you.'

'And you. Bye.'

'Bye.' As she clicked her mobile off, Ellie sighed. She so hoped it would work out for them, that Dan would make a full recovery. They were trying to be so positive, to make the best of such a horrible situation.

In Deana's office, four o'clock. The teashop had been hectic, and this was Ellie's first chance to get away.

Deana's emergency kettle was coming to a boil; a strong brew was definitely in order.

'Right then. I take it you've had another call. Where are we with Bridezilla now?' They didn't bother using the girl's real name, Chelsea, any more. *Everyone* at the castle knew who Bridezilla was.

'Well, two days ago I had a request to change the wedding cake. I'd already made all the fruit cakes for the three tiers, got them steeping in brandy, and now she wants a rainbow multi-layer sponge cake that she's just seen on some fancy wedding makeover program. *And,* even better, get this, she wants to make a grand entrance by coming down the driveway on a unicorn.'

'Unicorns and rainbows – sounds like some My Little Pony-inspired do.'

'Possibly, I have no idea. But I've told her I'll have to charge for both cakes, at least the un-iced version of the first. I can't afford to waste all those ingredients, not to mention the time I've spent. Anyway, she seemed fine with that.'

'More money than sense, that one . . . But how the hell are you going to get a unicorn? Does she know they aren't actually real?'

'Heaven knows. But apparently they had one at a celebrity wedding featured in *Hello* recently.'

'Oh.' Deana poured some water into the teapot for two. Ellie had brought across two slices of her signature Choffee Cake, anticipating the need for something sweet in a bid to boost them both.

'We need to think of a plan.'

'Oooh, plan for what?' Derek, one of the castle tour guides, popped his grey-haired head around the door frame.

Malcolm, his partner in visitor-information and life, appeared beside him, sporting a yellow and red spotty bow tie. 'It *has* to be Bridezilla.'

The tour guide team stood waiting for the response.

'You got it in one,' Ellie answered.

'What *are* they up to now then, girls?' Everyone in the castle had had some obscure request from the bride or her mother, and mostly not in the politest of forms.

'They want a unicorn at the wedding,' Deana stated.

'You're joking.'

'I wish I was.'

'A unicorn?' Derek's mouth stayed partially open, 'Horned horse that doesn't exist . . . has anyone actually told her that yet?'

'I tried . . .' Ellie's tone was exasperated, 'but if it's good enough for Plush and Becks, then it's good enough for her, apparently. And we're here to make her dreams come true.'

'Jeez.' Derek stood with his arms folded.

Malcolm was grinning, or was it a grimace, Ellie couldn't quite be sure. 'Leave it to us. We like a challenge, don't we, Derek? The Malcolm-Derek think tank is about to leap into action,' he announced.

'God help us,' Deana muttered under her breath.

'Well, have you got any better plans, Deana? Or a fairy godmother to hand?' Malcolm was getting a bit flouncy.

A second of silence. Then Ellie gave a wry smile, Derek slipped her a grin, and the penny dropped with Malcolm on his final comment, as the group collapsed into laughter.

'Well, it'll be one thing less for me to think about, so thank you, Malcolm.' Ellie gave a wry smile. 'I've got a teashop to run and apparently a seven-layer rainbow cake to design and create. Hmm, it'll be interesting to see what you two come up with.'

'Hah, I can't wait.' Deana's eyebrows were raised. 'Cuppa, gents?'

'No, but thanks, we need to go round and check all the visitor rooms are empty, before we shut up for the day.

Don't want any stragglers stranded in the drawing room, or such like.' That had actually happened in the past.

'Another time, Deana. Thank you,' added Derek.

'Right, that's me off too,' said Ellie, a yawn creeping over her lips. It had been a long day. 'Better see how the tearooms are getting on, and then get ready to close up for the night.'

4

Evening settled over the castle, the long, lazy shadows of summer dusk finding their way through the leaded windows. Ellie liked the shift from the bustle of the daytime visitors, the steady stream of orders, the splutters of the coffee machine – she'd invested in a second-hand Gaggia coffee machine and loved it; it filled the teashop with a gorgeous fresh ground aroma. Doris, believe it or not, had turned into her barista! After a little encouragement and a few lessons, she became the queen of the coffee machine, no less. Though of course, no one could make a cup of coffee *quite* like her now. Irene was relegated to baking and tea duties, which she was quite happy with, to be fair. But now, with only the soothing noise of her radio, when the order row was empty, and she had a chance to take a slow breath, there was a sense of peace. Time to plan for tomorrow, and to look forward to getting back to their apartment and to Joe.

Ellie turned off all the appliance switches in the kitchen, bar the fridges and freezers. A routine she'd kept to since the dramatic and devastating fire that had ravaged her lovely teashop and kitchen at the end of her first year there. It had happened just when she had managed to turn the business around, and it all seemed like her dreams were finally coming true. The memories of that night still haunted her; how scared she had been when she realized Joe was still in there. How very different life might have been . . . If Joe hadn't made it through . . . it still made her feel sick just thinking about it.

She could really feel for Lucy and Dan, and all that they were going through right now, having been so close to disaster herself.

Right then, everything seemed in order at the tearooms. She'd be down to make a batch of chocolate brownies first thing tomorrow. And, as she and Deana had nearly polished off the Choffee Cake, she'd better get the coffee and chocolate sponge layers for that made early on too. Irene would make the scones for her, and they'd need another four quiches made for lunches too. Then, she mustn't forget there was the ordering to do. The list in her mind just seemed to build. But for now, she needed to turn off the lights, check the real fire in the teashop was settled to a gentle smoulder – it never quite went out being big enough to fit a couple of tree trunks in, and could happily sit a dozen people around its hearth.

She made her way across the courtyard and up the circular stone stairwell to the living quarters she shared with Joe. The only other person who lived in the castle was Joe's father, Lord Henry, who preferred a pretty isolated existence, so all was quiet of an evening.

Every now and again, the reality of her surroundings took her breath away. The doves cooing in the battlements above her. The evening sun washing the cream sandstone walls with a blush of colour. A glimpse of the walled gardens neatly laid out with short box hedges, colourful blooms and herbaceous borders from a portcullis window. She wasn't used to any of this, having been brought up in a red brick terraced house in a suburb of Newcastle-upon-Tyne. But more than this amazing castle with its centuries-old walls and gardens, it was going back to Joe every night that warmed her heart.

Three years of marriage hadn't dimmed the love she felt, it had just cemented it. Like the stone walls of this castle, she felt they were built to weather the storms, to hold firm over time. At least, she hoped so.

He was already there in the apartment, when she opened the heavy wooden door from the stairwell landing.

'Hi, gorgeous. Everything okay?'

'Yes, not bad.' Today had been a busy one, and she still felt a little vulnerable and emotional, what with Lucy and

Dan's terrible news yesterday, and of course her period coming on like that. She still felt the dull ache of it in her back, a reminder of her non-pregnancy. Oh well, onwards and upwards. She tried to smile, but wasn't a good enough liar, obviously. Joe knew just what to do. He held his arms open to her with an understanding smile on his face.

But that just made her feel even more emotional. She didn't know quite what was up with her, to be honest. A silent tear slipped from her eye as she went to him and pressed herself against his shirt, relaxing into his warm embrace, breathing in his aftershave smell that she knew so well. She stayed there in his arms. This was definitely one of the best parts of being married; having that other person to share things with, the bad times as well as the good. Things weren't that bad, she knew that really, people were going through far worse in the world. It had just prodded an emotional raw-spot, that was all. But to get this comfort from Joe was just beautiful.

'Love you, Mrs Ward,' his warm, mellow voice spoke into her hair.

She pulled away very slightly to be able to look at him. 'Love you, too, Mr Ward.'

'Come on, I'll get us some dinner started if you want? You look shattered.'

'Aw, th-anks . . .I'm just tired.'

'Well, after a day of working in the kitchens again, I'm

40

sure you'll want a break from the oven. But . . . you know the score, if it's over to me then the repertoire is either pasta, frozen pizza or chili con carne.'

'Pasta it is then.' Something warm and comforting would be just fine, especially if it wasn't cooked by her.

'I'll do my creamy chicken sauce one then. I popped out to the Co-op earlier, so I have all the ingredients to hand.'

He had a proud glint in his eye.

How sweet, he must have thought of that after their heart-to-heart on their walk up in the hills yesterday. She didn't know quite what she had done to deserve him, but she was going to make the most of it.

'So, put your feet up, madam. And I shall pour you a glass of vino.' Joe slipped into an over-the-top Italian accent. 'Rosso or Blanco.'

She had a feeling he was making up his own words, but it made her smile. 'White would be lovely. Thanks.'

It was nearly time for *Coronation Street*, her favourite soap opera. So she did as she was told, sat down on the very cosy if worn sofa, slipped her shoes off, and curled up her legs. She was feeling a bit brighter already.

After a supper, eaten casually on their knees on the sofa, she leant in against him. She couldn't wait for an early night and a bucket-load of sleep. But cuddling up for a little while longer here with Joe would be lovely too. She felt a glow inside, realising how much she loved this gorgeous man beside her. His long lean legs stretched out, his arm angled casually, yet protectively, around her. Heaven knows how Lucy must have felt when she had heard the awful news about her fiancé's accident; Ellie remembered that sickening lurch in her own stomach like it was yesterday, when Joe had got trapped in that fire in the castle. How easily the things you loved could be taken away.

5

Five days to go until Bridezilla's big day.

At the Monday Meeting, where the castle employees got together to discuss the week and tasks ahead, there was a tension in the room that was palpable. This week's list was particularly long!

'Have you sorted that bloody unicorn yet, gents?' Deana asked Malcolm and Derek.

'Well, we've had a brilliant idea, haven't we, Derek . . . we just need to test it out.'

'That sounds ominous,' Lord Henry quipped with a wry smile. He knew his tour guides only too well. They certainly seemed to get themselves into all sorts of capers.

Ellie *really* didn't want to ask what they were up to, but she did need to know that whatever it was, was right, and wouldn't spoil the start of the big day for the bride. 'Well, try it out today, and let me know, as soon as. If it doesn't work, then we'll need to come up with an alternative, and fast.'

'Time's running out,' added Deana, 'So it'd better be good.'

'Anyhow,' Ellie took up. 'The orders are all in for the wedding buffet. We've got oysters coming across fresh on the day from Lindisfarne, and prawns and dressed crab. The bread's going to be delivered on the wedding morning from the local bakery. Irene's helping me make the two hundred mini quiches to go with that, and I've got three whole salmons to cook, two gammon joints to boil, which are roughly the size of Usain Bolt's thighs, as well as a pile of salads and coleslaws to prepare. Most of the catering can't be done until last minute, so the teashop team are going to have a hectic end of week. We've got mini scones to bake for the cream tea for the mid-afternoon, *and* with the wedding cake being changed last minute to sponge, that will have to be made fresh just two days before, and then iced.' Ellie felt tired just talking about it all. So much to do, so little time.

'Wow, you'll be busy. It all sounds well organized though, so that's great.' Joe tried to keep his tone fairly formal at the Monday meeting, addressing Ellie the same as the other staff, rather than as his wife. Ellie preferred it that way.

Joe took a sip from his coffee mug. It had a Batman motif on one side and 'Kapow!' the other. He had a bit of a Batman thing, loved all the films, old and new. And if you needed passwords to get into his laptop, a variety of Holy Smoke, Boom or Kapow might just do the trick.

'Oh,' Ellie continued, 'and I've got five extra staff recruited for the day before and on the day, to help with food prep and the waiting on. As well as Alan and his team from The Swan who'll be setting up the bar as per usual in the Drawing Room, and then later in the marquee, plus serving the champagne cocktails on arrival, and for the toasts.'

Wendy, the florist from their neighbouring market town of Kirkton, was at the meeting too. 'The flowers are all ordered for the bridal and bridesmaid's bouquets, the chapel, the Great Hall, for the balustrades at the castle entrance, and I have sourced the however-many-hundred white roses I'll need for the latest petal-scattering demand. And there's now a rainbow theme going on, after the bride's sudden switch-about, so it's been rather interesting changing the bouquets to multi-coloured flowers.'

There was a general eyebrow raise and groan around the room. They were all praying that Bridezilla didn't have yet another change of plan in the final few days.

'Let's just hope a new copy of *Hello* doesn't come out in the next couple of days, and give her a load of new ideas.' Deana voiced their concerns.

'Hah – well, the castle will be closed to visitors on the day of the wedding, so it'll be an *exclusive* here.' Derek commented drily, 'Maybe, the *Hello* team will arrive here to cover *the* wedding of the decade.' His tone was ironic.

'Or more likely the *Kirkton Gazette*,' Malcolm quipped.

'You never know what might happen with Bridezilla, but some press coverage might be likely, actually.' Joe's mood was serious, 'So, we need to make sure everything goes by the book and is absolutely tip-top.'

Lord Henry was obviously still mulling over the initial conversation. 'A *unicorn* . . . I hope you two haven't come up with a bloody pantomime horse.'

The pair of them looked slightly shady.

Oh, bloody hell, thought Ellie. 'It's not, is it, Malcolm?'

'No, no, it's a real live animal, that's all I'm saying 'til we test it out.'

'Why does that fill me with a sense of dread?' added Deana.

The others just laughed, except for Joe and Ellie who were feeling decidedly nervous about the whole event. This could really make or break things at the castle, and their relatively fledgling wedding event venture. They had been up and running for four years now as a wedding venue, but it took a good while to establish a sound reputation. It had been building nicely so far, and they'd had some lovely events and feedback, but a few mistakes, and a disgruntled wedding party, especially one as verbal as this lot, could really spoil all the hard work they'd put in to build themselves a positive profile.

'Well, the last thing we need is bad-mouthing in the press, or the wedding party holding back on the final balance, so everything has to go smoothly and be spot-on, okay.' Joe looked deadly serious, cutting the laughter short.

'Of course, boss,' replied Derek earnestly. Malcolm was nodding.

'We'll pull out all the stops and do our best, Joe,' Deana added.

There was a real respect for Joe and Lord Henry amongst the staff. And, though they joked about sometimes, they did all take pride in their castle work. They were a good team. And they had become to feel like family to Ellie.

'Right, well then, there's still the day-to-day work to get on with; the teashop, the castle tours, the shop, and keeping our regular visitors happy. I need to get across to the farm, to see how that's all going too, so thanks everyone. Just call my mobile if you need me, and if any further support or advice is required throughout this week, just shout.' Joe stated. 'Right, well if there's no more questions or comments, then it looks like we've all got a busy week ahead. So let's crack on with it, then.'

As the room emptied a small sigh escaped Ellie's lips. Yes, she'd been doing this for five years now, and the tearooms were becoming second nature, but a big, demanding wedding was still rather daunting.

* * *

Irene had stayed in the teashop kitchens baking her daily scone selection, whilst the meeting was on. There was a delicious smell as Ellie and Doris walked back in; sweet, warm and doughy, and a tray of cherry and almond scones stood cooling on a rack.

'Cup of tea, ladies?' she asked.

Was that woman a mind reader? 'Oh yes, that's just what I need. Thanks, Irene.' And I might just have to split one of those scones, with a generous dollop of butter. Anyone fancy sharing a half?'

'Yes, please.' Doris had no fear of expanding waistlines. *No point baking all these lovely goodies if you're too afraid to eat them,* she'd often mutter.

Five minutes later, Ellie was sipping her tea whilst preparing the ingredients for a batch of salted caramel cookies – a new addition to her range. Ellie liked to shake things up every now and again, and they'd been going down a treat with the customers; all chewy toffee with a crunchy, crumbly edge.

Irene had already baked a tea loaf and a chocolate cake to go on the counter display. Ellie would do a couple of lemon drizzles next too. They were expecting a minibus trip from the old people's home in Kirkton for morning coffee at 11 a.m., so it was going to be a fairly busy day.

The supplies delivery was due in shortly too; her fruit juices, fresh salad stuff, vegetables, sliced bread for toasties, milk and more. The teashop days just seemed to flow. There was always something to keep them active.

Ellie also wanted to make a couple of batches of vanilla cupcakes ready to ice. It was still summery out there, early September and the sun was shining today, so she'd decorate one half with a swirl of butter icing, a chocolate flake and some hundreds and thousands, so they looked like the top of a 99 ice-cream cone. For the rest she'd add some soft-pink colouring to the frosting and scatter the tops with pretty sugar icing flowers. She liked to make seasonal changes to the food on offer so her regulars didn't get bored with the same old selection, and it kept it fun for her cooking too. She felt so much more experienced now, but she still loved her baking. And, seeing the customers' faces light up as they tucked in to one of her creations, still gave her a buzz and made it all worthwhile. She hoped to goodness she'd see a look of delight on Bridezilla's face at some point (hopefully several!) over the weekend.

But, there were so many things that might go wrong . . . Ellie felt a bit shaky. Normally, she was pretty calm about her up-and-coming wedding events. Over the past four years the castle had hosted over forty weddings, and she had grown into the role of wedding coordinator. She had really begun to enjoy it, trying her utmost to make the wedding couples and their families' days as special and unique as they wanted. They'd hosted a medieval banquet where all the guests dressed up, and they'd hired in a huge hog roast, they'd had a funfair wedding with clowns, stalls and fair rides, they'd even had a *Strictly Come Dancing* themed event with plenty of sequins, scooping necklines, and a ballroom-inspired reception. Yes, sometimes there were minor hiccups, but nothing Ellie wasn't able to overcome with the help of the castle staff and Joe.

But there had been so many twists and turns on the lead up to this particular wedding, not to mention the tears and tantrums already! Ellie was catering for over 200 people with a 'buffet to die for' – Bridezilla's words. Often they contracted out the catering, especially on the bigger events such as this, as it was such a lot to take on, but this time the bride had insisted, so Ellie was doing all that as well as coordinating the wedding day throughout, making sure every last request was met, *and*, she was certain some new requests would appear on the day too.

They really needed the income from this event. They were being paid far more than any previous wedding they had ever booked, basically as they were providing far more, with all the demands that had kept rolling in. But, if it all paid out, then Ellie and Joe might finally draw some good wages, and have enough to do up their apartment rooms, and finally get the central heating system in there working properly. There was one room in particular that Ellie wanted repainted and decorated, fingers crossed that they might be needing it soon, to make it into a nursery. She could dream still, couldn't she? And plan a little for now, at least.

Boy, she couldn't wait for Sunday night to come around – when the whole event would be over, the bridal party and guests all away, and she could curl up on the sofa next to Joe, with a large glass of chilled white wine.

Right Ellie, *cool, calm, and collected,* she reminded herself of her mantra of old. She had the castle team on her side, and several years' experience now. She could only do her best for the wedding weekend ahead, and that would hopefully be enough to pull them all through! Go girl!

After a flurry of lunch orders, Ellie popped in to see how Irene and Doris were getting on out front in the teashop. There were still several tables occupied. Ellie waved across at a lovely old couple, who came in most weeks to share a toasted teacake and a pot of tea. She walked over to them.

'Hello, Jim, Mavis. Are you both keeping all right?'

'Oh yes, pet. We're doing grand, thank you. Mavis has finally shifted that cold she had, so we're back out and about again.'

'That's good. I missed seeing you last week.'

'Lovely cup of tea, pet.' Mavis raised her china cup with a smile.

'I'm glad you're enjoying it.'

'Our Sarah is coming home for the weekend, bringing the two grandchildren.'

'Oh, that'll be nice for you all. When did you last see them?'

'Over a month now, back at the start of the school holidays. They live down in Lincolnshire, so it's quite some drive.'

'Oh well, it'll be lovely to all catch up.' That reminded Ellie, she'd have to go and visit her own family soon. The Bridezilla wedding and summer season in the teashop had taken over a bit. Time seemed to rush on, and weeks went by before you knew it. Her parents had popped up one Sunday a few weeks ago, but Ellie had been so busy in the teashop that she hadn't had long to stop and chat with them. And they'd had to get back sharp, as Ellie's dad had an early start on a big plumbing job for a housing company in Gateshead the next morning. But they did speak on the phone every few days, and yes, after the wedding of the century was over, then she'd arrange a couple of days off with Joe and go down to Newcastle and see them.

'Well, we'd better not keep you, pet.' Jim brought her back to the present.

'Lovely to see you both. Have a super time with your family. Take care.'

Doris was bustling about refilling the sugar bowls,

Irene taking through a new Victoria sponge, and topping up the cupcakes on display.

'Everything been okay here, ladies?'

'Fine, thank you,' Irene answered happily.

'No problems,' Doris added from behind the counter, 'other than a couple of screaming kids . . . Now we've just got rid of all the big ones back to school, we're invaded with toddlers and babies.' She gave a grimace.

Irene just raised her eyebrows at Doris's moaning; there was always some complaint or other.

Ellie shook her head, used to it by now. 'Well, I hope you were nice to them, Doris. They're all our customers, small or large.'

With that Doris's gaze shot pointedly across the room to a rather plump lady sat on her own in the corner, and gave a nod of her head. Ellie wished she hadn't used that turn of phrase now.

'*Two* slices of Victoria sponge *and* a cookie,' the waitress mouthed, looking very like the comedian Les Dawson in his heyday.

Oh dear, Ellie tried her best to ignore her. 'Right, well I need to nip out to the village shop and get some more milk to tide us over 'til the morning's order comes in. We seem to have had a run of milkshakes and lattes today. Anybody need anything?'

'No, thanks.'

'All fine.'

Ellie had her car keys in her pocket, so headed on out. 'I'll not be long.'

She went out of the side delivery entrance, got into her trusty old Corsa car, started it up, and turned out through an old stone archway onto the main driveway. She slowed, as she spotted something up ahead that seemed to be blocking the road. A few tourists had stopped to take a look at whatever it was, and were gathering on the grass verge. Ellie approached cautiously, then had to divert off the driveway, pulling over on to the verge. A white pony seemed to be the cause of all the bother, doing a bit of a jig, its ears back and its rider hanging on for dear life. And, oh dear God, there was Malcolm tugging the poor thing along by a lead rein, like it was some kind of bellpull, with Derek trying to keep up alongside.

Ellie got out of her car. 'What on earth . . .?'

It was then she spotted the long pointed appendage, that looked like some kind of *Blue Peter*-style, papier-mache probe, which was strapped onto the poor creatures noseband, sending it cross-eyed and into a bit of a pony-strop. No wonder it was tossing its head about irritably.

The rider then leapt off the animal, probably just in time, as she was about to be bucked off by the looks of it. She snatched off her riding hat. Ellie recognized Lauren, one of the girls from the local village, who also helped as a waitress at the teashop.

'There's no way I'll be riding that thing again,' she shouted. 'It's bloody dangerous. It's like Buckaroo up there. There's no way you can put the bride on that thing. You'll kill her.'

Oh dear God, this must be Malcolm and Derek's masterplan for the unicorn. In hindsight, maybe they hadn't been the best couple to put in charge of this particular task.

Malcolm was looking rather flustered, holding on to the pony's rein for dear life, muttering, 'Well, the bride insists she's going to be *riding* the unicorn down the driveway.'

It wasn't just poor Patrick the Pony – Ellie recognized him now from the farm down the road – who was unhappy. This was never going to work. Ellie shook her head in despair. She might have laughed along with the tourists who were watching it all with much amusement, had she not realized how much Bridezilla was likely to flip out if she didn't get her unicorn grand entrance. There were only five days left to sort out this mess.

6

It was the day before the big Bridezilla wedding and Ellie's mind was on a running loop of to-do's: check all the deliveries came in, boil and glaze the hams for the buffet, bake as much as she could in advance for the afternoon-tea goodies. Oh yes, there was a buffet lunch *and* an afternoon tea to prepare for, as well as the outside caterers coming in for the evening event. She also had to make sure all the guest rooms were ready and looking tip-top – especially the suite which the bride would be using to get ready in, and the bridesmaids' rooms that were along the same corridor. Oh yes, the advance party of bride and bridesmaids were arriving today, and Ellie had to be prepared.

The water began to run lukewarm and the shock of the cool water made her realize she'd been off in another zone. She'd better shampoo and condition quickly before the shower decided to totally run cold, which happened fairly regularly at the castle. Bloody hell, she hoped the hot water system would hold up for all the guests. Another concern to add to her list. Though the main guest wing had recently been given its own new boiler system, at last. Hopefully, it would all be fine.

She turned off the shower, and as she went to step out, realized Joe was stood there. Oh wow, stark naked in fact, holding a towel ready for her. He smiled at her as she stepped into the warmth of the towel and his arms, where they engaged in a surprisingly sexy kiss for this time of the morning. He was *very* naked just on the other side of that towel. Shame they both had to go to work. She pulled back gently from the kiss, smiling back at him.

He started towel drying her. She could feel his palms through the soft material moving over her body, loitering just a tad longer than was necessary on the breast area, which she had to admit was on the generous side. It used to annoy her that she was curvy and had trouble keeping the weight off of her hips and boobs, trying all sorts of faddy diets in her late teens and early twenties. But it never seemed to worry Joe, it was a positive bonus on his book. He often told her so.

Looking at him then, she realized that in the rush of everyday life, sometimes she forgot just how gorgeous he really was, dark hair still morning-tousled, toned physique, lean, fairly tall – no, not *forgotten* that wasn't quite it, but she just didn't *notice* like she used to. But moments like this could still take her by surprise, remind her how very lucky they were to have found each other. To be able to love each other.

She felt the nudge of an erection the other side of the towel, pressing low against her tummy, stirring something deep within her.

But there *really* was so much to do. A Bridezilla wedding to start cooking for, as well as all her Friday teashop routines. Damn. 'Later . . . sorry, Joe. I really have tons to do.'

'Such a shame. But I'll take the *later* as a promise.'

She grinned at him. It was one promise she'd be more than happy to keep later on that evening. And the thought of it would keep them both smiling through what was bound to be a long day.

'They're here!' Malcolm announced, poking his head around the teashop kitchen door. He'd been on lookout duty.

And so, the wedding weekend was about to begin. At least she'd got through all the lunch orders before Bridezilla and co arrived. Ellie quickly took off her apron, and ran from the teashop, across the courtyard, to the main castle entrance. She was just in time. A huge dark blacked-out windowed limousine pulled up at the bottom of the castle steps, followed by the biggest black stretch-Hummer vehicle she had ever seen. She could almost imagine the president of the USA stepping out from there, with his team of bodyguards.

But instead it was something far more intimidating. Platinum-blonde long curls and a short, rounded body, shrieking, 'Get me the hell out of here. I feel car sick after all those bloody winding lanes.'

The limousine driver, who was now holding open the rear door of the vehicle for her ladyship, plus her mother, looked rather frazzled. Ellie smiled sympathetically across at him. That must have been some journey.

The bride-to-be and her mother were in the first vehicle, whilst out from the Hummer poured nine bridesmaids, who were stretching out their rather stiff joints, and then leaning back in to gather up a festoon of huge gowns, wrapped in special carriers. The last dress out was immense, layer upon layer of white taffeta and silk was apparent through its clear cover. It took two of the girls to carry it. No wonder the bridesmaids had been crammed in. The dresses would have filled the back of the vehicle alone.

Malcolm offered to help manoeuvre *the* gown into the castle, after phoning Derek quickly for backup.

Ellie smiled broadly at the arriving party, looking far more confident than she felt, 'Welcome Chelsea, everyone, to your wedding at Claverham Castle.'

* * *

'We *need* prosecco!'

It was 6 p.m., that same Friday evening. The Bridezilla bridal party had arrived at the castle two hours earlier. There had already been several demands; one being that an extra guest room was essential . . . for the dresses. The gowns were in fact the size of small houses, being of the Gypsy Wedding fashion style. The bride's mammoth dress, and nine (yes, *nine* bridesmaids) only slightly smaller versions in . . . oh yes, you've guessed it, a selection of vivid colours to make up the colours of the rainbow (with a couple of repeats). They were certainly going to catch the eye tomorrow. Ellie had helped carry the robes into the spare room and was nearly flattened by the sheer weight of them. She seriously wondered how all ten of them were going to fit into the chapel aisle. It would be a squeeze.

And there was no way Bridezilla would be getting on a horse (or unicorn) dressed in that, or anything else to be fair. Ellie had already had to break that particular piece of news, highlighting the fact that a helmet would also have to be worn for health and safety reasons, which would of course ruin the bridal hairdo. The bride had finally conceded that riding in like Lady Godiva was maybe not such a good idea after all. Phew! Ellie had also explained the alternative suggestion for the unicorn entrance, which had been trialled only yesterday, and seemed to work fairly well – fingers crossed. Lauren had come to the rescue in that respect, with an alternative that looked the part at least.

And so, the wedding weekend had begun. Ellie's mobile was unfortunately on speed dial.

'So?' Chelsea was shouting at her down the line.

'Yes, right, prosecco . . . Well, I can certainly get that organized. I'll just need to pop to the local shop in the next village.'

'What do you mean you don't have any here? What *is* this place?'

'There's plenty ordered in for tomorrow, which the landlord from the village pub will be bringing across. He'll also be running a full bar service for the day, but we don't have a bar of our own here all the time. But I can certainly fetch some for you, if that would help. It's no trouble.' It was hard trying to keep up a smiley voice through gritted teeth.

'Yes, well don't be too long. We're getting parched here.'

'So, how many bottles are you thinking?'

'Ah, a dozen or so will do.'

A dozen. There were only eleven of them staying over tonight. Bridezilla, her mother, and the bridesmaids. The groom and all the guests were heading up first thing in the morning. Well, a bottle each then, nice going for a *pre*-wedding night. 'Of course.'

Ellie had had fifteen minutes crashed on her sofa, with a *small* glass of chilled Sauvignon; she had definitely needed it, but that was all she was allowing herself, as she had to keep a clear head for the big day ahead and all of its many challenges. After having put the finishing touches to the wedding cake, and checking all the grand buffet arrangements, she had finally headed up to their apartment. She supposed it was a miracle she had managed fifteen minutes.

'I'll be back with you in about twenty minutes.' She told Chelsea.

'*Twenty* minutes? How's that?'

'Well, the nearest shop is five miles away, and I'll need to nip in and pay.' *And that'll be added to the ongoing bill.*

'Right then. Well, I suppose that'll have to do.' She sounded very disgruntled, and not even a mention of a thank you.

'I'll deliver it up to your rooms as soon as I'm back.'

'Can we have ice buckets too?'

'Of course.' There were one or two stacked away in a cupboard in the teashop. She'd buy a big bag of ice at the shop too.

Still no thank you. *Since when did Wedding Coordinator equate to slave?*

Joe walked in from the apartment kitchen, where he'd just popped a pizza in the oven for them both. He'd obviously overheard the conversation. 'I'll go if you like. You'd better get something to eat. The pizza will be ready in about ten minutes. Just save me some.' He smiled.

'Thank you. You're an angel.'

He gave a big grin.

'An angel in a very sexy body,' she added.

He grinned wider.

'It's on one condition though.'

Damn, she remembered her earlier promise. She may now be too tired to fulfil those particular needs tonight. 'Yes?'

'I don't have to take the wine to their rooms. I have a feeling they'd eat me alive. It'd be like entering the lion's den. I don't think even my Batman underpants could protect me.' He actually looked fearful.

'Hah, you flatter yourself.' But yes, he did have a point; ten hens pre-wedding. It could be a dangerous situation for any man!

'Okay, twelve bottles of prosecco, actually make that sixteen, you never know.' She could imagine a further phone call when the last bottle was emptied at midnight. 'And a large bag of ready-made ice. Ring me when you get back, and if you help me get the bottles upstairs, I'll take over at the threshold to the bridal suite.' She laughed.

'Deal.' He flashed her a smile. 'And you make sure you eat something while I'm out. Big day tomorrow and you'll probably be working flat out.'

'O-kay.'

Prosecco duly delivered, which seemed to settle the group down a bit, there was one more call-out to attend to an hour and a half later: a '*horrific* noise issue'. It was an owl; good old Hooter (or his offspring probably) was still on form out there in the woods. Not actually a lot Ellie could do about that, except offer cotton-wool balls to shove in their ears (Bridezilla did actually take her up on that) and a reassurance that it wasn't an axe murderer out there, just normal nature doing its thing at night.

And then she managed six hours of rather unsettled sleep before her alarm went off at 5.45 a.m. It was going to be a hectic day and she wanted plenty of time to get organized. She had Irene coming in at 8 a.m. to bake two hundred mini scones for the afternoon tea. Doris (who'd been wrapping cutlery in ivory napkins till seven-thirty last night, bless her) was to be in at 8.30 to help set out the Great Hall with the assistance of Malcolm, Derek and Joe; there was to be a rectangular top table, and circular tables of twelve places set for the guests. The long antique wooden table that was usually the centrepiece of the room was to be covered for the buffet and set to one side (now, that'd take some moving – an all-hands-on-deck job), the French doors could then be opened out to the gardens where there was a marquee already set out for the bar, disco, and the hog roast company who were hired in for the evening. At least Ellie and her team got a break from the catering for the night do. But that didn't mean she wasn't still on call! And, she was going to be back cooking on Sunday morning, doing a hundred breakfast rolls of sausage and bacon for the no doubt worse-for-wear revellers who had stayed over.

Wendy was coming in early morning too, to decorate the chapel, the balustrades into the castle, and the tables in the Great Hall with her floral magic. The displays and table decorations were then to be transferred out for the evening event to the marquee. The whole event had taken mega-organising skills, an ongoing (and ever-changing list) on a Word doc on Ellie's iPad, and nerves of steel.

As she got down to the teashop kitchen Ellie was relieved to see that the three separate tiers of the iced wedding cake were still in one piece and looking perfect – she'd been fretting about it overnight. All she had to do was assemble them, but she was going to do that in the Great Hall. There was no way she was going to risk carrying it as a complete whole up the winding stairwell; so, she'd put the final touches to it in the next hour or so in situ, ready for the Wedding Breakfast. The delicate icing flowers, the unicorn modelled from sugar paste, and the arch of rainbow for the top, were all made and placed on greaseproof paper; with some rainbow piping and with a delicate hand it would look . . . well, like a rather gaudy rainbow cake to be honest, but pretty good. And it was what the bride wanted, so who was Ellie to judge.

An hour and a half flew by as she began preparing the buffet food. The Wedding Breakfast gourmet-buffet was to be served at 1.30 p.m. after champagne in the garden.

The chapel service was booked for 11.30 a.m., and was usually just under the hour. She knew she'd be dashing about like a mad thing at that point, when she'd have a narrow window of free time to put final touches to the catering and check the Great Hall was ready, whilst the bridal party were otherwise occupied getting married. Then, she'd be back on call as maidservant to the bride. She was running a tight ship today and so far, by some miracle, hadn't been called up to the bridal rooms as yet, though she had made a quick phone call to check all was well, and that they hadn't needed anything at that point.

She'd spotted the hairdressing team and make-up artist turn up about an hour ago, so the ladies were probably busy getting preened. Deana was primed for reception duties, ready to meet and greet and show any guests through to the drawing room where they would congregate initially, and then to file them on to the chapel area. Ellie's stomach gave a little churn. She sent up a little prayer to the heavens that today would go well.

7

The kitchens were a hive of activity. The oyster, salmon and prawns delivery had turned up, phew, another check on Ellie's list. She and Irene had a quick cup of tea, which Ellie forced herself to have a slice of toast and butter with, or she'd be at risk at forgetting to eat. Nanna's voice had already appeared in her head that morning nagging her about that.

Ellie headed up to the Great Hall to see how things were going. Joe, Colin – the gardener, Malcolm and Derek were trying to shift the heavy banquet table to the side of the room. There was a lot of huffing and puffing, and the gents were obviously struggling. So Ellie took up one side and nodded to Doris to help too. That seemed to add to the momentum, and they shifted it the few feet across it needed. Boy, was it heavy!

'Crickey, that'll do my back no favours at all, Malcolm,' Derek muttered.

'You'll be fine, Derek. If Ellie can lift it, I'm sure you can.' Malcolm seemed to have lost his patient edge this morning. This event was testing everyone.

'Thanks, folks.' Joe was trying his best to keep them all motivated.

A couple of minutes later, Wendy bustled in bearing two large boxes of flowers. As she opened the lids, the scent was gorgeous, filling the room.

'We're nearly there, Wendy. If you can hold fire for about fifteen minutes, we'll have the other tables in and set up ready for you. Come on lads, step to it.' Joe said.

Malcolm just raised his eyes to the heavens. 'Slave labour.'

'Tell me about it,' Ellie added, with a wry grin.

'So masterful though,' Malcolm mouthed silently to Ellie over Joe's shoulder, much to the amusement of the room.

Ellie's mobile went off. Her eyes flicked to the screen, *Chelsea* calling. Here goes . . .

She walked to stand by the leaded windows that overlooked the rear gardens; the signal being better there.

'It's a total disaster! The electrics have all gone off, and we're in the middle of blow-drying my hair. You'll need to sort it out immediately,' Chelsea shrieked, her voice so loud, Ellie had to hold the phone away from her ear.

It was probably just the trip switch. They would no doubt have an array of hair straighteners, hairdryers, nail dryers, music systems playing, the works, all on at the same time. The ancient castle electrical system just couldn't cope sometimes. She'd go check it out and call in Joe if it seemed more complicated than that.

'We've run out of prosecco, too. We'll need at least four more bottles. I'll need to calm my nerves after this fiasco. I'll never be ready in time, now.'

'O-kay. No problem.' They had indeed drunk all sixteen bottles last night. But Ellie had seen Alan arrive to set up the Reception drinks in the drawing room. She'd call by and see if he had any spare bottles on the way through.

'Okay, everything all right here for now, then? I'm off to the bridal rooms. Some electrical crisis. I should be able to handle it.'

'Good luck.' 'Yes, best of luck.' 'Call me if you need,' Joe added.

'Will do.'

There were looks of empathy as she headed out.

Ellie tried to smile as she knocked and entered the bridal zone, but already the act was hurting her cheek muscles.

She was carrying the four bottles of bubbly as instructed, and popped them down on the side.

'About bloody time.'

Manners maketh a man, echoed in Ellie's mind. *Some*

71

people, goodness . . . It was Nanna's voice. Ellie bit the inside of her cheek.

'Right, if you just give me two minutes, I'm going to check the fuse box for this area of the castle.'

She scoured the room before she left. Yes, guilty as charged; on the first glance, she saw a kettle plugged in, an iron set up on an ironing board, two pairs of ghd straighteners, three hairdryers, some kind of gel-nails drying machine, several iPods charging, and goodness knows what else was tucked away out of sight. 'You can't have all that equipment on at once, I'm afraid. The electrical system just can't cope with it. Whilst the hairdryers and straighteners are going, maybe hold back from boiling the kettle, and charging your phones.'

There were groans all round.

'Anyone would think we're in the dark ages,' Chelsea muttered, with a scowl.

'Well, it is a *castle* venue.' Ellie tried to hold her frustration at bay. 'There are naturally some limitations. I'm sorry, but there's not an awful lot I can do about it, other than warn you not to overload the system, or it may well trip off again.' She felt like adding that electrics just weren't in the original castle designs, and to remind them that they had *chosen* a rural castle venue specifically and not the bloody Ritz Hotel, but she thought the rebukes would just be too much.

Joe and the team did their best to keep the castle

infrastructure as modernized as possible, and of course they were careful to keep everything up to date safety-wise, but rewiring and upgrading a whole ancient building like this would be a logistical nightmare, as well as running into many thousands of pounds, which they just didn't have.

'Sorry . . . Perhaps you could spread yourselves over a few of the rooms you have, that'd help too.'

'Aw,' Bridezilla pulled a face, 'but it's all girlies together, that's the whole idea. Anyway, what are you waiting for, stood around here. Get it sorted. My hair'll be a frizz-ball else. And I know who'll to blame.'

Ellie pursed her lips as she turned to go, to stop the torrent of home truths that were threatening to spill out at that very second. Instead they burned in her brain, including several swear words.

She reached the fuse box down the passageway, and used a chair to climb up and take a closer look.

Damn.

It wasn't just the trip switch gone. There was a suspicious smell of burnt plastic and one of the switches looked rather frazzled. This was a job for the experts, *and* there was no way they would be turning any electrics back on in this section of rooms for now. At least the other switches on the row seemed okay, there was no smoke, and the rest of the castle was still up and running.

She needed to get in touch with Joe ASAP, and get

him to call out the local electrician; with any luck they might be able to get it fixed through the day, so the girls could at least come back and use their bedrooms that evening.

But for now, there were hairdryers, curlers, straighteners, and goodness knows what to get back into action. As well as a bride with a very large bee in her bonnet.

Ellie wasn't quite sure how she was going to tell her, and felt her throat tighten and her mouth dry. Maybe she should go and put on the full metal suit of armour from the Edward I Chamber first . . .

'Chelsea, I'm sorry, but I'm going to have to move you and the girls. The electrics are burnt out at the trip switch and I need to get a qualified electrician to check and repair that before I can turn anything back on for this section of rooms.'

There was a second of silence and a glare that would melt steel.

'Well, that is just *ridiculous* . . . You are joking!'

'I have the rooms ready for you right now.' Deana was already there, giving the guest rooms on the corridor above them a check over right now. Ellie had made a plea for help, phoning after seeing the damaged fuse box. The rooms could have a quick refresh during the wedding service, ready for the wedding guests who should be in them for this evening. Needs must.

'I knew I shouldn't have trusted this tinpot of an organisation with the most important day of my life,' Chelsea shrieked. 'Can't you just bring in a generator or something? I'm not moving now.'

'That might work, but not in the timescale we have. By the time we could possibly get one hired and set up, you'd need to be ready and at the chapel. The only option is to move upstairs. I have staff ready to help you transfer everything across.'

'Humph! Well, I shall be letting my contacts at the *Daily Star* know about this shoddy hole of a place. *And* . . . I have an old school friend that works at *BRIDES* magazine.'

Ellie could see all her dreams of the castle becoming one of the best wedding venues in the area tumbling before her very eyes. Bad press would be disastrous. She swallowed the knot in her throat, and was determined not to shed the tear that was forming in her eye. 'Right, Chelsea, we still have an hour and a half before you need to be at the chapel. We can move everything up in the next five minutes. What are the most important things you need to move across with you? We'll get right on with it.' Ellie tried her best to sound professional, though her heart was pounding.

'I cannot believe this. So, I'm going to have to move across to another poxy room in my dressing gown on my wedding day. It's shambolic.'

'Come on Chelsea, let's just let them move our things.

I don't think we have a lot of time or a lot of choice.' The head bridesmaid tried to coax her friend to get going and get on with it.

Just then the bride's mother waltzed in. Ellie felt her heart sink even further.

'Chelsea sweetie, what's going on here? Have you been crying?!' She then fixed a cold stare on Ellie, her voice turning to stone, 'What's happened now?'

'It's a problem with the electrics,' Ellie felt her voice quaver, 'I'm so sorry.'

'Sorry isn't good enough though, is it? You've made my poor daughter cry on her wedding day. We won't be forgetting this . . . will we, Chelsea sweetheart. In fact, we might just have to sue . . . There, there.' Her voice went back to a simpering tone. In her bold black-and-white mother-of-the-bride two-piece there was a definite look of Cruella de Vil about her.

Deana marched into the room.

'Okay folks, apologies. But let's just sort this out as quickly as we can, and get you ladies and everything you need, to the other rooms as swiftly as possible. They are all ready for you. Malcolm and Derek are here to take up what you need. It's just one flight up the stairwell. The day can go ahead exactly as planned, and we have an electrician on his way at this very moment. So bridesmaids, your rooms should all be ready again for this evening. And Chelsea, be assured that the bridal suite for you and

Kelvin is unaffected.' Deana gave a calm, confident, we're-in-control look around the occupants of the room.

Ellie managed a smile, but still felt a bit shaky. She was so grateful for Deana's calming influence at times like this. She realized she had much to learn about dealing with a crisis. 'Thank you, Deana.'

Ten o'clock. Crisis resolved, and less than an hour until the moment of truth when the 'unicorn' was due to make its appearance, ready to transport the bride down the castle driveway for the start of her big day. The weather was holding fine at the moment, though there was a forecast of sunshine and showers. Ellie had moved the girls, dresses and the equipment, worthy of a whole hairdressing salon, up and into their new rooms with the help of Deana, Derek and Malcolm. So, the bridal hairdo was all finished, and teased into perfect place. Please, please, please let it stay dry, at least until Bridezilla got back into shelter of the castle.

8

Ellie was stood anxiously on the castle steps. Once the 'unicorn' was in sight she was to go straight up to the bridal suite and fetch Bridezilla to be ready on the castle steps for collection. The unicorn entourage were to do a loop, out through the side entrance of the castle, up the hill and through the little hamlet. Ellie had even primed some of their neighbours to stand at the roadside ready to wave and cheer, as Bridezilla had wanted a Royal Wedding feel. They would then come back in to the estate through the very impressive wrought-iron gates of the main castle entrance, down the tree-lined avenue, to meet with her bridesmaids who were to be dutifully waiting on the same steps for her, along with her father. They would then all troop on up into the castle and to the chapel, where hopefully the groom would be ready, or else.

Crickey, there were so many things might go wrong with this part of the day's events. Tractors blocking the road, animal antics, always unpredictable, Malcom and Derek – enough said. At least Lauren was in control of the action now, *and* a certain ex-jockey racing stable owner, apparently, which had put Ellie's mind more at ease. She still hadn't seen the final plan in action herself, but was assured it would be a hit with the bride.

Ooh look, there was something happening away in the distance. A rattle of carriage wheels maybe? Ellie wasn't sure whether to be excited or distraught.

There was a small procession coming down the tree-lined driveway. Leading the way was a rather magnificent white horse, and as it neared, Ellie could see it had a very impressive horned head – certainly not the same papier-mache article that Malcolm had created. Leading the horse was a rather handsome chap that Ellie had once met in the village stores – ah, so *that* was Anthony from the racing stables then. He was in full riding attire, tight beige jodhpurs, smart navy velvet riding jacket, over a crisp, white shirt, and stylish cravat. In fact, he looked rather like a character out of a Jilly Cooper novel – wow. He flashed Ellie a broad smile as they approached the castle steps.

A small gathering had followed them along the driveway, including Derek and Malcolm who were walking beside a rather quaint wooden carriage, *and* guess who was pulling it – Patrick the Pony. Lauren, was master-fully driving the little carriage, holding the reins confidently, with a unicorn-horn free Patrick, who at this point anyhow, seemed to be behaving himself.

'Good morning,' greeted Anthony in a lovely, warm Irish accent. If that voice, on top of the white-stallion unicorn and the Colin Firth-style riding breeches, didn't have the bride as putty in his hands, Ellie wasn't sure what would. She began to relax, just a little.

'Morning. Thank you so much for helping out at late notice. Right then, I'll just go and fetch the bride.' And off she dashed, feeling a little like Cinderella herself.

Across the courtyard she scampered, and up the stone stairwell to the second-floor suite of rooms that the bride and her bridesmaids were now in. She knocked, with her fingers on the other hand crossed behind her back. *Here goes.*

'Who is it?' came a bark from the far side of the door.

'Just Ellie, we're ready when you are Br . . .' Ooh, she nearly let it slip, 'Chelsea.' She opened the door to be greeted by hair tongs and straighteners, nail varnish bottles open at precarious angles on the furniture, hand-bags, jewellery, discarded underwear, empty bottles of prosecco, half-filled flutes, bouquets in rainbow-coloured hues, a heavy scent of ladies perfume, and twelve very glamorous, if slightly (she was being kind) over-the-top, ladies, plus a ragged-looking hairdresser.

Chelsea was stood in the middle of all this in her silk and taffeta dress, which seemed to take up the whole room by itself.

'Just need my tiara fixed on. Amy, are you ready with it? I need it *now*,' she shrieked across the room. The poor hairdresser flitted to her side, though it was hard to reach the bride's head now with the meringue-gown creation in full expanse. Two bridesmaids and Bridezilla's mother had to hold it down like it was some kind of caged animal, to let the hairdresser get to Chelsea and secure the tiara with its short, very sparkly train in place. The bride's platinum blonde curls had been corkscrewed and then partly pinned-up in a sweeping mid-section on the top of her head. Ellie noted that her make-up was extremely heavy, in a trowelled-on shade of orange – if it rained out there now, they were in big trouble.

'Have you got your something blue on, Chels?' one of the bridesmaids asked.

Bridezilla flashed a lacy blue garter in response.

'Oh, and don't forget your clutch bag and bouquet.'

'Got it. Are you all ready, my girls? I need you on the steps to see me off, and then you have to wait there while I do the tour. I hope that unicorn's ready?' She flashed Ellie a don't-you-dare-get-anything-else-wrong-here stare.

Ellie felt her stomach shudder, but held her nerve. 'Of course. It looks stunning. Just perfect.'

'Good.'

Ellie and the maid of honour lifted the expanse of skirt to help Bridezilla get out of the room and down the stairs, whilst she was muttering, 'Should have got this staircase widened, knowing there were going to be brides in their wedding dresses coming down here.'

Oh yes, knock down a thirteenth-century stairwell to accommodate a multi-meringue layered dress. Good idea. Ellie bit her tongue.

There was a clatter of stilettos on stone, it sounded like they were storming the castle, as they trooped carefully down and out across the courtyard. Joe was under strict instructions, keeping a careful eye on the drawing room holding area where the other guests were being plied with champagne, to make sure that neither the groom nor any of the other guests ventured out and caught sight of them. Derek was also acting as sentinel on the doors out to the courtyard.

Anthony, and the white-stallion unicorn (well, it was a gelding but no one was going to say anything!) were waiting patiently at the bottom of the steps. By some miracle Patrick, Lauren and the cart, were positioned in the right place just behind them – after doing two loops round the block to keep the restless pony happy.

'Oooh.' Bridezilla seemed quite overwhelmed. Ellie prayed this was in a positive way, but couldn't be quite sure.

'So, do I ride this gorgeous creature?' Bridezilla looked teasingly across at Anthony.

'If only,' he replied smoothly. 'But, my lovely lady, a riding hat would be essential, and that would so spoil your beautiful hairdo. *So*, your carriage awaits.'

God, he was a charmer. Ellie held back a wry grin.

He gestured to Patrick and his cart. Since Ellie had nipped upstairs, the carriage had had a quick makeover and been gorgeously decorated by Wendy, with floral twists of pink and orange roses, sprigs of delicate white gypsophila and greenery. There was a rainbow-coloured throw in place on the seat, and Patrick himself now sported a pink rose on his head collar, which thankfully he hadn't seemed to have noticed.

Was this going to be the moment Bridezilla flipped? There seemed to be a universal holding of breath.

'Oh, how lovely, and isn't the donkey sweet.'

Thank goodness Patrick didn't speak human, or *he* might have flipped – donkey indeed.

Anthony handed the lead rein of the white horse across to Malcolm, whilst he gestured for the bride to take his arm, ushered her to the carriage, and yes actually made a step out of his two hands, fingers locked together, for her to climb up to the seat. Bridezilla had a stunned and rather mesmerized look on her face, as she gazed back down at him. Ellie hoped she wasn't now regretting her choice of groom.

The official photographer was snapping away in a photo frenzy.

'And so, let the wonders of the day begin!' Anthony announced.

The bridesmaids cheered from the castle steps as he took up the lead rein of the unicorn-stallion who began to walk steadily beside him ready for their village tour, Patrick plodding dutifully behind. Perhaps he was in awe of the unicorn too! What a marvellous pair they both made.

And, Ellie spotted, as the carriage set off, Bridezilla was grinning from ear to ear. Ellie nearly jumped up and made a huge air punch, but reined it in. Result! Thank you, Lauren, and *thank you*, Anthony.

When they returned twenty minutes later, Bridezilla was still smiling and waving regally (she'd obviously mastered the Queen's technique on the way round). The two equines, Lauren as carriage driver, the rather gorgeous Anthony, and a beaming Malcolm (who was taking all the credit of course) brought her back to a halt outside the castle steps once more. The only problem was when Patrick lifted his tail, farted and did a superb pile of pony poo right in Bridezilla's eyeline, just as she was about to dismount. Her face dropped for a nanosecond, but Anthony saved the day, reaching his hand out at just the right moment to help her down and take her mind right off what had just happened. Lauren was giggling, and

Malcolm was cursing Patrick between gritted teeth for taking the shine off the whole event at the last moment.

Anthony gave the bride a very gentlemanly kiss on the back of her hand, and passed her back to the gaggle of bridesmaids, who Ellie was certain were swooning on the steps. She gave him a grin and a thumbs up as she mouthed, 'Thank you, so much.' Then she was ready to take over for round two; the safe delivery of Bridezilla to the chapel and her groom.

The bride's father was here on the steps now too, which had initiated a quick exit from Bridezilla's mother. Apparently, the maid of honour filled Ellie in briefly, there had been a *very* bitter divorce some years back. Ellie might need to have a quiet word about the seating plan for top table then, and a quick rearrangement, or that might prove interesting. Why on earth hadn't they thought to tell her beforehand?

Right, all she had to do was get the bride, her father, and her bridesmaids in the right line-up and to the chapel. She checked her watch, 11:27 a.m., perfect. They had a couple of minutes' walk across the courtyard and up the steps into the main castle building. Then a further short walk along the corridor to the chapel, and that was it.

She'd give the bridal entourage a minute or two to gather themselves for now, and be a fashionable few minutes late . . . without panicking the groom. Mind you, if he had any sense at all, he'd have run a mile by now.

9

It still got to her, at every wedding she had attended as either a guest or coordinator, that moment when the music started up and the bride set off down the aisle (even if it was a Bridezilla!), all heads were turned expectantly and it was the groom's look that usually said it all. *And*, after all, there's someone for everyone, and *yes*, even this groom had a look of awe and love on his face. So, maybe it might work out well for them after all; though this groom was going to have his work cut out, bless him.

Ellie breathed out with a slow sigh of relief to have made it so far in the day relatively unscathed, and turned to see Joe beside her. He gave her a wink and squeezed her hand. She felt herself melt just a little. She hadn't realized, until that point, just how tense she must have been. Mind you, there was still plenty to do – a buffet to put the final touches too, and a top table to quickly rearrange, before it came to fisticuffs. Deana was staying in the chapel to keep an eye on things with the bride and groom, which released Ellie to make a quick dash to the Great Hall, and check on all the catering arrangements.

'Gotta go.' Ellie squeezed Joe's hand back.

'Already? I've only just caught up with you.' He looked a little disappointed.

'Sorry . . . I've still got loads to do.'

'Well, I'll go and check on everything in the marquee for later, in that case. I spotted Alan just before, he'll be setting up the bar for the evening in there. Just give me a shout if there's any last minute things you need for the Great Hall, too.'

'Will do. Catch you later.'

She sighed. They'd been ships in the night for the past few days. In fact, it seemed like they hardly had time for each other in the last few months, but she'd had so much to do on the run up to this demanding wedding, and with juggling the needs of a busy teashop too. Late nights, early starts, ordering catering supplies, making lunches, buffets, cakes and bakes. But she wouldn't complain, she loved her role, it was so far from her boring insurance work and her hemmed-in city life of five years ago. Usually the weddings took some organizing, but they were also fun and very satisfying to be part of. But this time, well, she couldn't wait for it all to be over and to just crash out on the sofa with Joe tomorrow evening. It might well end up being a tv and take-out night, and that would be just bliss.

The buffet was ready and looking quite stunning, she had to admit. Whole salmons, gammon joints, dressed crab, prawns and oysters, salads, new potatoes, an array of desserts. They just needed to lift the clingfilm covers away. The staff were all in place, ready for the off. And there was plenty of spare food made, ready to ferry up from the kitchens to keep the platters and salads topped up. It was self-serve, except for the top table, so they'd organized it in table order to keep the flow even. Okay, all was going to plan so far. She'd nip back to see the happy, (hopefully) just-wed couple coming out of the chapel.

There was to be a short lull after the service to give everyone a chance to chat, relax, and take a toilet break, before the official lineup where greetings and congratulations were given to the bride and groom. To do this, they would all file past the happy couple as they went into the Great Hall.

Malcolm loved taking over as master of ceremonies at this point, taking charge of the Wedding Breakfast, speeches, cutting of the cake – which gave him free rein to be theatrical, darling, and also gave Ellie a bit of timeout. Well, time to get the next mountain of food prepared – a late afternoon tea of scones, cake and delicate sandwiches to keep everyone going.

Ellie was one of the first to congratulate the couple and hung around subtly in the sidelines, in case she was needed to help in any way. Sure enough, just as the bridesmaids nipped off en masse to the loo, no doubt the morning's prosecco taking effect, and a need to reapply lipstick and tweak hairdos, Bridezilla started complaining about her shoes killing her. No wonder; Ellie had spotted the stilettos earlier when she'd hiked up on to the carriage via Anthony's palms – killer heels, six inches tall, and a spike that could do serious damage.

'Ellie,' she hissed. 'Ellie . . . my bloody feet. It's these wobbly stone floors, and all the bloody steps everywhere. Castle's a friggin' nightmare. I'm gonna have to swap my shoes. I've got some of those butterfly pumps in my handbag back in my room. Can you go and fetch them for me?'

'Yes, no problem. Which is your bag, in case there's more than one?'

'Black Mulberry, gold chain strap.'

'Okay, I'll just be a couple of minutes.'

'I don't know if I can last that long. I'm getting blisters.'

Ellie dashed off, leaving Bridezilla chatting with the best man. She had master keys, and flat shoes on, so got there in no time, located the bag and the pumps, and rushed back. Some of the bridal party had drifted across the landing towards the Great Hall. The large wooden doors to the hall were still closed at present, so as to make an impact and allow the last-minute preps to be completed. Two waitresses were stood either side of the entrance with trays of buck's fizz flutes ready to hand out to the guests, who would then file past the bride and groom, to greet them as a married couple. For now, guests were still mingling in the corridor and filing out of the chapel.

'Made it.' Ellie offered up the shoes, with a smile.

'Where's my chief bridesmaid, for Christ's sake? Hah, should have known it, look at her down there, it's *my* day and she's off chatting up the bloody ushers. *You'll* have to do it.' She thrust the butterfly pumps back at Ellie. 'Well, there's no way I can reach my feet in this dress.'

Ellie crouched down on her hands and knees to one side of the bride, trying to be discreet. The things you have to do as a wedding coordinator, honestly. She pulled up the massive hoop of the skirt, and popped her head in under; it felt very like a huge tent. A foot poked her, the pointy toe nearly hitting her in the eye. Bloody hell, she should be paid danger money. Right then, she carefully took the shoe off, and rolled the pump over the bride's slightly sweaty stockinged foot.

Just don't look up, she advised herself, *keep your mind on the task and get the hell out of here ASAP*. Who the hell knew if commando was in style for this particular bride?

Suddenly from under the muffling layers of taffeta and

silk, she heard Malcolm's boom, 'Ladies and Gentleman, please make an orderly line to greet your bride and groom.'

With that the whole skirt dropped down over and around Ellie. She received a kick, yes a *kick*, damn her, from the other stiletto, a prompt for her to get on and change it. Then, she heard muffles of 'Congratulations', 'Well done', 'You make such a lovely couple' and mwah, mwah kisses, from above. The bride was leaning over her now. *What the . . .*

Ellie lifted the other shoe quickly and slightly abruptly took it off, and slipped on the second ballet-style pump. *Now what . . .?* She'd need to get out somehow, but it would look awfully weird if she crept out into the waiting lineup of guests from under the bridal skirts, and possibly a bit pervy. She stayed put, still not looking up.

The file-by was in full swing, more mwah-ing, and a big hug from a male relative, it had to be, as there was a smell of stale beer and sweat from outside the wedding dress tent, accompanied by the bride being lifted off her feet – now that was interesting. As daylight entered Ellie's zone, she wondered if anyone might have caught a glimpse of her crouched under there. She stayed put for a while longer, feeling like a child playing a particularly embarrassing game of hide and seek.

Good God, this was going on forever. She *really* needed to get inside the Hall now, and check that everything was ready and absolutely perfect, as the guests began to take their places.

Right that was it, she was going to make her move. Still on her hands and knees, she shifted around the back side of the skirt, far less room here under the bridal buttocks, and she was getting a cricked neck. Slowly but surely, Ellie crawled out backwards. She darted a look around; only a small boy dressed in a cute navy suit had spotted her; he was holding onto his mother's hand in the line-up. Ellie gave him an 'It's our special secret' shushing-finger sign across her lips. He smiled shyly, and bless him didn't say a word, not then anyhow. He was definitely going to get extra cake later!

So, she was out. She stood up, partly shadowed by the bridal gown and shifted along to slip out from beside the groom, past the waitresses, into the Hall. Doris gave her an odd, and slightly relieved glance.

Joe quizzing, 'Where on earth have you been?'

'Don't ask . . . you *really* don't want to know. And if I did tell you, you probably wouldn't believe it.'

The buffet seemed to go to plan and there were lots of positive comments and 'mmms' as the guests tucked in. Yay!

There was the usual bustling, refilling of platters, clearing of plates, cutlery, topping up glasses, and general buzz as the staff dashed about whilst trying to look calm and orderly. Ellie gave a huge sigh of relief as she took a two-minute breather and a cup of strong tea at the teashop, served by Irene, who had stayed down in the kitchens, bless her, on a mammoth washing-up mission – she'd been matching the dishwasher plate for plate in speed.

Back up in the Great Hall, later, it was time for the speeches, orchestrated by a rather magnificent Malcolm, literally, his arms were going like the clappers every time he spoke. Ellie wasn't sure if it was nerves, or just general over-exuberance. And, then it was the moment for the wedding cake to be cut. Ta-da-daaah! Ellie held her breath.

It was a three-tiered, circular, rainbow-layered sponge cake, iced with white frosting and decorated with a scattering of coloured hearts and flowers that formed a rainbow-fade effect and increased in size as they wound down the cake tiers. The top tier had large icing letters of C and K (Chelsea and Kelvin) intertwined under an arch of icing rainbow, as requested by the bride, alongside a sugar paste unicorn. Rather gaudy, but pretty too; Ellie had given it her best shot. Each sponge cake had seven separately baked layers, of single rainbow colours, so when sliced through, you got a full rainbow sandwiched together with white frosting.

The bride and groom were there hand on hand ready to make the first cut. Ellie was anxiously waiting with a plate, ready to receive the first slice. It felt very like the showstopper moment on *Bake Off* where Mary Berry cuts into the creation, and the audience hold their breath waiting for the verdict. An even bake . . . moist sponge . . . soggy bottom . . .?

The knife went in smoothly to the top layer. Ellie tensed.

The cake came out in an even rainbow-layered slice, Bridezilla smiled broadly at her audience and her gaze settled on Ellie, who breathed again. *Yes!* Thank heavens for that, one more hurdle over.

There was a slight hiccup when one of the young waiters tried to carry too many plates, whilst clearing up, managing to drop the top three with a noisy smash that echoed around the hall. His face blushed crimson as Doris bustled in bearing a dustpan and brush, tutting, as she cleared the mess away swiftly.

Then it was time for everyone to either spill out into the gardens, pop back to their rooms for a nap or touch-up their make-up and hairdo. Alternatively, they could just stay in the Great Hall and help themselves to a cuppa, with tea and coffee urns and crockery set up at the far end of the room. Whilst that was going on, the staff rallied to clear the Great Hall, to get it set up once more for the afternoon tea at 3.30 p.m., and also to prepare the marquee for the evening entertainment and disco. The guests would be fit to bursting by the time the hog roast was served that evening. Meanwhile, Ellie realized she hadn't eaten a thing herself since her one slice of toast that morning. She gathered the waitresses and helpers in the kitchen, and announced they could all take a short break, telling them to help themselves to a plate she'd put aside of spare sandwiches and quiches, whilst she made up a huge pot of tea. Irene put out cups, saucers and plates ready for them to tuck in.

Joe popped down, grabbed a mug of tea and a sandwich, and kissed Ellie's cheek as he muttered 'Got to dash'. He was in charge of getting the marquee bar, the hog roast man and the band all in the right place and ready to start by 6.30 p.m. for the evening do. A further forty guests were coming along then too. He had Colin, young James – who still worked for them at the castle, though he was doing a lot more on the farm these days – and a couple of lads from the village roped in, to set out tables, chairs, and more. The marquee people had erected a small stage area and a dance floor. Wendy was busy displaying even more flowers in the marquee, transferring some from the hall, and keeping them fresh with spritzes of cool water, as the day and the tent was turning warm.

The afternoon flew by and they were all back in the Great Hall before they knew it, serving afternoon tea. Plates and cake stands were stacked with dainty sandwiches, cakes, scones, clotted creams and jams, and beautiful cupcakes that Ellie, Irene and Doris had spent a couple of hours decorating with more rainbow-coloured hearts and tiny icing flowers. Unfortunately, some of the younger members of the party were getting bored by then, just as the older members were becoming fuzzy with champagne and prosecco. A cupcake fight had broken out on a table near the bride, three children launching the sugary missiles and giggling. Boomph, one landed on the feathered fascinator of one of the guests and slid down into her lap. She looked up aghast.

'Step away from the cupcakes!' Doris boomed at the two flower girls and the mini usher, who had started throwing the food. Food that *she* had helped bake and decorate no less!

Bridezilla intervened with a simpering, 'They're only children, they're just playing.'

The white-frosting smeared guest shook her head at the bride's comment, but seemed a little afraid to speak up for herself and her ruined outfit.

Doris fixed Bridezilla with one of her trademark stares, that was then aimed at each of the children in turn. Oh Lord, her hands were on her hips too, Ellie knew all the signs, she'd worked with her long enough. *Don't mess with Doris.*

'There are children starving in Africa, missy,' Doris's finger was wagging determinedly. 'So, I suggest you put that cake, that you have in your hand, back on your plate and eat it. *All* of it. And *you* young man, can go and fetch a napkin and pass it to the lady whose dress you have spoilt. And if you can point out your parents or whoever you're with . . .' Her voice raised, as he lifted his hand to point at a man and woman at the next table, 'Perhaps they can offer to pay for this poor woman's dry cleaning bill.' Doris gave one of her cool but meaningful smiles at the couple, who seemed to shrink under her glare, then her focus settled back on Bridezilla.

There was a stunned silence. Ellie waited for Bridezilla to blow. But no, she looked rather shocked, but said nothing. Perhaps she'd finally met her match.

'Right then, anyone for a top up of tea?' Doris offered. Matter closed, the room returned to a buzz of chatter again. The children sat back down and quietly ate a cupcake each, then went off to play outside in the gardens – a much better idea all round.

Other than a whirl of clearing plates, and tidying the Great Hall and the teashop kitchens, Ellie had it slightly easier for the evening event, being on hand for advice and general assistance if need be. The bridesmaid's wing had been reunited with its electricity supply, phew, so the guests all had their rooms back, and so far, all seemed to be well.

Ellie looked in on the marquee mid-evening, after finishing her mammoth, kitchen-cleaning session. The chords of 'Love Me Like You Do' by Ellie Goulding were striking up; she had got here just in time to see Kelvin take Chelsea's hand to lead her (and the dress) across the floor for the first dance. The bride was actually smiling, and finally seemed relaxed – possibly something to do with a bucketful of champagne. But, she looked happy and was enjoying her moment. Her groom was smiling broadly too, and after quashing down the many-layered skirt, took his bride into his arms and they started their slow, shuffle-dance together, lost in their world of two for a while.

'I'm awarding that man a medal.' Joe came up beside Ellie.

'Yeah, but, they look happy. There's someone for everyone. Good luck to them.'

'He'll need it.' Joe smiled.

The dance floor was a soft whirl of rainbow colours from the disco light, there were gorgeous flower displays, coloured ribbons twirled around posts, balloons, sparkles from the table confetti, and the marquee looked rather magical at that moment. The bar was bustling, and the guests seemed relaxed. The younger children joined in on the dance floor, and then other couples started waltzing on too.

Phew, they had done it – just about pulled off this wedding, Ellie felt, by the skin of their teeth. She held on to Joe's hand as they stood for a few minutes to watch the occasion.

There were fairy lights guiding the way between the

marquee and the Great Hall. And the stone-walled castle stood behind them, majestic and rather beautiful, even with its quirky electrics and trip-you-up winding stair-wells. It was just such an amazing place for a wedding.

Hopefully, Ellie's evening would be less stressful from now. To be honest, the bride had had that much champagne, she had mellowed. Unfortunately, the alcohol had the opposite effect on her mother. All appeared to be going well, the first dance, disco, hog roast, bar, until the obligatory wedding punch-up broke out. And no, it wasn't the adolescent young men who got carried away after too many lagers. It was in fact, Bridezilla's dad who ended up with the black eye and bleeding nose, as a parting shot from his ex-wife, for daring to bring along his latest 'floozy' to the wedding, despite the fact the young woman had actually been invited by Bridezilla in the first place. Families, hey!

After helping Joe move tables and stack chairs after the disco and band made their exit, and checking that the remaining guests seemed fine, Ellie finally got to bed at 2 a.m.. The duvet she snuggled into and the soft mattress beneath her felt *sooo* good.

10

'I didn't get a wink of bloody sleep all night.' Lord Henry trounced into the teashop at 8.15 a.m., where the morning-after wedding breakfast was to be served, but as yet none of the wedding party had made it out of their beds.

Ellie was setting out sauces for the bacon breakfast rolls and juice glasses on the tables, with jugs of fresh orange and apple juice waiting on the counter for the off.

'Why do they have to be so bloody noisy? All night. All *bloody* night. Boom-boom of the disco, the scraping of chairs, shouting, laughing, and then, just as I manage to get my first forty winks in, bloody fireworks, fireworks I tell you, at midnight. Well that was it, it sounded like shrapnel going off, like I was in some war film, woke me up and that was that. *Then*, I had to listen to the chatter of those damned bridesmaids in the rooms beneath me. Nightmare.'

'Sorry, Henry, it's a necessary evil. We really need these wedding events to finance the castle. They bring in more money than anything else we do.' Ellie tried to appease him.

'Well, I think I'm going to book a night in the bloody Swan Inn in the village next time. Get myself away from it all.'

'That might not be such a bad idea . . .' Ellie smiled. 'Cup of coffee, Henry?'

She had dropped the 'Lord' title, now she was his daughter-in-law. It had taken a while; it had just seemed wrong, too familiar at first, but gradually and after he'd insisted on it, it had become the norm. He was still a quirky old soul, very private; after his wife had died, he'd been very much a hermit at the castle for many years. But now, with the truth that he was Joe's father revealed, and having spent time with Joe and Ellie in recent years in a family-type environment, though a rather disjointed one, (he hadn't known of Joe's existence until after his son's eighteenth birthday), he had grown closer to them both. Every couple of weeks Ellie would cook for them all, and he'd come across to their apartment for a roast dinner, or some supper. He also popped into the teashop regularly, partly to see how things were going, but often leaving with some quiche or a filled jacket potato and a slice of cake for his lunch or supper. They rubbed along quite well really.

She wondered for a second, what kind of grandfather he would make. She hoped they would get the chance one day to find out.

'Yes, please, Ellen. Coffee would be lovely.' Though she had dropped the Lord, he had never lost her misnomer. From day one he had called her Ellen instead of Ellie – it was just one of those things, a quirk of his nature. It used to annoy Ellie, but she was fine with it now; it sounded more like a term of affection. 'May as well stay awake now,' he continued.

Doris came through, stifling a yawn herself. 'Morning, Lord Henry.'

'Morning, Doris.'

By the looks of it, they were all looking forward to a good night's sleep tonight, but before that there was a breakfast to serve, the kitchens to clean up, and the usual prep to do to get everything back to normal for tomorrow's tearooms. It was going to be another full-on day.

'I'll put the pizza on, shall I?'

'Oh yes, that'd be great. Do you mind? I've seen enough food in the past two days. We could have fed an army with it all. And there's still leftovers, but I'm really not in the mood for a prawn vol-au-vent or a rainbow cupcake.'

She felt shattered, but it was bliss to sink into her sofa

back in their castle apartment, knowing all the hard work was done, and thankful that it had finally gone well. Deana had told her not to worry about the *Daily Star* threat and *BRIDES* magazine, joking that the bride's so-called friend probably only made the tea there anyhow. And actually, before Bridezilla left in her Bentley, to be delivered plus groom to the airport for her honeymoon in the Seychelles (God bless the hotel staff she'd be staying with), she . . . yes, believe it or not, thanked them for her lovely wedding day. So hopefully, Ellie and the castle team had managed to turn things around.

In the end, the wedding had gone better than anyone had imagined. And the 'Happy Couple' had finally left the castle at 3 p.m., along with the last of their guests. Off to the Seychelles, lucky devils, ooh yes, Ellie could just imagine lying on a sunlounger with an azure blue sky above her, right now.

She'd have a bath in a while, soak her tired limbs, but all she wanted to do for now was stay on this squishy, oh-so-comfy sofa . . . and not move.

Joe walked back in from their kitchen with a tired-but-gorgeous smile on his face, and she realized with a warm, fuzzy feeling that she actually had everything she wanted right here. She patted the seat next to her. 'Come here you. I need a hug.'

He sat down beside her, wrapping his strong arms around her, and she leaned back against him.

'You okay?' he spoke softly above her head.

'Yeah,' she answered sleepily.

'You did a great job this weekend. It all went really well in the end, didn't it? Only blips were electrics and the fight, but hey, that last one was way outside of our control . . . The women in that family are pretty scary, huh?'

'Hmm.'

'You going to make it through 'til pizza?'

Ellie just nodded. Speaking was becoming too much of an effort.

He kissed the top of her head.

And she found herself in a world of baking/serving/rainbow-cake/unicorn dreams.

When she came to, it had got dark, there was just the glow of lamplight in the room. Joe had covered her with a soft blanket, and he was sat in the armchair opposite, so as not to disturb her. He looked so handsome sat there watching the tv which was turned down low, unaware at that moment that she had woken. His thick dark hair, the fringe which was a tad floppy but she loved, tumbling across his forehead – it was rather nice running your hands through that. Hazel eyes that were kind and sexy all at once, his tall physique, and long legs in denim jeans angled out in front of him.

He must have sensed her looking. 'Ah ha, and so she returns to the land of the living. Do you know you've missed three days?'

'Hah, very funny . . .' Her stomach then gurgled and groaned.

'See, told you. You're withering away.'

'Fine chance of that.' She had always been on the larger side of twelve, namely a size fourteen. It would take more than three days to wither, she knew that only too well.

'Well, I don't want any withering. Those delightful breasts need a preservation order on them.' He grinned.

She smiled back. Over time, she had learnt that he loved her just the way she was.

'So, it's just as well I saved you some pizza, then.' He got up and headed for the kitchen. 'Fancy it now?'

'Please, I'm starving.'

He handed her the plate which he'd warmed in the microwave, and sat down beside her whilst she ate. The pizza had gone a bit chewy, but was still tasty.

'Well, some event that was,' he said. 'Glad *that* wedding's over with, anyhow. At least it went fine in the end, didn't it? You did great, Ellie. Don't know how you kept your cool sometimes. What a nightmare she was to work with.'

'Our first Bridezilla.'

'Let's hope she's the last.'

'I wouldn't count on it. I think wedding planning and stress brings out the worst in some people.'

'Ye-es.'

'But then there's others who are so lovely . . .' She sighed. 'I wonder how Dan and Lucy are getting on?'

'Yeah, let's hope he makes a great recovery, and they get their big day soon.'

'They really do deserve that.'

He kissed the top of her head, as she snuggled in a bit closer. His arms were around her and he smelt rather gorgeously of aftershave and Joe, with a hint of pizza.

She turned, tilted her head towards his and their eyes met. She felt such a warmth, such connection, all her senses suddenly seemed alert. She pressed her lips against his, this was becoming so familiar now and yet more beautiful than ever in moments like these. The kiss, full, tender and passionate, awakening something within her even though she was tired and her limbs aching.

She pulled back to look at him, then placed her finger-tips on his cheek which was slightly rough with stubble. 'I love you, Joe.'

'I love you too. So much.'

The honesty in those words made her melt, and then ache a little inside.

She pressed herself closer to him. It was like the world had come down to just the two of them. And she suddenly realized that she wanted all of him, was ready to give all of her, right now. Slowly, she undid the top two buttons of his shirt, placing her palm against his chest, tracing fingertips over those lean, firm muscles.

She felt him stirring beneath her, in just the right place. They were still both on the sofa. She smiled at him, saw his grin back. Kissing, touching, her hands through his hair, his hands firm on her back, then tracing her spine through her clothes, reaching down to her buttocks. She felt the warmth of passion and her yearning for him unfolding within. The knowledge that he wanted her too, turning her on even more.

Her blouse now off, bra still on. He was touching her breast beneath its lace, couldn't hold back his gasp as her nipple hardened under his touch. She was tugging off his trousers, his boxers, kneeling over him, needing to feel him within her.

It was urgent, and sleepy, and sexy all at once.

She collapsed down against his chest, wrapped up in his arms, one of his legs propped over hers. They lay on the sofa in a sated, though slightly uncomfortable, heap.

'Well, that was unexpected . . .'

'Yeah, surprised myself there, too.' She was amazed how her energy levels had zapped up there.

'I have this effect on women,' he joked, his words murmured in to the top of her hair, as she lay against him.

'Tired now, though,' she muttered as she began to doze in the warm, safety of her husband's arms.

'Yeah, me too. Bed?'

'Bed. Definitely . . . Perfect.'

11

It was full steam-clean ahead.

Ellie popped her head around the door to the bridal suite, shouting over the sound of the vacuum cleaner. 'You okay, Sue? Anything you need?'

'Hey, hi, Ellie. I'm fine, pet. Head down and busy, busy.' Joe's mum switched off the hoover and smiled. She and her cleaning company, The Clean Team, had taken over the castle housekeeping after the bigger events, such as weddings. She'd travel from her home an hour away in Newcastle-upon-Tyne, with one of her trusted staff, stay overnight and blitz all the guest rooms over two days.

At other times, for the general cleaning of the visitor rooms and displays, they hired two ladies from the village to keep the castle spruced up.

Sue had been anxious about coming up to the castle at first – there was so much past history for her there. But now that her affair with Lord Henry was open knowledge, and with the passing of time, things had become easier. Coming back to Claverham Castle for Ellie and Joe's wedding, after all those years away, had broken the ice. The years had passed and eased old hurts. Life had moved on for all of them. She and Henry made conversation fairly comfortably now if they both happened to be invited to Ellie and Joe's for a family meal, or at other castle events.

Life could take you places you never imagined, and relationships evolved. This crazy, beautiful journey we are all on. There would still be memories, of course, some love affairs never really left you, not when the relationships had meant something special. And theirs, of course, had produced a child. And Ellie, for one, was so glad it had.

'Wow, I've found all sorts under this bed.'

'Don't tell me, I really don't want to know.'

Sue bent double, then from under the king-size bed frame, pulled out a scrap of lacy thong which she held cautiously between finger and thumb and dropped into a bin bag, along with a half-eaten bacon sandwich. They grimaced, then both laughed.

'It was an interesting wedding to say the least,' Ellie commented.

'This wasn't the Bridezilla one, was it?'

'Oh yes . . .'

'No wonder you lot are all looking shattered. I did think Joey was a bit pale this morning. And Henry, we had a chat in the corridor just before, he was in a right grump about not getting any sleep for two days.'

'A slight exaggeration. But yes they were a rowdy lot, and it was very full-on trying to keep them all happy. But hey, it's all done now. And the final cheque is ready to bank, so that's a relief.'

'They'll be coming back for the Christening party next.'

'Don't even go there . . .' And with that, Ellie felt that little pang of longing again. Though she hadn't even told Sue about them trying for a baby, and how difficult it was proving to be, she felt herself heat up, her face surely reddening.

And remembering last night, making love in every beautiful sense of the word, maybe, just maybe . . . She felt herself blush even more, thinking about Sue's son in *that way* in her presence seemed a little wrong. But, she was sure Sue would make a lovely Granny. Her mother-in-law was polite enough not to have ever mentioned anything or pushed for information on their parenting plans, but Ellie knew she would be thrilled should it ever happen. One day . . .

'Right, I'd better get back to the teashop. We open in half an hour, so it'll be all go, and I haven't had chance to bake my brownies yet. Going to try a new recipe today, melting-mint and dark chocolate. You'll have to take a break and pop in and try one with a cup of coffee later.'

'They sound divine. I'll crack on for now, but I'll definitely be there later on.'

'And come and have supper with us tonight, yes? I'll make a lasagne or something.'

'You sure? You've had loads on. We could get a takeout. I'm happy to pay.'

'Thanks Sue, but no. I'd like to cook for us. I'll prepare the lasagne at the teashop this morning. I'll be making some for there too. We'll have it as a special on the lunch menu.'

'Well, in that case, yes, it sounds lovely. Thank you, Ellie.'

Ellie felt lucky that she got on well with Sue. It wasn't that dreaded mother/daughter-in-law clash that some of her girlfriends had experienced. Gemma, her friend and ally from the insurance office years ago, had landed a rather ferocious woman as her mother in-law, who always seemed armed and ready with pointed remarks – no woman could possibly look after her little boy as well as she ever had. Gemma dreaded the monthly visit, saying it was like going to visit a temperamental Rottweiler most of the time. Yes, Ellie was very grateful for kind and chatty Sue. They had clicked from day one.

'Wow, that smells gorgeous! All minty and dark chocolatey at once.'

Ellie looked up from rolling out shortbread dough.

'Oh yes, it's my new brownie recipe, made with After Eights. They're on their last few minutes in the oven.'

'I'm gonna have to try one.' Sue smiled.

'Of course. You can be my official taster . . . Have you got time for a quick coffee?'

'Yes, I'd love one. That's the bridesmaids' rooms and the bridal suite all done, anyhow. It's amazing how much mess a few people can make in two days.'

'Tell me about it . . .' Ellie raised her eyebrows.

'Well, hey-ho, that's how I earn my living, so I'll not complain.'

'It's fairly quiet in the teashop for now, so I'll join you for a quick break. I'll make us a coffee from the machine. Just give me a moment to finish this shortbread.' She sliced up the biscuit base into fingers, laid them out on a papered baking tray and pricked them over with a fork.

She then checked her timer and took out a large tray of the brownies. She gave the bake a gentle prod, yes, just at the right stage where the top was crispy and slightly cracked, revealing the gooey mint-chocolatey middle. Perfect. Once they had cooled she'd cut them into squares. Her brownies were getting famous in the local area, and sometimes not so local. She'd had a request to send some down to London last year. She made dark chocolate and orange, raspberry and white chocolate, salted caramel was a newer addition, and the good old double-chocolate recipe.

Daniel, the poor chap who'd had the accident, had raved about the salted caramel ones. She'd make a batch of those next. She planned on a trip to Newcastle soon to visit her family, now that the wedding from hell was over. If Dan was still in the Royal Infirmary she could pop by and cheer him up with a goodie bag full of them.

Over a soothing cup of Americano with a splash of frothy milk, the two ladies chatted and tested out the new flavour.

'Absolutely delish!' Sue grinned.

'Pretty good with a cup of coffee, I must say.'

'And that melty-minty-middle, a delight. You're on to a winner there, Ellie.'

They broke off another chocolatey corner each. Good job she was always bustling about, Ellie mused, she'd be the size of a house with all these scrummy cakes and bakes around her day-in day-out. But boy, it was a just the best job sometimes. And *someone* had to try them.

'So are you and Joe okay, then? Looks like you've had a really busy time here lately,' Sue asked kindly.

'Yes, we're both fine. Thanks, Sue.' Ellie was aware she wasn't quite telling her the whole story. 'And how are you? How's the cleaning business been going?'

'Life at the sharp end of a duster and hoover. Ah, it's great. I've got so much work coming in, it's hard to keep up with it all though. Just taken on a new contract for the care home down the road in Heaton. Twelve bedrooms and all the main living areas too. In fact, before I go tomorrow, I'll buy some of that fruit cake you have there on the side, it looks great. The residents at the home would enjoy a piece of that.'

'It'll certainly make them sleep well.' Ellie grinned. 'Got a rather large splash of brandy in,' she explained. 'It was meant to be Bridezilla's wedding cake. Long story.'

'Aah.'

'At least you had your break away to Vegas.'

'Well, I've got my five lovely ladies that work for me. So they kept everything going at The Clean Team in my absence.'

'Yeah, it's so important to have a good team behind you. We're lucky to have some great staff here too. So, tell me all about the holiday then. The sights, the desert, casinos. Sounds like you had a fabulous time.'

'We did indeed, me and Marge had a blast. Did I tell you about the Texan tycoon in the gambling hall?' She chortled. 'Tycoon my arse, I'm sure he was a waiter from another hotel, posing as whatever, hoping for a good night, if you know what I mean ... A Stetson, an American drawl and a wodge of notes don't mean a lot. Well, I brought him a bit of luck at the roulette table, but that was the only lucky break he was getting from me. We dashed off when he nipped to the loo.'

Ellie could picture the pair of them, both well into

their sixties, best friends, no doubt giggling like school-girls as they made their escape. She laughed at the image.

'And you, Ellie. How are you, pet? If you don't mind me saying you look a bit peaky, darling.'

'Oh, I'm fine. It's just been a long week. I'm tired, that's all. It's been pretty nonstop lately.'

'Ah, yes. And you'll be on your feet all day.'

'Yep. But it'll ease off a bit now. The main summer season is over. We only have two more weddings booked now this year, one October and one mid-November. And they're much smaller affairs, thirty people at the next one, and only twenty-four for the one after. The first wedding want a full silver-service sit-down dinner, so we'll be hiring outdoor caterers for that which takes the pressure off me and the teashop staff. The second is fairly straightforward menu-wise. So, I'll enjoy co-ordinating them and making sure everyone has a great day. Honestly, they'll seem easy, after this weekend's malarkey.'

'Well, make sure you look after yourself. Or get my Joey looking after you, at least.'

'I will, and he's pretty good, really. He helps cook sometimes, and he's not bad with a hoover and duster.'

'Learnt something from me, then,' she grinned. 'Right, on that note, I'd better step back to it.'

'Me too. Catch you later, and this evening, just pop up whenever you're ready. Supper'll be around sevenish.'

'That sounds lovely. If you're sure it's not too much trouble. I brought up a bottle of wine with me just in case, so I'll bring it along.'

'Perfect.'

Sue stayed over in Ellie's old room, which was on the floor below their apartment. It was really handy for her when she visited, or came to work for them after the functions.

'See you later.'

Ellie took a plate of the now-cooled brownies through to the teashop to add to the counter display. It was a smaller selection than normal, after the hectic weekend they had had, but there was fruit cake – a tipsier version than usual, being the wedding cake Bridezilla had ordered and then cancelled in favour of the rainbow sponge. Irene had made some scones first thing; a savoury Red Leicester-and-herb, and her fabulous fruit ones packed with sultanas. Irene had popped home for an hour, after her early start and busy weekend of work, but was going to be back soon to make some of her quiches ready for lunchtime.

Doris was at the counter taking an order from a local couple who often came in with their little girl, Katie.

'Mint-choc brownies,' Ellie mentioned, as she passed behind Doris, 'Fresh from the oven.'

'Oh, we'll have to try one of those as well, then. So two teas, a juice, Katie's favourite chocolate cake with extra sprinkles and one of the brownies. Thanks.' The woman smiled across at Ellie.

It was lovely cheering people up with your baking creations.

12

The weather was beginning to cool. September turning autumnal as October approached. The leaves on the trees already turning golden, with a hint of russet. The apples were ripening in the castle orchard. They'd have a good crop by the looks of it, so lots of crumble on the menu, and some of her windfall apple cake, with brown sugar and raisins through it. Ellie liked the shift in the seasons. The mad rush of the summer tourists trade slowing to a steadier stream of customers, and she and Joe had chance to see a bit more of each other, to enjoy their nights in by the real fire.

The castle closed to the day-to-day tourists early November after their end-of-season fireworks event, opening only for weddings or functions over the winter months. Though that gave them some much needed time off, and Lord Henry was happy as he loved getting rid of the 'invaders' as he called the tourists, it meant in reality that funds were often tight, during that time. They really needed to think of something else to help tide them over that slower period.

They were in the castle Monday Meeting, the last Monday in September.

'A Christmas Craft Fayre, that's what we need. That'd draw people in,' Doris piped up.

Actually, it wasn't a bad idea. Far better than Malcolm's children's party venue suggestion. Lord Henry had nearly had a fit at that.

'Yes,' Doris was on a roll, 'we could invite local craft stalls to come along, Christmas cards, jams, there's a guy makes lovely wood carvings and decorations. I bet Wendy would do some nice Christmas wreaths. And I've a cousin makes wonderful knitted mice and hedgehogs, and such like.'

'Hmm, I could put on mince pies and mulled wine, as well as opening up the teashop with lots of festive favourites. Oh, and hot chocolates with cream and marshmallows.'

'Ooh, you could sell that fudge you make and mini shortbreads.' Derek added. 'I love that, I could get some for Mum and Auntie Glenda.'

'The Great Hall would be a fabulous venue,' Malcolm joined in. 'Tinsel and tiffin.'

Everyone bar Ellie gave him an odd look. 'You know, that biscuit stuff, could even be "Tinsel, tiffin and tray bakes".'

'Christmas at the Castle has a good ring to it.' Joe piped up, obviously warming to the idea.

'When do you think? Early or mid-November, whilst Christmas is in everyone's minds, but they haven't yet bought all their gifts?' Deana joined in the conversation.

'Yes, why not make it a couple of weeks before our last wedding booking. So, say the second weekend of November. A Saturday is always a good day,' Ellie added.

'Agh, blimey. I'll have even more people traipsing around the castle. They'll be here all bloody winter at this rate. We'll never get a moment's peace.' Lord Henry was rubbing his forehead agitatedly with his hand.

'It's actually a really good idea, Henry. It'll bring in some extra income just when we need it. And, it'll be good as a community event, bring everyone together. We could get the local schoolkids over to sing carols on the courtyard . . .' Joe said.

'I thought we were avoiding children?' Lord H was definitely disgruntled.

'Then,' Joe continued, on a roll, 'All the parents will come along and hopefully pop into the tearooms or buy some Christmas gifts too. It's a great idea, Doris, well done.'

'I suppose you'll be wanting me to dress up as bloody

Father Christmas next,' Lord Henry grumbled, sarcastically.

'Well . . .' Joe pretended to consider it.

'Hah, no chance. You'd frighten all the kids away,' Malcolm was grinning. 'Come Christmas Eve, they'd all be terrified of you coming down the chimney.'

They all laughed.

Meeting over, they came away with lots of ideas for a Christmas event on their minds, then it was back to work as usual. A normal week lay ahead in the teashop. It was nice just to have time to catch up with some of her regular customers, Jim and Mavis were in a couple of times, so Ellie took the chance to chat with them. There was also a pair of young mums who came in for tea and cake every once in a while, with their babies in their prams. Ellie often said hello and had a chat with them. This time, one of the little boys became unsettled and Ellie offered to hold him for a while. She enjoyed her cuddle, taking in that gorgeous baby-lotion smell. She was soon able to settle him again, giving his mum a few minutes peace to finish her slice of coffee and walnut cake.

It was lovely to have the time once more to really enjoy the teashop, to bake without any pressure, try a few new recipes, and to get a good night's sleep at the end of the day. She and Joe usually took a Tuesday off, generally being the quietest day at the castle. Doris and Irene managed well between them, and in high season they'd often have an extra waitress in too. In the summer months Joe and Ellie would just take the one day, and at the busiest times none at all, but as the autumn drew in, it was lovely to be able to take two days together. The chance for a proper chill-out, or to go walking in the countryside or on the wonderful, windswept golden beaches nearby, or to have a cosy pub lunch at one of the local villages. It also gave them the opportunity to go a little further afield.

'I'd like to pop down and visit my family soon, Joe. Maybe next week? We could stay over on the Tuesday night or something? What do you think?'

'Fine by me.'

'I'd really like to go to the hospital to see Dan too. I spoke to Lucy in the week and she says he's back in the RVI for a further operation. His leg's been shattered in that many places, it's going to be a long process. He's not been able to go back to work, or anything yet.'

'What a bloody shame. Must have been a horrendous accident. Yeah, we should go see him. Definitely.'

13

Rows and rows of brick terraced houses, the slow crawl and drone of traffic, a convenience store, coffee shop, people milling about the pavements; suburbia.

Ellie hardly noticed these things when she lived here five years ago, but already she felt a bit hemmed in. She was missing the wide-open spaces, the green, brown and golden hues of the countryside, and those big blue-grey Northumberland skies. Her life at the castle seemed a world away from where she had been brought up.

Heading along the Chillingham Road now, pausing for the traffic lights, then a final turn into Fifth Avenue. They parked up in a space just along from No. 5, Ellie's family home in the Heaton area of Newcastle-upon-Tyne. They walked the five paces through the small square of front garden that dad had paved and put welcoming pots of geraniums and petunias on. It was neat and tidy, and cheery.

No need to knock. Dad was already there with her brother Jason too, both in their work-wear navy boiler suit, the sign on the van outside now proudly sporting, J Hall & Son, Plumbers. Dad scooped Ellie up in a bear hug as always, lifting her feet off the ground; even at the age of thirty-one, she didn't escape his demonstrative affections. And that was fine with Ellie.

'Good to see you, 'wor lass.' He put her back down. 'My, you're as light as a feather. You looking after yourself all right?'

'Yes, of course, Dad. It's you getting bigger, not me getting smaller.' There seemed to be rather a lot of tummy inside that boiler suit.

'Ah, it's my six-pack. Well could be more like an eight-pack nowadays?' He gave a wink.

'Think it's more like a buy one, get one free,' Jason taunted. For which he received a sharp clip round the ear, despite the fact that he was now twenty-six.

'Joe. All right, son?' He grasped his hand in a firm shake, whilst giving him a resounding pat on the back with his other palm.

'Yep, fine.' Joe sounded slightly winded.

'We were just passing on the way to another job. I said to Jay, we'd pop by on the chance you were here already. We'll stop for a quick cuppa with you, and then get on again. We're working at that new housing estate down past the old gas works.'

'Oh, okay. Good.'

'Hi, Els, Joe. You okay?' Jason was still a man of few words.

Jason had joined his dad in learning a trade, and they now worked together in their plumbing business, which seemed to mostly go fine. He had ambitions to train up as an electrician too, widen his skills. His hair had been cut recently, short sides, long top, gelled carefully across. He seemed to be taking far more care of his appearance lately, and his aftershave was fresh and full-on to say the least. No doubt something to do with the new girlfriend, Carmel, who'd actually lasted a few months now. Ellie had met her on her last visit back, and she seemed a really nice girl; bubbly, friendly and with feet well on the ground, which would suit Jay.

'Hello, hello. Come on in. Shift out the way lads, let them get through. I've just put the kettle on.' Mum beckoned them through, and gave them both a neat-but-happy kiss on the cheek.

The five of them sat at the kitchen table, with a nice strong cup of tea in front of them, and a plate of biscuits. Somehow Mum still managed to find those Garibaldi ones that Dad loved but no one else seemed to – the 'crushed-fly' biscuits that Ellie and Jason used to avoid in their childhood. Luckily, there were also some custard creams put out, so Ellie helped herself to one of those. They watched as Dad dunked a crushed-fly into his tea; Ellie and Jay shared a grimace and then a wry smile. For a second or two, she felt like she'd been transported back to when she was twelve again.

'I've got a nice cottage pie in the oven.'

Oh yes, it would either be cottage pie, a stew, or a roast for visitors depending on the time of year or the occasion. Ellie would probably have fainted if mum had offered her a Thai curry or some fajitas. And in fact, that predictability, that routine, was fine and kind of reassuring.

'Thanks, Mum.'

'Sounds lovely, Sarah.'

There was bound to be an apple crumble ready for dessert too, with lashings of tinned Devon Custard, mmm. It was great not to have to cook for once, a whole day off from the tearoom baking and prepping, though she genuinely loved it there, was wonderful. They were at that slightly jaded time in the season, at the end of the summer, when you'd been working long days with only one day off a week for months. And, with the wedding events getting busier, though that was great for the castle finances, it all took its toll on the small team of staff.

'How's it all going, then? How's life at the castle?'

'It's great. All going well, thanks Mum.'

'And how did that big wedding go off? I was thinking

of you over the weekend. Wasn't that the one with the stressy bride?'

Bridezilla's reputation had gone before her.

'Yeah, she was still a bit stressy, but it all went off fine in the end. Wouldn't want many more like that one, mind.'

'Sounds like you're doing a great job, lass.'

'She certainly is,' Joe confirmed.

'Bet that big castle keeps you busy too, Joe. Lot of land with it to look after, and everything. How's that boiler system getting on, by the way? Never seen anything quite like that one. I'm usually fixing up three or four bed-roomed houses. That was a different kettle of fish. Like something out of the Victorian era.'

'Yep, well it probably is. Has its challenges. '

Ellie's dad had offered to help with the various castle plumbing issues over the years. He was always fascinated by what quirks the system turned up, and the issues they faced. It wasn't so fascinating to Ellie, who often had to put up with the hot water running out at just the wrong time, mid-shower being the classic. They had invested in a new system to cope with the refurbished guest wing, but their own quarters still left an awful lot to be desired.

'Still playing your footie, Jay?' Joe asked.

'Yeah, just in the local Saturday league. We're second at the moment. It's a good group. Bit of banter with the lads. I like it.'

'I need you working this Saturday by the way son, big job at the new housing estate.'

'Agh, Dad.'

'Work comes first, son. You need to earn your keep.'

'Saving up for his own house, so he is,' Mum added.

'Ooh, that's news.' He'd lived at home for years and was now twenty-six, but was always happy to be cooked and cleaned for, and looked after by mum. 'Is Carmel anything to do with this new state of affairs?'

'Might be.'

'Hah, you loved up old thing you.' Ellie gave him a friendly punch on his arm.

'She's a lovely girl is Carmel. It's about time he settled down.' Mum gave her seal of approval.

'Be wedding bells soon, son. You'd better start saving some more. I've got plenty of overtime for you.'

'Thanks.' He was blushing.

Must be serious. Ellie thought of the other wedding that should have happened back in the summer. 'We're going to pop over and see Daniel in the morning.'

'Oh yes, that lad who had that terrible motorcycle accident you were telling me about? How is he?' Mum asked.

'Well, not so good. But he is making a slow recovery. He's back in the RVI hospital for a follow-up operation. Had to have his leg pinned and everything. Sounded really nasty.'

'Bless him. Motorbikes are such dangerous things though. Glad you never got into it.' She gave Jason a sharp look.

'I don't think it was Dan's fault, to be fair. Lorry veered too far across the road on a bend, clipped him and took him right out,' Ellie explained.

'God, that must have been frightening,' Jason commented.

'Yeah.'

'My mate Nick's got a bike now. He's always saying how people are right idiots on the road. They're just not aware of other road users . . . off in their own little worlds. That's what's dangerous.'

'Yes, but on a bike there's no protection around you, whoever's fault it is,' Sarah continued. 'It's just you and the road if you come off, doesn't bear thinking about . . . that poor boy.' She shook her head, worried about the state of the world and the poor people in it. 'Another biscuit anyone?'

Dad headed for a second garibaldi. Joe and Ellie declined.

'Well, on to happier news, your cousin Lynn's just had her new baby. A little girl, and she's absolutely gorgeous. Seven pound nine ounces . . . Her first . . .' she added for Joe's benefit. 'You must call in and see them, Ellie. I've knitted a cardigan. You could take it around for me.'

'Yes, okay. Oh, how lovely.' Ellie felt a prickle in her throat as she spoke. *One day . . .*

14

'Go right on in.' The young nurse smiled, as she gestured towards the side room of the ward.

The door they faced was pale turquoise; the exact shade of an egg that Ellie had found in her back garden as a child. Her dad had told her it was most likely a robin's, dropped out of the nest. The shell was fragile, so pretty. Ellie had kept it stored in cotton wool in a warm place at the bottom of her bedroom cupboard; it never hatched. The balance of life was so delicate.

She took a slow breath, felt Joe's gentle hand on her shoulder, as she pushed the door handle. Through the circle of safety glass she could see Daniel, propped up in bed. As she stepped into the room, the full impact of his injuries were apparent. Grazes were healing on his face even now, and one wrist was bandaged. But it was the sight of his leg laid out on the bed before him that took

Ellie's breath away, making her feel giddy for a second or two. Protruding from the skin of the lower shin right up to the knee, she could see about sixteen metal rods and bolts keeping it all together, fixed on to some kind of metal brace. It looked more like an instrument of torture than healing. It must have been drilled right into the bone. She winced just thinking about it. Brutal, but necessary. She tried to cover her shock.

'Hi . . .' she rallied. 'Good to see you.'

'Sorry, it's a bit of a shock first time, I know.' Dan looked down at his leg, then was smiling back at them. He sat propped up against white hospital pillows.

'Okay, mate.' Joe went to shake his hand.

Dan held up a bandaged wrist. 'I'll pass, if you don't mind.'

'Ah, sorry pal.' Joe gave him an extremely gentle pat on the shoulder instead. 'So how's it going?'

'Great.' There was a second of silence among them, and then the tension in the room burst, as they couldn't help but give a gentle laugh. It didn't look that great. 'Well,' Dan continued, 'In the scheme of things, it's going okay. I'm slowly on the mend. *And*, I'm here to tell the tale, that's the main thing.'

'Yes, thank heavens.' Ellie responded. 'It looks nasty though. Must have been one hell of a break.'

'Multiple breaks, unfortunately. It's the ankle that's most messed up . . . Docs said if it had happened ten years ago, they'd never have fixed it. I'd probably have lost the lower leg. So these pins and bolts are doing a good job . . . I'm trying to look on the bright side.'

'Yeah, wow. Good for you, mate.'

'Yep, it was pretty messy. One minute I'm biking along happy as Larry, then woomph, lorry's veered across my side of the road on a sharp bend. I clipped it. Couldn't do anything about it. Ended up sliding across the tarmac and wrapped around a tree apparently . . . I don't quite remember that last bit. Felt like forever and all in a flash, right at the same time.'

'Jeez. That must have hurt.'

'Weird thing is, right at the time, no. Must have been the shock or something. It was only afterwards in the ambulance it all kicked in, 'til they got some morphine in to me.'

'Bad luck, mate.'

'Yeah, what a bloody shame,' Ellie added. 'So how long are you in the hospital for this time? It's the second op isn't it, Lucy was saying?'

'Yeah, just a few days, all being well. They have to tighten the rods, joy. Then I get a load of checkups and stuff, and the Ex-Fix . . . this thing . . .' He pointed to the metal brace. 'Comes off in around four weeks. Then there's physio, strengthening exercises to do. They've warned me there's a chance I still might not be able to walk on it. We won't know for a while.'

'That's so tough, Dan. I'm sorry.' Joe was shaking his head.

'Well, it's frustrating but hey, one step at a time . . . hopefully. And, the good news is that I've got some feeling back in the right leg now.' He smiled, but he looked sad too, like it faded on his face. Ellie noted the irony in that phrase. 'But hey, Lucy's been great,' Dan continued. 'I just feel so awful letting her down about the wedding and everything. All her dreams, and all those hours she'd spent planning for our big day. You guys too, sorry about that. I feel like I've messed it all up for everybody.'

'It's not your fault, Dan. I'm sure Lucy realizes that. And we're fine about it. Hey, no worries, honestly,' Joe reassured.

'She'll just want you to look after yourself, and to get better,' Ellie added.

'Yeah, I know . . . but one day, I'll give her the wedding she deserves. Not too long I hope. That's what's spurring me on, to be honest.'

'Good for you. And let us know. Give us a ring when you're ready, however long that is,' Joe spoke. 'We'll help coordinate with everyone to get it all set up again. Once you have a date in mind, just contact us. We'd like to make it really special for you both.'

'Second time lucky, hey.'

'Yeah, definitely,' Ellie said. 'Oh, I've brought you some goodies. Hopefully, they'll help cheer you up a bit.'

'Or if not, fatten you up,' Joe chipped in, with a wry smile.

'Mmm, sounds promising.'

Ellie lifted a gift bag up onto the bedclothes. Daniel dug in, pulling out carefully-wrapped bags of fudge, in three flavours – traditional, rum and raisin, and chocolate. Then, some mini salted caramel brownies and mini shortbread packs, all made by herself. There were also a couple of slices of lemon drizzle, and some grapes for good measure.

'Hey, great stuff. That'll supplement the bland hospital food nicely.'

'It'll keep you going for a while, at least,' Joe said.

'Cheers, Ellie. I really appreciate it, and you guys coming in.'

'You're very welcome. We just want to see you get back on your feet.'

'Yep, me too . . . ' His voice dipped. With that he wiggled the toes on his injured foot that was sticking out the bottom of the metal brace; they moved very slowly, as though they weren't quite keeping up with his brain.

They were stood outside in glorious sunshine, which seemed extra bright after being in the artificial light and hush of the hospital. The sounds of traffic from the nearby city streets and the sound of birds tweeting around them were vibrant, life-affirming.

'Phew, that was harder than I thought.' Ellie let out a slow breath.

'It was a bit of a shock seeing that metal brace attached to his leg like that. Must have been some major damage.' Joe grimaced.

'I'm so glad we went to see him though.'

'Absolutely. Me too.'

'Hope it's not too long a job for him, and that he gets to make a full recovery. It'll be such a bugger if he can't walk properly.'

'He mentioned that he wasn't sure when he'll be able to get back to work either, being a dentist. On his feet all day, I suppose. That isn't good,' Joe added.

'No. And his motorbike, he loved that. Do you think he'll even want to get back on it?'

'Who knows? It'll certainly be hard either way. Makes you realize how fragile we all are, hey. One split second and boomph.'

'I know. And, how lucky we are too.' There was a mistiness in her eyes. She took Joe's hand.

'We'll make sure we give them a really special wedding, when it's the right time.'

'Yeah, we will. I'd like to do that.'

Aw, she was so perfect. Her gorgeous face, with dusky blue eyes struggling to focus on the world around her. Tiny fingers and hands. The pale-pink Babygro snug over her body. Her feet in little bootees. And to think she wasn't even in this world, well not in her own right, just a couple of weeks ago.

'She's beautiful, Lynn.'

Another visit, this time to her cousin Lynn's, to meet the newest member of the Hall family.

'Do you think I can have a cuddle?'

''Course.'

'Are you sure? She looks so peaceful there. I don't want to disturb her.'

'Na, she'll be fine. She doesn't seem to mind being passed around.'

Lynn took her daughter out of the wicker Moses basket, and passed her across.

Ellie was super-careful taking her, supporting her fragile head and neck. 'Hey, little Emily. Nice to meet you.' Ellie's voice was hushed, not wanting to unsettle her.

That new baby smell, milky, baby bath, lotion and new peachy skin. Her hair was soft, downy, and dark. Ellie just gazed at her. As she looked up for a second she saw Joe watching the pair of them intently.

'She is just beautiful, Lynn,' Ellie repeated, with a gentle smile on her face.

'Thanks . . . not so beautiful around 3 a.m. when she's crying for her feed,' her cousin laughed. 'But yeah, most of the time she is pretty adorable.'

'I bet James is over the moon with her,' Joe said.

'Oh yes, major Daddy pride going in. He's even been wearing a T-shirt with 'I'm the Father' on the front. It was a joke from his mates, but he loves it. He's just nipped out to the shops, to get some more milk. Won't be long. You should catch him.'

'She'll have him wrapped round her little finger very soon, I bet,' Ellie added.

'Already has . . .'

'Just wait 'til she's a teenager,' Joe added.

'So, it'll be you guys, next then.'

Ellie felt her heart give a little throb. 'Hope so.' Her voice came out high-pitched.

'Ooh, so it's on the cards then? Fab.'

'Maybe.' Ellie didn't want to say any more, didn't want to risk the tremor, that was sure to be there in her voice. And feeling a little shaky with a baby in her arms was not a good thing. Joe gave her a reassuring smile. *So,* swiftly moving the conversation on, Ellie asked, 'Is she feeding well?'

'Yeah, seems to be doing fine. Putting on a little weight this week. Lost a couple of ounces last week, but apparently that's pretty normal when they're just born.'

'She does looks gorgeous.' Joe had taken a seat on the sofa.

'Do you want a turn?' Lynn asked him.

'No, thanks, she looks great but I think I'll pass. She looks so settled there with Ellie.'

'Anyone for a cuppa then? You sit down with her Els, she'll be getting heavy else, and I'll get the kettle on.'

'Yes, that'll be lovely, then I get to cuddle her for a while longer.'

She sat down next to Joe, who gently reached across to touch a tiny finger, and then took the whole hand gently between his thumb and forefinger.

'Wow, I didn't realize quite how small they are. I've never really had chance to see any brand new babies. It's awesome and a bit scary all at once.'

'Yes.' The little face started screwing up a bit, so Ellie rocked her in her arms, which seemed to soothe whatever it was that was bothering her.

'You look like a natural though.' He smiled at her warmly, lovingly.

One day. That thought felt like a beautiful weight in her mind and her soul.

They had tea and some shortbread biscuits. James appeared with the milk just in time and they chatted about work, the castle, babies, lack of sleep. James was a postman and used to being up at all hours.

'We'll be having a Christening in a month or so, just need to get it booked. You'll have to come down for it. All the family will be there.'

'Wow, that'll be noisy then,' Joe joked.

After being brought up by a single mum with no siblings, Ellie's household and family seemed chaotic to

Joe. Everyone talked over the other, as well as there being a telly or radio on, and no one seemed to bat an eyelid.

'Hah, yeah, of course.' Lynn agreed. 'She'll be meeting the whole tribe, cousins, aunties, uncles, nannas.'

'She'll have a baptism of fire then, better get her some earmuffs sorted out.' Joe smiled.

'Or else, she'll be bawling along with the rest of 'em,' Lynn added.

'We're hiring a hall out for a bit of a do. Mam and Auntie Joyce are going to help me put on a bit of a spread.'

'It sounds good. I'm sure we'll come down . . . Oh, I've got a gift for her in my bag. Joe, could you pass it to me?'

He lifted her handbag onto the sofa next to her.

'Thanks.'

She managed to rummage one-handed and found the parcel. She had spent ages in the children's department of Next just looking at all the outfits. All the mini clothes were so gorgeous it had been hard choosing, but she'd gone for a cosy all-in-one, it had a pink applique rabbit on it, and a matching hat. She'd gone for a 3–6 months size, for little Emily to grow into.

Lynn unwrapped it. 'Aw, that's so sweet, Ellie. I love it. She'll look so cute in it. Thanks, hun.'

Emily then started to wriggle in her arms, and her tiny mouth screwed in to a ball. A small bleating cry started up, that tugged right at Ellie's heart. 'Oh, dear.'

'It's fine. She's due a feed, so it'll be hungry mode kicking in.'

'Well, we'd better be getting on anyhow. Got another round of visits to do yet. We haven't seen Joe's Mam yet. And then we'd better spend some time with Mum and Dad. And we head back first thing in the morning.'

'Well, thanks so much for popping in.'

'I couldn't have missed seeing this little one. You all take care now.'

'Yeah, you too.'

Ellie passed her newest relation back over to mum. 'Aw, she'll have grown so much by the time I see her next, bless her.'

'Cheers, James.' Joe stood up.

'Bye, Ellie, Joe.'

The men shook hands. Joe then kissed Lynn on the cheek, who now had a bawling but still-gorgeous infant in her arms.

'We'll go. Let you get her sorted. Lovely to see you all,' Ellie said.

'Happy families.' Joe gave a wink.

'Thanks. Great to see you.'

There was one more place Ellie needed to go this afternoon, and before that she needed to buy some flowers.

'Hi, Nanna.'

She sat down in the grassy verge beside the grave that

was well-tended. It had little chippings of grey granite all over the base and a solid headstone that read, 'In loving memory of Beryl Simpson. Mother, grandmother, and wife of Arnold Simpson. Much loved. Rest in peace, Nanna.' Granda was laid beside her in the next plot, just as it should be for them.

Ellie took the flowers out of their cellophane wrap and gently displayed them in the glass vase they kept here. She'd just filled up the water from the cemetery tap that was in a stone wall nearby. She'd chosen some nice carnations, in a mix of peach and red that looked bright and cheery.

'There, that's better.'

She let out a small sigh, wondering where to start. Good news was always nice. 'Went to see our Lynn's new baby today. I expect Mum's told you already, or maybe you can see it all anyway and this is old news, but I'll tell you anyhow. She had a little girl, Emily, and she's absolutely gorgeous. You'd have loved her. It's dad's side of the family so not one of your lot, but you'd have loved her all the same.'

Ellie remembered that little heavy-bodied cosy warmth, nestled against her. 'Just gorgeous. All fine. I think she was 7lb 9oz – quite big for a first.'

Ellie looked up at the sound of bicycle brakes screeching to a halt. A couple of rows across from her, two youths in hoodies slammed down their bikes to the grass, making Ellie feel quite uneasy. They disturbed the calm of the cemetery with their loud banter. 'Go there, then Jake. Yeah.'

Ellie wondered if they were up to some mischief. Maybe coming here to wreck the gravestones or bash up the flowers. They only looked about thirteen; she'd have to have words if they started something, but was a little afraid too, but she couldn't let them damage Nanna's grave and all those other people's final resting places who had been much loved and passed away. Damn them. She had her mobile phone; if it got too bad she could ring the police, she supposed. She wasn't quite sure if they had seen her yet, as she was sat low down. Nanna's headstone a visible shield.

'Damn. It's those "villigain" types, Nanna.' Nanna was great at getting words wrong and creating her own mash-up new versions. She'd been thinking of villain and hooligan at the same time, and out popped 'villigains' one evening when she and her nanna had been coming out of the local convenience store in Heaton; there were a gang of youths, smoking and dropping their empty beer cans to the ground then kicking them about. She was indignant, had to have words – she was so brave Nanna, didn't want anyone spoiling her neighbourhood. 'I'd pick that up, young man. There's a bin just there.' Unfortunately, he just growled at her, 'What's it to you?' She had the sense, at that point, to walk on. Probably because Ellie's little hand was tugging at hers. If she'd have been on her own, well, who knows. She might have tackled them with her handbag (which always had the potential to be an offensive weapon) or something. Good old, Supergran. Now there was another tale . . . Ellie smiled remembering the legend that was her Nanna. She'd have to tell Joe that one when he came to pick her up.

One of the youths wandered off with a circular glass vase in his hands. She hoped he wasn't going to smash it up. He trekked off to the stone wall. Then, she heard the sounds of water splashing. Next thing, the other lad was unzipping and removing something from under his hooded top – a bunch of yellow flowers that looked like roses. They must have been prickly against his chest! Ellie smiled – looked like she'd got it wrong about them, then.

'There you go, Gramps.' She heard as the two lads stood there, faces serious, looking down at one of the graves for a second.

She heard her Nanna's voice loud and clear then. 'To assume makes an Ass Out of You and Me.' One of her many wonderful sayings. Ellie smiled. Felt herself relax again.

The boys gave each other a firm pat on the back. 'Football back on the field?'

'Yep.'

Ellie watched as they remounted their bikes, and sped

off. She *so* wished Nanna was here still. That she could go and have a cup of tea with her, sat in her galley kitchen in her terraced house. The kettle was always on the boil at Nanna's literally (she must have had the highest electricity bill in the street!), and the door always open. If you were lucky she'd have just baked, too. They could have had fat wedges of Choffee Cake or one of her fabulous Victoria sponges, whilst they chatted. She missed her so much.

She realized that she wanted the teashop to feel like that; like Nanna's kitchen. For her customers to come in and feel more like friends, and sit and have a chat between themselves or with the staff, eat something gorgeous and comforting and just feel a bit better about the world, put their worries aside for a little while.

'Nanna . . . I haven't told anyone this. Only Joe knows that we're even trying. Well, obviously he knows . . . but I can't share how I'm feeling with him or anyone really, but I know you won't mind. Holding Emily today was beautiful, but I just feel so sad. It's not happening, you see. We want a baby, our own child, been trying for six months now. I know it's not that long, and the doctors won't even look at you 'til its past two years . . . But what if I can't, or Joe can't? I don't want to worry anyone or go on about it, but inside I just feel so sad. It's weird.'

Ellie sat staring at the leaves blowing on the trees. They were just starting to tinge with russet and golds, autumn creeping in. The breeze cooler now, she wrapped her cardigan tighter around her.

'Ah, maybe I'm just too impatient and worrying about nothing . . . But I just . . . want it so much. I know not everyone can have children . . . It's not a God-given right but . . . you just hope, don't you.'

And a little voice in her mind spoke up, 'Just give it time, lass. It's nature's way. If it's meant to be it'll be, and if not . . . Well, you'll always have each other. That's a precious gift in itself.' And she didn't know if it was her subconscious talking or Nanna's sound advice, but it soothed her.

She hadn't heard the footsteps coming along the grass, until a figure stood before her.

'Oh, hi.' She looked up. 'Get on okay at your mam's?'

'Yep, great. She's fine.' Joe had popped across to see Sue for a while, leaving Ellie to her graveyard chitchat. He knew what she was like, and sensed she might just want a little timeout too.

'You okay here?'

'Yes. Nearly done. Just need a couple of minutes.' She patted the grass next to her, signalling for him to come close.

'Hi, Nanna, Granda,' he said aloud, as he sat down. It only seemed polite.

They sat quietly for a minute or so, listening to the sounds of the birds, watching a rabbit hop along the next row of gravestones, eyeing up his next flowery snack, no doubt.

'We've been busy, haven't we' Joe said.

'Yeah, there's always so many people to see when we come back down. Nice though to catch up with everyone,' Ellie commented.

'Yeah, of course.'

'And little Emily, aww, she is just so adorable.'

And he knew she was thinking of their future, their dreams for a family, and he took her hand gently in his own, and gave it a little squeeze. She lay her head on his shoulder. No words. They didn't need words.

15

Ellie snuggled up next to Joe. Mum and Dad had bought a new bed for her little room. It was a single, but had a pull-out section from the base that made it into a double, for when Joe and Ellie came back to visit. It just about filled the whole room when it was extended, and her bedside table had to be moved out to the landing.

'You okay?' Joe asked.

'Yeah, you?' They found themselves whispering. The walls were so thin in this house, they'd be chatting away with her Mum and Dad who were just in the next room otherwise.

'Yeah, fine.'

'Did you feel all right, about holding the baby today?'

'Yeah, she was so adorable. Just made me want it for us even more.'

'Me too.' He turned and gave her a hug. Skin to skin

in her childhood bedroom. How times had moved on from sighing over pictures of Justin Timberlake when she was fourteen. She had a real live, very gorgeous man in her bed. Suddenly she could feel his erection nudging up against her.

'Joe,' she whispered. 'Stop it.'

'I can't help it, it's just a natural male reaction. Don't get so close then,' he whispered back.

'You'll have to wait until tomorrow.' A hug would definitely be all he would be getting tonight. It still felt weird back at home, in *this* room, with Joe beside her, knowing that her parents were lying parallel to them just next door. The walls were as thin as eggshells and still painted the same shade of pink she'd chosen at twelve, for goodness sake, and her teddy bear collection was still lined up on the shelf!

'I'll hold you to that promise then, Mrs Ward.'

They were nearly asleep, when Ellie started laughing. The bed was shaking with it.

'What's up with you now? You'll be waking your mum and dad up, at this rate.'

No answer, still more shaking and giggles.

'They'll think we're up to something, the bed's rattling that much.' His voice had laughter through it too, though.

'Just remembered something . . . It's a story. I was going to tell you when you came to pick me up from the graveyard.'

'What? Spill the beans. It must be a good one.'

'Ah, it's a classic. She's a legend, that one . . . Supergran, in fact.'

More rattling.

'Go on, then.'

'Right, well . . . a while after my Granda died, Nanna decided to go off and have a holiday with her best friend, Jean.' There was a pause, while Ellie shuffled in the duvet. 'So off they went to Paris, the pair of them. She hadn't done a lot of foreign travelling. They'd been warned about pickpockets and to be careful about people trying to sell you things in the street.'

'Right.'

'Anyway, they're over there one evening, on their mini break, when a young woman comes up to them . . . flick-knife in her hand, pointed right at them.'

'Uh-oh.'

'Exactly.'

'Well, Nanna being Nanna comes out with, "Oh no, we don't need one of those, hen. Not much need for a knife like that. What do you think I am, Supergran or something?"'

Joe was chuckling then.

'The girl didn't know what to do with these two old dears from the Toon,' Ellie continued. 'Who were either naïve or stupid, or both. Maybe she thought of her own gran then or something. She just dropped the knife and ran . . . It was about twenty minutes later, in some café down by the Seine, it hit home. The pair of them got a bit shaky, realising they'd been about to be mugged.

'Wow.'

'Good old Supergran, must have taken the wind right out of that girl's sails. Saved by her Geordie wit and unbelievable naiveté.'

'How fantastic. What a woman . . . it's such a shame I never got to meet her.'

'Yeah, I know. She'd have liked you, very much . . . . And yeah, she'll always be Supergran to me.'

16

Time to get up, face the day, and head back to the castle.

'Thanks for everything, Mum. It's been so nice to see you all. You'll have to come up and see us at the castle again, sometime. You can always stay in one of the guest rooms, you know.'

'I'll have to see how your dad's work pans out. But yes, that might be nice.'

'Thanks, Sarah.' Joe gave his mother-on-law a kiss on the cheek.

'You're always welcome, Joe.'

Dad took Joe's hand in a firm grasp which grew into a full man hug on the step; although Joe was the taller, he seemed to be engulfed.

'Good stuff, nice to see you lad. Take care of our Els.'
'Will do.'

'See you, mate.' Jason and Joe shook hands.

Ellie gave all her family kisses and hugs.

In the car now, Joe driving, tooting the horn as they went, Ellie's hand waving out of the passenger side window as they travelled down Fifth Avenue's terraced street. Houses, shops, small businesses, large supermarkets, traffic lights, roundabouts, offices, schools, more houses, until the road opened out on to the A1 heading north. Patchy blue-and-white cloudy skies, fields each side of the road, many ploughed back now to a muddy brown. Early October, and the main harvest finished for another year.

An hour later, back to the patchwork green and brown fields of their valley, with the dusky rise of the Cheviot Hills in the distance, Claverham Castle appeared from its shelter of trees. Home – yes, it really did feel like home to Ellie now. The driveway was catching falling leaves, their colours the earthy warm tones of autumn.

They had to get straight back to work that day. With Joe being the castle and estate manager, and Ellie running the teashop as well as her wedding coordinating, there was never a dull moment, and always something to plan for.

'Everything been okay, Doris?'

'Oh yes, pet. No bother. Except we've got a booking for a busload coming in this afternoon, so we'll have a busy day.'

'At least they've let us know, I suppose.' Often they just

turned up out of the blue, and made an onslaught on the tearoom goodies. It always led to a mad hour or two afterwards, trying to bake as quickly as possible to replenish stocks, or improvise with some 'ones-I-made-earlier' from the freezer.

'All hands on deck then.' Ellie rolled up her sleeves, and washed her hands at the sink.

'Yep . . . your family all okay? Trip go well?'

'Yes, thanks. Nice to catch up with them all again.'

Ellie spotted Irene across the kitchens, taking out a tray of delicious-smelling cheese scones. She let her set them down safely on the side. 'Morning Irene, how are we doing for cakes and the like? Doris says we've got a coachload coming in later.'

'Well, I made a large Victoria sponge yesterday and a couple of tea loaves. That's all the scones done. Two batches of eighteen, so we've got savoury, and cherry and almond on the go.'

'Great stuff, I'll pop out front and see how we're doing, and find out what's left from yesterday.'

There was a half a coffee and walnut cake, a third of a chocolate, a whole gingerbread loaf, two slices of lemon drizzle, (all under their glass cake domes) and about a half-dozen cookies that had been stored in a container overnight.

She headed back to the kitchen, 'Did the order come in okay, yesterday?'

'Yep, all here . . . except there wasn't any cucumber for some reason, so we improvised with grapes in the salad, seemed to work okay,' Doris answered. 'So yes, there's plenty of paninis, jacket potatoes and salad stuff.'

'Okay, so have you got what you need to make up two large quiches, Irene, no better make that three?'

'Think so, I'll just check the pantry cupboard.'

Sometimes, Ellie felt like she was running a food army. Strategy in sandwiches, and battle of the baking. But she loved it too, even though after a long day her feet throbbed, and her back ached. It was so much better than her humdrum job working in the insurance offices back in Newcastle. She couldn't imagine being back there now, sat at the desk in that open plan office with its grey partitions, with all that paperwork and phone calls all day. Here at least, she created something, and made people happy with her food and her hospitality.

She wanted to make Dan and Lucy happy again, too. The shock of seeing his injuries, the image of him lying in that hospital bed, battered and held together by metal rods. The way he was trying to be upbeat in the face if it all. She so hoped they'd get their wedding soon. And, that the castle would get the opportunity to do them proud.

'Earth to planet Ellie?' Doris was flapping a tea towel near her face.

'Oops, yes. Was away there . . . just thinking for a moment.'

'Well, that's always a dangerous pastime.' Malcom marched in through the swing door. 'Any chance of a quick cuppa and some lemon drizzle to start us on our way.'

'Yes, of course. Doris, can you pop the kettle on please, we'll all have one to set us up. It looks like it's going to be a long day.'

'Gents, did you know about the coachload coming in at twoish?' Doris asked.

'Yes,' Derek, who'd followed Malcolm in, answered. 'Deana's just let us know, on our way in. That'll be fun. I quite like a crowd, as long as they're interested in the tours.'

'Well, it'll keep you out of mischief, I suppose.' Irene shouted across mid-pastry making.

'Never get chance to get in any mischief nowadays. Chance would be a fine thing.' Malcolm quipped with a wink.

Derek just shook his head.

Ellie fetched the last two slices of drizzle cake for Derek and Malcolm; she'd make another four of the lemon cakes today and freeze a couple, they were always popular, as well as some more cookies. Then, it'd be full on for the coachload and lunches. Five minutes and cup of tea would be bliss first, though.

It was in the teashop kitchens an hour or so later, whilst she was poking small holes into the sponges ready for the lemon-sugar drizzle to soak into, a thought struck her. It was something Doris said about people hanging around too long at the end of the day, and didn't they have homes to get back to. Several weeks ago, just that scenario, when Ellie had had to dash off to the loo, hadn't she.

When *was* that exactly? Because a little glimmer of realisation was dawning . . . like a fragment of crystal catching the light in her mind . . . that that was when her last period was. They'd been so busy lately, what with Bridezilla's wedding, and visiting her family back in Newcastle. So when would that have been? Maybe towards the end of August? It was now the second of October.

Ellie felt an amazing surge of hope.

But, it could just be a false alarm. She'd only be a week late . . . She was never a week late. A few days, yep . . . never a week. Oh My God. Oh, wow.

When she'd not been thinking too much about it, or particularly trying for it, could it have really happened?

She put the lemon drizzles to one side, and silently crossed her fingers. *Could this really be it?* She felt a mistiness in her eyes. *Right, keep the excitement down.* She needed to confirm with a test to find out for sure. No point getting all her hopes up for nothing, *again.* She might end up with that all-too-familiar nagging lower back pain by supper time, and be back to square one.

But still, her mind was having its own little party in

there, bouncing up and down and doing air punches. She tried to focus on a tray of jacket potatoes that were ready to pop into the oven, though she felt slightly giddy. She felt like she'd downed a glass of champagne in one on an empty stomach.

She'd have to get away, nip to Kirkton, and get a pregnancy test. But it'd be far too busy with the coachload due in, until after the lunch session. And, it would certainly raise alarm bells, especially with the gossip-loving Doris, if she dashed off unexpectedly. No, she'd just have to stay calm and carry on as normal for a few hours yet. But every now and then she found herself gazing at the wall, daydreaming, with a glimmer of a smile on her lips.

Joe popped in for a quick cup of coffee late morning, and it took Ellie all her effort not to fling herself into his arms and tell him her *maybe* news, but that wouldn't be fair, not until it was definite. There'd only be two people to disappoint then. But how lovely would it be to be able to tell Joe tonight, if it really was real.

'Right, thanks for the coffee, got to go over to the farm next, there seems to have been some problem with the driller for seeding. Might need to get the engineering company out to check it.'

'Oh, okay. See you later. Have a good day.' She quelled her excitement.

'You too.'

He gave her a quick peck on the cheek. He smelled lovely up close, a mix of cool blue aftershave and him. She so hoped she'd be sharing some amazing news with him later.

For the next few hours she tried her best to carry on as normal. She held hope inside her like a trapped butterfly, trying to keep it safe. She made a batch of dark chocolate and orange brownies, and then prepped the salad ready for the lunches, making some homemade coleslaw too. Minutes seemed like hours. She needed to know.

By 3.30 p.m., she came up with the excuse that she needed to buy baking powder for her next batch of cakes, despite the fact that a new lot had been ordered for the delivery tomorrow, and finally she got away. It was only ten minutes' drive to the small town of Kirkton, which nestled in the foothills of the Cheviot Hills. She parked on the traditional main street of stone and brick properties, and popped to the Co-op first to get the baking powder. She'd better take some back with her, or Doris would be on to her!

Her rural community were lovely, and she'd got to know so many friends locally over the past five years, but honestly it was hard to keep anything private. If someone spotted a pregnancy test in her hand, well that'd be it, it'd be all over North Northumberland within the hour. Honestly, there'd be no need to go and announce the news to Joe later that evening, he'd already know! The rural grapevine could be very speedy – there may as well be a carrier pigeon flying direct to the Castle in seconds.

Ellie scoured the high street like a sleuth. She had to time her visit to the chemist's shop to perfection. Look left, look right. No one she recognized was on either side of the street, for now. She ducked across the road and darted in, scanning the shop. Just one old gentleman was in, who nodded politely at her; she'd never met him before. Perfect.

She located the tests, checked no one else was about to come in to the shop, and took one to the till. It felt like a promise in her hand. A little flutter of excitement hit her stomach as she paid for it. The woman behind the counter popped it thoughtfully in to a white paper bag, and off Ellie went.

Driving back, she felt excited and scared all at once. Could she get away with nipping up to their apartment and doing the test straight away? Or would she have been away from the teashop for too long already? She supposed she'd better nip in and at least check they were getting on okay, in case a surprise coach trip had turned up or something exceptional. Joe should still be out of the apartment at the moment though, at work around the estate somewhere. It would be an ideal time. She needed that quiet and privacy just to take in the result, either way.

Could this really be it, after over six months of trying?

'Everything okay, ladies?'

Both Irene and Doris were out front in the teashop. Only a couple of tables were taken, and it all looked in control.

'Yes, fine thanks, lovey. Just been steady here,' answered Irene.

Doris nodded in agreement, as she cleared a table that had obviously just been vacated.

Okay, so this was it. Her chance. She knew she wouldn't settle until the test was done. 'Right, I just need to pop up to the apartment, then I'll be straight back. Thanks.' Ellie felt her cheeks burn. She was just waiting for Doris to ask what she was going upstairs for. Or, for her nosey waitress's extrasensory gossip perception to click in, and for her X-ray eyes to bore a hole through her handbag to find the pregnancy test lurking there.

But no, all seemed normal, except for Ellie's insides which were bubbling up like Mount Vesuvius.

Stay calm, Ellie. Stay calm.

She walked across the courtyard, but then skipped up the stone steps of the circular staircase two at a time, then reminded herself to go steady, just in case this really was it.

'Hel-lo?' The door was to their apartment was locked, but she checked loudly as she let herself in. A welcome silence. She opened the pack in the safety of the bathroom, briefly read the instructions, got the small pot ready, laid the white plastic stick out, and managed to pee mostly over her hand, before catching some in the pot, typical.

Pot half full, the stick now in. Wait five to ten seconds . . .

A door slammed. The apartment's?

Shit. She didn't know the result yet. It was only matter of seconds, but what if it was a 'no'? She'd need a few quiet moments to compose herself. And it didn't seem right to raise his hopes just to dash them. That's if, it was in fact, Joe. She stayed perfectly still, hearing the sounds of her own breathing which seemed so loud. Then there were footsteps, a rustling in a drawer, a jangle of keys.

A half-hopeful 'Ellie?' was launched from the other room. Joe's voice.

She stayed silent. The bathroom door was closed. She spotted that her own keys were here in the bathroom with her, luckily. She didn't think she had left anything of hers out in the lounge to give herself away. He didn't have to know she was here at all. Okay, it might seem a little strange that the apartment door was unlocked, but not totally unusual, as they were often both in and out. And for the odd five minutes, or later in the day when the visitors were due to go home, they didn't always feel the need to lock it.

'Oh . . .' his voice drifted. Footsteps that faded, the bang of a door closing.

Hiding again, half out of breath, behind a gorse bush and some fern fronds. Phew, that was some climb. She'd sped on up there, after closing the teashop, to be the first to arrive. She sat down to catch her breath, popping the rucksack beside her that she'd filled with two small bottles of raspberry lemonade from the tearoom fridge – those were the best pink bubbles she could think of – and two slices of lemon drizzle cake, Joe's favourite.

It was a beautiful, clear evening. She looked across the valley; now an autumn patchwork of rich browns, tramlines ploughed in, green grassy fields, and another field that had recently been cut with fat round bales of straw looking like sausage rolls, ready to collect in. The blue of the sky was starting to fade, streaking with blushes of pink and orange. On the horizon, the majestic outline of the Cheviot Hills was becoming darker, more prominent. It wouldn't be long until dusk.

Yes, this was the perfect place.

She heard footsteps pacing up towards the brow of the hill.

'Ellie?'

She wondered why she'd hidden now, this wasn't ever

meant to be hide-and-seek; he'd found her years ago, there was no need to hide.

'Here.' She stood up, brushing rust-coloured pieces of dried bracken from her jumper.

'What on earth are you doing up here? And why all the mystery? Texting me: "Meet me on top of our hill, 5.30"? Come on, what are you up to?' He was smiling.

She couldn't stop the grin that was spreading across her face.

'So, are you dragging me up the top of this hill to ravage me or something? Making me work hard for it?'

She laughed. 'Not quite that . . .'

He eyed her quizzically.

'I've got something to tell you, Joe.' Her voice went all serious.

He looked concerned for a second, then saw the beam that she couldn't hide from her face.

'Ye-es . . . ?' His eyes were wide, hopeful.

She was nodding. 'Yes, you're going to be a daddy, Joe.'

'Oh, wow. That's amazing. That's just . . . .' And he got all choked up. He had a glint of happy tears in his eyes. 'Bloody amazing!'

He swept Ellie into his arms. Spun her gently around. 'I'm going to be a dad.' As he dropped her softly to her feet again, he placed the biggest kiss on her lips, still grinning as he finally pulled away. 'Kapow! Hey . . . do you think it was the Batman underpants that finally did it?'

She'd bought him a couple of pairs for his birthday, back in August.

'Of course, has to be,' she laughed.

He stood behind her then, both looking out at the glorious Northumberland view, and he placed his arms around her so they reached protectively to hold her stomach. You couldn't really feel any difference there to be fair. She'd checked earlier, having never been a flat stomach kind of girl, there was nothing obvious as yet.

'Our baby is in there,' he whispered behind her. She felt the words catch in her hair.

'Yes.'

'Hi baby . . . look after yourself, see you in a few months.'

Ellie smiled, feeling such an overwhelming sense of love, for him and for this new life. This was possibly one of the most perfect moments she had ever experienced.

17

In their apartment the next morning, the news was still sinking in.

'Oh my goodness, my mam'll be over the moon! And can you imagine your family when they hear?' Joe said, grinning.

'Yeah, I know. Mum's been hinting about a grandchild for years, and going on about all the wonderful antics of her friends' grandchildren. But, I must only be about five or six weeks pregnant I think, so can we keep this just to ourselves, for now?'

'Yeah sure, of course.'

'Don't want to tempt fate . . . maybe just leave it 'til we get past the first couple of months. Then, it'll be lovely to share the news.'

'I wonder how Henry will take it?'

'Hmm, I'm still not sure myself. Once he's got used to

the idea, I think he'll actually make a good, if slightly grudging, Grandpa.'

'It might mellow him,' Joe said.

'Yep, I could see that . . . He might want to make the most of what he missed with you.'

'Maybe. Hah, the bear with a sore head might really turn out to be a soft teddy bear underneath it all.'

They sat on breakfast stools in the apartment kitchen, spooning up cereal and drinking tea before heading off their separate castle ways for the day's work. They still had to carry on as normal, but, every now and then one or other of them would look up and smile knowingly.

It was going to be hard keeping it quiet, especially with extrasensory Doris about. But it seemed wise for now. At least Ellie wore an apron at work, which should hide any growing lumps and bumps for a while.

It would be their special secret to harbour for a little while longer.

The day flew by. They were busy with a large group of ramblers, as well as several tourists, and a few of their regular locals. It was 4 p.m. before Ellie knew it, when she finally had chance to catch her breath and have a bite of late lunch herself.

Deana popped her head around the door. 'Busy day?'

'Yeah, you could say that, this is my lunch.' Ellie gestured to her cheese toastie, which was going down a treat with a nice cup of Earl Grey. 'You'll have been all go in admissions too, I bet.'

'Oh, yes.'

'Joe'll be happy anyway, all good news for the castle takings. We might even get a smile out of Henry at this rate.'

'Now come on, don't take things to extremes. Lord H. might like the income, but he certainly won't like the fact that they're all trooping around his home. It'll be a grin and bear it, not a smile.'

'True enough.'

Lord Henry still struggled with the fact that he had to let people in to his country estate. But finances had diminished, as well as the property itself over the years, and like so many stately homes, this was the only way to keep it going. It had been more than ten years since they had had to open the castle to the public, but it still was a bug he had to bear.

'Fancy a coffee or anything, Deana?'

'Sure. If you've got time?'

'I'll make time. I need a five-minute breather, anyhow. Haven't had a break since nine o'clock this morning.'

Doris trooped in with a tray of dirty cups and saucers ready for the dishwasher.

'Blimey, that last lot we had in were a stingy bunch. Never served so much hot water! Tea for two and there were six of them. Kept wanting top-ups of hot water. I think they were just about wringing the teabag out at the end.' She was shaking her head animatedly.

'Oh well, I suppose some people are on a budget.' Ellie was trying to be considerate.

'Funny how the kids had new phones then, and those Nintendo thingies. Didn't hardly speak to each other, heads down in them all the while. With all this fabulous history around them too. Think they should be banned from using them in the castle. Then they'd have to look up and see what's here. They might actually learn something then.'

'True,' Deana agreed.

'Oh, I've been thinking some more about the Christmas Craft Fayre,' Doris piped up. 'While you were away, I had a word with the committee on the Kirkton Country Show, the one that's on in the summer. They always have a craft tent, you see, and it's lovely. They've put an e-mail out to all their past stallholders for us, so we'll see if we get some interest. I've already heard back from knitted toys, the jam and chutney lady, the honey farm and a hand-made soap company.'

'Sounds great . . . Good idea, Doris, thanks. I'll put my mind to it, too. I'm sure there's lots we can be doing in the teashop for the event, making up foodie gifts and the like.'

'Oh, can you make up some of that gorgeous fudge you do, Ellie? I can put it in the Christmas hamper gifts

I make up for my Mum and Auntie Dora.' Deana was smiling.

'Hampers . . . now there's a thought.' Ellie's brain was ticking over. 'The Teashop in the Castle Christmas Hampers with all sort of goodies in. We could even raffle one off for a good cause.'

'Brilliant.'

'We could make a few up for display, with all the longer-life things, but then for all the fresh cakes and the like we could take orders for collection nearer Christmas time . . . Hmm, Christmas cakes. Bet people would love a homemade Christmas cake, without all the bother of having to do it themselves.' Ideas were popping in to Ellie's brain thick and fast now. 'Do you fancy a coffee at all, Doris? I'm just making one for Deana.'

'No, ta. Need to get on. Our Simon's popping over for his tea tonight. His Stacey's on a night out down to the cinema with the girls. I'll just get this lot loaded up, and then wipe over all the tables. That's me done, then.'

'Okay, thanks, Doris. I'll mop the floors in a minute, so no need to do that.'

'Thanks. Oh, I meant to ask you before, did you go and see that lad? The one in the hospital?'

'Daniel? Yes.'

'How's he getting on? Been thinking of him. Nice boy.' *Boy,* he was well into his thirties.

'Not too bad. Going to be a long job though. His leg

must have been really smashed up. Got more ops and a lot of physio to go through yet. He's still all wired up to some metal leg brace.'

'Oh, poor thing,' Deana commented. 'I remember them, a lovely couple. Bikers, weren't they? Not at all like you'd think bikers are, though. Wasn't he a dentist or something, and she's an accountant?'

'Yes.'

'Riding a motorbike doesn't make you a thug, Deana.' Doris tutted.

'No, I know that. Of course, it doesn't. It's just a few of those Hell's Devils mobs give it a bad name.'

'Well, most motorcyclists I know are just out for a road trip, some fantastic scenery, a bit of company, and a good time. Our Simon took it up for a while. I did use to worry about accidents, mind. It's just you and the road if you come off. You need all the right gear. And thank God helmets are compulsory these days. There's still some bloody awful accidents though.'

'I know.'

'Right, I'll wipe over these tables, and then I'll be away home, Ellie.'

'Thanks, Doris. And, thank you for all the help on my days off this week.'

'You're welcome, pet.' There was even a trace of a smile.

Ellie had got to know Doris's dour ways over the past few years, but they had warmed to each other too.

Underneath the slightly miserable exterior lurked a heart of gold.

Irene was already away home. She tended to start early, cracking on with the baking in the morning before they opened, and then left as the customers tailed off later in the afternoon. It seemed to work well. On busier days, Bank Holidays and weekends, they had Lauren and a couple of the girls from the village in too. Together they made a good team.

Ellie felt shattered by the evening.

'Busy day out on the estate?

'Yeah, and you?'

'You could say that. Deana said we'd had about a seventy admissions through.'

'That's great for early October. Feeling okay?'

'Yeah, bit tired but that's nothing unusual.'

'Yeah. By the way, I saw Dad earlier . . . up on the roof believe it or not, long story.'

'Oh, blimey. That sounds dangerous.'

'It was. He was checking the roof tiles above his rooms, some kind of leak appearing apparently. Wanted to check it out himself, first.'

'He's in his seventies.'

'I know. Bloody nuts sometimes. But I don't think we're going to change him now. Anyway, I got him to come down, as quickly and safely as I could. He'd climbed across from the viewing tower . . . As we'd been away, I thought we'd ask him to supper.'

'Oh, okay. That's fine. When did you say?'

'Tonight.'

Ah, so there went her lazy evening sat in her PJs. 'Jo-oe.'

'Sorry, he just seemed a bit lonely, and God knows what he cooks for himself these days. He said he had ham sandwiches for the last two nights.'

She'd been so busy, and with her exciting news, she hadn't thought to check how he was since getting back from Newcastle. She softened. 'Okay, it's all right.' It was just that she was so damned tired herself, and hadn't even begun to think about what to eat that evening. Something easy from the freezer on their laps had appealed, but that wouldn't work now. But, she was a cook after all, she could come up with something for sure. Maybe she could wander back down to the teashop, and hijack one of Irene's quiches. She thought she'd spotted half a salmon and asparagus one left. She'd ask her nicely to make some more tomorrow, lovely Irene. It would certainly save cooking from scratch. With a few new potatoes and some salad, they'd be sorted. She could even warm three slices of chocolate cake, pour some cream over and that would be pudding organized too. 'It's no problem,' she repeated.

'You're a star. Thank you. Sorry to dump that on you. I know you've had a long day.'

At least her husband wasn't a heartless soul, who didn't care if his dad ate cold sandwiches in his lonely room across the courtyard. She gave him a hug.

'Sure we can't say anything yet? Our big news . . .

'No, not just yet. It's such early days. Let's just enjoy it as our little secret for a while longer at least.'

'Okay, yeah, that's fine . . . I'm just so chuffed, I feel like telling the world. But yeah, might be a bit of a shock, to find out that he's going to be a grandad. I'm not quite sure how he'd take it.'

'I know. He's not generally the fondest of children.'

'Oh well, time will tell.'

'Yeah, when's he coming across then?'

Joe glanced at his watch, sheepishly. 'Five minutes.'

Oh shit. No chance of sitting down yet then. 'Jo-oe.'

'What was it like here in the castle years ago, Henry? Back when you were a little boy?' Ellie was curious.

'Well . . .' Henry paused as he was about to spoon up some chocolate brownie and ice cream. 'Quite amazing in some ways. Living in a castle, the grand rooms, the gardens, woodlands . . . It was all like an enormous adventure playground. I had a fabulous go-kart and used to head off up and down the driveway, thinking I was at the grand prix. You took it all rather for granted as a young child . . . But, it was rather isolating too.'

'Yes, I can imagine that.' Ellie was thinking of her own

terraced house upbringing in the Newcastle-upon-Tyne suburbs, quite a world away.

'I had no siblings, you see. So it was always exciting when guests came. Though some of them were more interesting than others. One ghastly girl turned up, she may have been a princess of sorts, that's what my father had told me. I think it was a warning to be nice to her. The family were from Asia, ex-pats I think. She was a spoilt brat as far as I was concerned, though my life was pretty coddled too. We never had to *do* anything as such; never had to clean our rooms, boil an egg, light a fire. It was all done for us.

'But anyhow, this particular girl was dreadful. I remember her ripping up one of my favourite books, because I was reading later that day and not paying her enough attention . . . Actually, I much preferred it when I could sneak off and play with Derek, that's our tour guide, Derek. His father was my father's butler.' Henry leaned back in his chair. 'We had some grand old games of hide-and-seek, took us bloody hours to find each other. You can imagine, in a castle this size, and all the grounds too! Sometimes the one hiding would have to give up and go and find the other one.' He smiled.

'What about your parents, what were they like?' Ellie was fascinated, and very much thinking of her own lively, slightly batty, close family.

Joe gave her a glance, surprised at how Henry was

opening up. He had never heard any of this, with his father being so quiet, such an introvert. It was often difficult to dig too deep, and Ellie *was* being rather blunt in her questions, risking rebuke in fact, but Henry seemed more relaxed than usual this evening. Joe was curious too, they were his grandparents, after all, a whole part of his life that he hadn't had a clue about – they had died before he ever had chance to know them. He'd only got to know his father in the past few years as it was. And it seemed even more relevant tonight, knowing there was soon going to be another new member to this aristocratic, quirky family.

'Well then, it was in the days of children having very much to be seen (and then only occasionally) and not heard. It was Nanny who brought me up really. Nanny Ida.' Henry smiled, thinking back. 'A lovely, rather plump, Irish lady. I did see Mother and Father of course, but only in short bouts. Mother used to pop up and read to me sometimes, that was nice. But yes, my parents always seemed rather distant, somehow.'

That might help explain his own distance. Ellie mused. It was such a different life than her own.

'Then later,' Henry continued, 'like many other boys in my position, I was sent off to boarding school down in Yorkshire, and saw even less of them.'

'Oh,' Ellie was finding it hard to take in, hardly seeing your parents, being sent away.

'It's all very different nowadays . . . our lives are very different.' He looked across at Joe.

Their own father-son experience was another world away from that privileged, yet rather closed, upbringing. Joe had been brought up in a rather deprived area of Newcastle-upon–Tyne in a hard-working, single parent family. Ellie was thinking that he was yet another son who hadn't really known his father. But they were learning to know each other, slowly but surely. And that was rather lovely. It was never too late. And it seemed so important to be making those bridges, even more so now they were about to have a child of their own. A new member of this family.

The evening had been pleasant. And, Ellie felt she knew her father-in-law just a little better.

'Would you like a coffee, Henry, or some whisky?' Joe asked.

'A tot of malt might go down rather nicely. Thank you, Joe.'

As the two men shared a smile, Ellie noted how similar they looked.

18

October rolled on with mellow, misty days; the nights now drawing in. Being quieter at the teashop now, there were moments where Ellie could look around her and enjoy the ancient stone castle and its wonderful setting. The first tower of the stronghold was built back in the thirteenth century. The building had seen many battles and bloodshed in its time, with earls and dukes as warriors, the infamous border wars, even Kings had stayed there in their way to Scotland. Later, in more peaceful times, it had become a family home. Their family home. It was strange to think of all that history in one place, of all the people who had been there before you. And then, your little piece of history, your story unfolding right now. Ellie held her palm to her belly instinctively, as she looked out from their apartment window across the front driveway.

The huge old trees of the driveway which seemed to

stand guard, were now cloaked in golds, russets and browns; the leaves tumbling down like bronze-coloured confetti, the estate lands stretching out as far as you could see. If you were lucky whilst walking in the woods, you might spy the herd of deer who had made this rather magical place their home too. It was so beautiful and peaceful, a world away from the bustle of city life, and had captured Ellie's heart. It was no wonder it was becoming popular with couples choosing it as the venue for their wedding day. A countryside castle, yours for the day.

The weeks soon passed, Ellie was feeling well, if a little tired at times, but oh-so happy. With the usual teashop routines, the Christmas Fayre to think about, and also coordinating another wedding for the first Saturday of the half- term week mid-October, Ellie was kept busy.

This wedding couple were great, a breath of fresh air after Bridezilla and co; they were just so relaxed about everything. They were both teachers from Leeds, and had wanted a small, intimate do, with just thirty close family and friends for their special day. Maddie, the bride, arrived at the castle in a gorgeous, old-fashioned cream limousine for their 2 p.m. wedding in the castle chapel. Stepping out of the classic vehicle, Ellie loved her outfit – she wore an elegant, cream-satin dress with a neat strapless bodice and long flowing skirt that skimmed her slim curves. With her dark hair swept up into a loose bun with strands of curls framing her face, the bride looked stylish, elegant, yet still very natural.

The bouquet that Wendy had created for Maddie was just perfect; with ivory roses, sprays of white gypsophila and bold greenery that framed the flowers. It was striking yet simple, with long dark-green sprigs trailing from it. The groom was smart and handsome in a dark grey suit, white shirt, ivory rose buttonhole and the most gorgeous smile, as he waited for his bride to come down the chapel aisle.

After the service, the guests chatted amiably in the drawing room, as the champagne flowed. Soon they were ready for their four-course sit-down dinner at the antique mahogany table in the Great Hall. It was large enough to sit all thirty guests and was set out with an ivory satin runner, white china plates, cut-glass goblets, and six of Wendy's floral displays which echoed the bride's bouquet – with roses, gyp and those trailing sprigs of greenery in tall vases. The Hall looked wonderful.

Ellie had hired in outside catering for the meal, as the menus the couple wanted were slightly complex; her level of cooking wasn't quite up to chef standard and certainly not for a silver-service style event like this. She knew her limits. But that freed her up to coordinate the occasion in a more relaxed manner, and to ensure that every little detail was just right.

Instead of a disco or band, they had hired in a string

quartet, who played beautifully, the classical music filling the room. Ellie felt like she had walked into a period drama. The Hall felt very much like it might have done centuries ago, with the soft glow of candlelight from the grand table, the sound of people chatting, the smells of gorgeous food, the main course being Beef Wellington, the clinking of cutlery and glasses.

There was only one problem earlier, when the catering company hadn't realized how the food had to be brought up from the kitchen via a flight of winding stairs, which always proved a challenge, but was aided by Ellie lending them her 'hostess'-style food-warming trolleys for the corridor outside the Great Hall, and also offering Derek and Malcom as spare runners for the chef and his team.

After the meal, and the speeches, the bride, who was in fact a music teacher, hitched up her satin skirt and sat at the cello to play. Along with the violins and viola, she played a piece which she dedicated to her new husband. The music was hauntingly beautiful, and vaguely familiar, and Ellie found out from the Maid of Honour that it was 'The Secret Wedding' theme tune from the movie *Braveheart*, a film that was apparently special to the couple.

It was so lovely when a wedding came together like this, and Ellie could feel proud that she had played her part in the hopes and plans for their big day coming true. All the wedding couples who had come to the castle for their big day were unique, and in love in their own special way.

That promise they were making for life, that commitment to their relationship *should* be celebrated, and though the world was sometimes cynical, and yes, some relationships did break down, where would we be without that hope, that bond, that love.

With only a few weeks remaining until the 'Christmas in the Castle Fayre', as Joe had aptly named it, (the catch-phrase seemed to be working well on the posters and adverts they had started putting out, and there had been a lot of interest locally), the next Monday meeting was focussing on planning the details of the event.

'Right then, what have we all got to bring to the table on the Christmas Fayre so far?' Joe started.

They were sat at the large, oval, table of the meeting room, which had originally been the old dairy. The walls were now whitewashed over the old stone, one wall still having the original white dairy tiles, the ancient beams above them painted a soft grey. Ellie could almost imagine the original dairymaids here, with their milk urns and butter churns, working hard. Perhaps it wouldn't have felt so very different from her dashing around in the kitchens at times.

Ellie looked around the members of staff assembled, for a fleeting moment she had a flashback to a Vicar of Dibley scenario, scarily familiar with a host of quirky characters, who were all rather noncommittal, and not responding to Joe's question about the Christmas Fayre at this point.

She thought she may as well set the ball rolling, 'We're organising Christmas Hampers full of goodies from the Teashop, made to order for pre-Christmas delivery, locally and further afield if they cover postage. I've already got a quote with Parcel First for £10, which considers the average weight and size of the filled box, and we can deliver in the local area ourselves for just a small fee. We'll also be making lots of shortbread, spiced cookies, brownies and fudge and chocolate truffles to make up into small gift bags for sale at the Fayre. I'm going to make loads of mince pies for the day, along with snowy topped iced-coconut cupcakes which will look really festive. We could also offer mulled wine as well as the usual tea and coffee type options.'

'Thanks, Ellie. Sounds good.' Joe commented.

'What about baking some plain biscuits or gingerbread and having the children ice them on the day?' Deana suggested. 'We could hold a competition and see who makes the best design, have a small prize or something. They could pay 50p to enter? We could put the money from that to charity. My grandchildren would love doing something like that.'

'Well, that's bound to make a fine mess everywhere. *Marvellous* idea, Deana.' Lord Henry was frowning, his tone heavy with sarcasm.

'I actually think it's a really good idea,' Doris spoke up. 'My grandchildren would love that too. Fits with the idea of a Craft Fayre, making things and all that. If we are doing something for charity, what about helping that chap who had the motorbike accident. The one who had to cancel his wedding here.'

'That does sound a nice idea Doris. But, it'd be better to give the money to a verified charity rather than an individual, but yes, a cause that's helped Daniel, maybe the ward in the hospital he's in, or the physiotherapy unit he'll be using. In fact, the air ambulance might be a good one – he was airlifted from the scene of the accident. They help so many people, especially in this type of rural community.' Joe was thinking practically.

'Yes, some charity fundraising would be great. The air ambulance sounds a fabulous cause,' Ellie agreed. 'We could hold a raffle on the day; we could ask local businesses for donations of prizes, if they didn't mind. Maybe each stallholder might give something too, just something small. I'd gladly put in a hamper from the Teashop.'

'Yes, that does sound a decent idea.' Lord Henry was warming to the concept, despite the thought of sticky fingers all over his antique furnishings.

'Which stallholders have confirmed so far then? Doris, you were taking names weren't you?' Joe asked.

'Yes, I have a list, hang on.' She dug around in her immense handbag. 'Right, candles, the card lady, a hand-made soap company, jams and chutneys, Doggie Delights – pet gifts. Wendy's coming along to make Christmas wreaths on the day and to take orders for festive flowers.

There's a micro-brewery selling bottled beers from the Kirk Valley. Oh, and my friend who does the knitted animal toys; she's already made some really cute Christmas mice.'

'We'll probably need a few more stalls for variety. Anybody else know of anyone who might be interested?'

Silence descended on the group.

'Well, does anyone want to pop to Kirkton market next week and take a look at what type of things are there? Ask any of the stallholders if they might be interested?'

'Oh yes, we'll do that. We quite like browsing market stalls, don't we Derek,' Malcolm piped up.

'Yes, I'm fine with that,' Derek agreed.

'Well, it'll take you all of ten minutes at Kirkton market. There's only about a half dozen or so stalls left, nowadays,' Deana said.

'It's worth a try.' The gents were not put off. 'We'll see if we can charm them to come along. Variety is the spice of life, so they say. So, we'll see who we can get on board. If the market's a bit thin on the ground, we might have some other contacts we can call on too. There's a lot of creative talent in this area. I was once a member of the Kirkton Art Society, I'll have you know.'

'Oh, I didn't know you painted, Malcolm,' Doris commented.

Derek was pulling a wry face, saying nothing.

'Not painting so much as sculpture, Doris. Well, I tried.

I wasn't that good. I gave up after my work went on display in the summer exhibition. I heard one woman saying what a lovely sculpture of a dog I'd done. It was a self-portrait, head and shoulders in clay, and it wasn't even meant to be modern art or anything. I had a bit of trouble with the eyes, very tricky, and the hair. Suppose it did look a bit shaggy. Lost my creative confidence then.'

Derek was holding back a snigger.

'Thanks for the support, you.' He gave his partner a terse look.

'Right, back to the Christmas Fayre. We've still a lot too plan.' Joe tried to get back on track.

'Are we charging a fee per stall? Just so we know when we're trying to recruit people,' Derek asked.

'Yes, I think we should. It seems to be the done thing, nothing too expensive, don't want to be putting stallholders off, but we need to make some revenue. I'd thought £20 per stall. They'll get a trestle table and an area each for that. The main event will be held in the Great Hall, and depending on numbers, we could overflow into the Drawing Room. Actually, that reminds me,' Joe added. 'We'll need to borrow the trestle tables from the village hall.'

'Not a problem,' Deana replied, 'Landlord Alan's on the village committee. He'll get them organized for us, for sure.'

Colin, the gardener, who'd been sat quietly up to this point spoke up, 'Do you need a Christmas tree for the Hall that day?'

'Oh yes, good idea, that'll look lovely. We need to make the event as festive as we can.' Ellie could picture a gorgeous pine tree all decorated with tinsel and baubles, and lit with fairy lights.

'Yes, Colin, you can go ahead and take a fir from the estate grounds. There'll be something suitable out there in the woods for certain,' Lord Henry offered.

Ellie could picture it all then, the Great Hall looking festive, with a touch of sparkle, the twinkle of lights, it would be a wonderful room to have a Christmas makeover. They had lots of tree lights and decorations up in their apartment. Ellie loved Christmas, and it had been extra magical since she had lived here at the castle. It was just such an amazing setting, old stone walls, latticed-leaded windows. Wendy could display some ivy and holly in the windowsills of the Hall, as they had loads spare in the grounds, Ellie had spotted it on a recent walk. And there could be storm lanterns and tealights –actually they might have to buy some of those battery-operated fake ones for safety. She was extra-cautious now after the devastating fire in the tearoom kitchens. That still made her heart sink when she thought of it . . . what she might have lost.

'Are we having a Father Christmas? My husband, Clifford, has offered to dress up if you'd like. He loves kids, and he's even got the Santa outfit stored at home from last year's Rotary event. Loves it, the fake white beard and everything. We could wrap up gifts, and put them in sawdust in some old bran tubs, like the good old days.' Doris was getting quite animated.

And so the plans were well afoot. The Christmas Fayre was taking shape, and it would hopefully be a rather lovely event, as well as bringing in some extra revenue. Ellie realized she had a stack of baking and sweet-making to do in the coming weeks that way, but she'd have help from Irene, and to be fair it was so much quieter in the Teashop just now, it should mostly get done in normal working hours. She noticed she'd been feeling more tired these days, early pregnancy stuff no doubt, but on the whole she felt well, full of hope and happy. She'd get on fine.

The next day, she woke up feeling pretty shattered even after a good night's sleep. It might well be the end-of-season thing, she mused, when you'd worked like crazy all summer, kept going on a mix of adrenalin and coffee; actually she'd cut the coffee right back since finding out she was expecting. Then boomph, often in October, the minute you had time to relax, you got floored by some cold virus or fatigue. She hoped that wouldn't happen this year. In fact, she'd better start listening to her body and pacing herself, making sure she took a few more breaks here and there. Joe kept checking up on her too, asking if she was feeling okay. Mind you, she wasn't ill was she, just pregnant, but maybe the mix-up of hormones might be a factor too.

Oh well, she had too much to do to dwell on it – with the Christmas Fayre coming up there was more baking than usual this time of year. The mornings were darker now, autumn creeping steadily on, which made it more of an effort to get up at the six-thirty start she needed, to make headway with the day's baking before the teashop opened.

She headed for the shower. As the hot water splashed her body, she started on her mental to-do list: she needed to bake several batches of plain and chocolate-chip shortbread for the gift bags she was going to make up for the Craft Fayre, gingerbread stars too – yes, they'd look pretty and would keep well. She could ice them nearer the event, but they'd keep well sealed in airtight containers up until then. She could picture batches of her bakes in pretty cellophane bags, with red, gold and silver strings curled at the ends, which would look so festive yet could be reasonably priced, so a child could buy a pack for their granny, or the like.

Today's baking for the teashop would include a carrot cake, and two lemon drizzles. Irene was in, so she'd make the scones, some nice cheese ones would go down well. It was the weather for the 'Winter Warmers' now. Soups, scones, toasted tea cakes, hot paninis, jacket potatoes. After wandering the castle, where the ancient heating system was dodgy at the best of times, along with the fact that Lord Henry kept the boiler on budget mode

– it would cost a small fortune otherwise – the visitors often needed warming up, literally. The teashop had its huge stone fireplace, where logs burned (the size of small tree trunks, *honestly*) all day. Ellie thought her teashop looked even cosier in the colder months, with the wrought iron chandeliers lit above them, the cosy crackle of the fire and the warming, rich smell of coffee and just-baked cake.

Okay, time to have a quick wash. She rubbed the shower gel over her torso, felt the gentle rise of her tummy under her fingertips, firming now, sheltering that new life. She smiled. Might be time to tell the family soon, and then the castle staff – she'd been thinking that Deana would make a lovely godmother. She couldn't wait to ask her. She shampooed, rubbed in some conditioner, and gave her hair a quick blast with the dryer, before kissing a sleepy Joe – who was still in bed – on the cheek, and heading down to the teashop, where she'd grab some tea and toast before making a start.

'When do you think it will be a good time to share our news?' Joe asked her that evening.

'Just a few more days. Maybe next week. I should be about eight weeks by then . . . I suppose we'll need to tell everybody on the same day, within the same hour ideally. Your mam, my mum and dad, Henry. You know what the grapevine's like, even between here and Newcastle. It'll spread like wildfire, especially once my mother gets hold of baby news.'

'It'll be exciting telling them, mind.'

'Yeah . . .' Ellie felt emotional just thinking about it. 'Makes it seem really real.'

'Right then, young lady. In your condition, I need to make sure you're eating well and getting plenty of rest. So, after such a busy day, I will concoct a supper of chicken curry and rice. Okay, so it might only be a jar of cooking sauce over some fresh chicken cubes, but it will prepared by my very own hands.'

'Do we have any naan breads? I'm feeling famished.'

'Indeed we do, I picked some up yesterday at the Co-op.'

'Perfect, you're coming on, Joe Ward.'

'Anything else I can get for you, madam?'

'Don't think so, I'm fine now I'm finally sitting down . . . oh, actually, can I book a foot rub for later, ple-ease?' She grinned hopefully.

'Okay, how can I resist . . . Used to be requests for rampant sex, now it's foot rubs. It's all going downhill fast.' But he was smiling as he spoke.

He ducked to avoid the rolled-up magazine that Ellie had launched at him.

19

Ellie spent the next day baking shortbread, brownies and gingerbread stars for her gift packs for the Craft Fayre. It was a Sunday. There were a few visitors in, and when Mavis and Jim called through for a spot of light lunch, Ellie had a chat with them, but generally it was quiet. So at four o'clock, she sent Doris home early and she decided to have a good tidy up without interruptions.

She made sure the kitchen and the tearooms had a thorough disinfectant-spray wipe down. She then felt a sudden burst of energy so scrubbed the two big ovens, which she hadn't had chance to do for a while, then carefully mopped the floors right through. By five o'clock, her back was beginning to nag. Maybe her cleaning efforts hadn't been quite as leisurely as she'd imagined. She sat herself down on a stool in the kitchen for a moment.

She decided to call it a day and head up and find Joe.

Hopefully he'd get an early finish too. They could chill out – bliss. She had some salmon defrosting, ready to pan fry for a cosy supper later.

Her stomach started grumbling, along with a dull ache in her lower back. Damn, maybe she'd got some kind of tummy bug coming on. She tried to think if she'd eaten anything unusual. But she'd been extra careful lately to be fair, making sure her eggs were well-cooked, avoiding pâté and soft cheeses.

She stood up, suddenly feeling like she'd better head for the loo; a warm wetness starting between her legs. What the hell was going on? Jeez, this was some bad tummy upset. She'd never lost control like that before. She had no time to get to the apartment, so she headed for the ladies toilets that were down the corridor next to the teashop.

Outside the door of the teashop she started to feel a bit giddy, held on to the stone wall to steady herself for a second, then carried on walking. She entered the ladies, found a compartment, where she sat down still feeling a little woozy.

'Oh, no, no, no, no, no.' She wasn't sure if she said the words aloud, or if it was all in her head.

There was blood. Bright red blood, all over the tissue paper.

This was no stomach bug.

She sat a while, afraid to move, afraid of what was

happening within her body. Though deep inside she already knew. The flow was heavy, like a bad period. A couple of big cramps, that snatched her breath, and then a clot or two.

Her baby. She was losing her baby.

She should try and get some help, but what could anyone do? She'd left her phone on the counter in the teashop, anyhow. She just had to try and stay calm, sit it out, the last thing she needed to do was to get up, and faint or something. She'd sent Doris home, the lads and Deana had probably gone by now too. There was no one left working in the castle at this time of day in the autumn other than Joe, and Lord Henry would be no doubt be tucked away on his rooms upstairs. She couldn't imagine asking him for help in this state, anyhow.

Tears began pricking her eyes, as the reality of what was happening began to hit home. She was miscarrying. A terrible sinking feeling took over her. Then, a sense of devastation that felt like a lead weight in her soul.

'Joe?'

She'd heard the apartment door go, the sound of his footsteps.

'Hey, where are you? What's up? I've just seen the missed calls – I was out on the estate, out of signal.'

'Here . . . in the bathroom.' Her voice sounded weak,

weary. She'd managed to get herself upstairs to the security of their apartment, but had had to stay on the loo since.

'Shall I come in?'

'Yeah.' She didn't want to have to say it.

Joe poked his head cautiously around the door. 'Are you okay?'

She shook her head. The tears forming, catching on her words. 'No . . . I-I think I'm having a miscarriage.'

'Oh Jesus, Ellie, no . . . Is there anything I can do?' He rushed over, knelt down at the side of the loo, and held her gently.

She sobbed into his arms.

'Are you losing blood, are you in pain?'

The pain was still griping on, but worse was the emotional pain – the devastating sense of loss.

'Yes, a bit. The blood's heavy. It must have been going on for about half an hour or so now.'

'Okay, we need to get you to see a doctor, Ellie. You're looking really pale. We need to know what's going on. Get some help.'

'It's a Sunday,' she replied. 'The doctor's will be closed.' She'd been thinking of options whilst she sat there, wondering if there was any way the baby could be saved. If this might all be a false alarm, the baby was still there, and it could work out okay in the end.

'Hmm, it'll have to be A & E then. Do you think you're

okay to move? I really think we should get you seen to. Check things out.'

'Maybe.' She still felt a bit weak, but with Joe around, she could try and get up. Then she realized she'd be in a bit of a mess, would need a sanitary towel. 'Look, give me a minute. I just need to sort myself out a bit.'

'Sure you'll be okay?'

She nodded.

'I'll just be outside the door.'

'Thanks.'

He came back in, a few minutes later. 'Right then, let's get you to hospital, my love.'

20

Eight thirty on a Sunday night, and everything felt out of kilter. They should be at home, in their apartment, snuggled up on the sofa watching *Poldark* or something. Instead, they were waiting their turn, sipping cool, milky tea from polystyrene cups, sat on hard plastic chairs in the A&E department of Cramlington Hospital. The waiting area was all shiny and new, having only been opened a few months ago. Along their row sat an elderly couple, the husband coughing and coughing; it wasn't his fault, but it was beginning to make Ellie feel sick. Just opposite was a boy of about ten sat with his mum, trying to hold back sobs. She'd had to carry him in; Ellie had heard her explaining his football injury, possible broken ankle at the reception desk. And a baby had been rushed in with a high temperature and a rash just before, and been allowed to go straight through.

That had made Ellie's heart ache even more, for them, for her.

All these broken lives, illness, gathered in one place. It was a pretty long wait; they'd been over an hour so far, but she had to admire the nurses and doctors who dealt with all this day in, day out.

'You okay?'

'Might need to go to the loo again in a minute.' The flow was still quite heavy, and painful. She'd wondered about taking some paracetamol that happened to be in her handbag, but then, if there was any chance the baby was still viable, she shouldn't be taking any tablets.

'Mrs Ward?' A young nurse, in blue uniform, came out from the double doors. She was holding a clipboard.

'Yes, here.' Joe stood up first. Ellie more slowly.

They were taken through the swing doors and into a side room, where the nurse, who introduced herself as Rachel, asked Ellie to describe her symptoms. She then did some initial observations on Ellie, and took a blood test, and said the doctor would be along shortly.

The lights were too bright. Smells, clean and clinical, hushed voices. Soft padding of shoes, and a slight squeak as they gripped the disinfected flooring. Joe took her hand as they waited. Neither of them knowing quite what to say for now. The doctor was a tall woman with grey-ish-blonde hair, who looked in her forties. Ellie wondered if she had children at all; if she knew what this was like.

They discussed her symptoms again, Ellie mentioning her positive pregnancy test a few weeks ago, the doctor nodding seriously, then checking the observation details on Ellie's chart.

'Ellie, I'm sorry to say, it does appear that you are undergoing a miscarriage . . .' The doctor's voice continued kindly, but Ellie was finding it hard to concentrate.

'Oh.' Ellie was trying hard to take it all in, but it was all a mix of words and terms, and there didn't seem to be anything the doctors could do other than let nature take its course. She and Joe were advised to go home, get some rest, and call back down to the hospital the next morning for a scan. It all seemed a world away from their joy and excitement at the top of that hill just two weeks ago.

They drove back mostly in silence. Ellie felt so tired. She had no words left. Closed her eyes for a while.

Joe concentrated on driving.

They had just turned off the A1, nearing the hills and valleys of home.

'Joe, what if it was me? What if I did too much? I'm always dashing about in the teashop. And now, getting ready for the Craft Fayre. I hardly stop, and I spent ages cleaning the kitchens this afternoon. I didn't have to do it all at once . . . Do you think it could be my fault?'

'Don't go blaming yourself, Ellie. Didn't the nurse say

earlier, that if a miscarriage was going to happen there was very little you could do to cause or stop it?'

'Maybe.' There had been so much to listen to. 'But what if . . .'

'Don't go there, Ellie. Don't put yourself though any more. We'll get through this, and we'll find out tomorrow what next, okay?'

'Okay.'

They parked up, walked in. Same castle, same walls, same courtyard, yet everything felt so very different – a little emptier. Back in the apartment she decided to have bath. Let herself soak in some warm bubbles, it'd ease her back pain that was still nagging.

Five minutes later, Joe knocked, 'You okay in there?'

She hadn't locked the door, just in case. 'Yeah, I'm all right.' The words flowed reassuringly, whilst emotionally she felt a bit of a wreck.

'Just shout if you need me.'

'Will do, I'm fine. Thank you.'

She towel dried, and wrapped herself up in her fleece robe. She felt a little calmer now. She snuggled up, next to Joe, on the sofa. His arm around her was just what she needed right now. But she still felt so very empty. Nestled together, he stroked her hair, as she let her head rest against his chest. She sighed softly against him, feeling the weight of her grief, *their* grief.

It was a weird sense of loss. As such, they'd had nothing

to show for it, just hopes and dreams and the knowledge of new life that had already been taken away, but already in her mind it had been her child.

Three-ten a.m., Ellie stood looking out a silver-white moon, through the latticed windows of their apartment lounge. She could see craters and scars on its bright creamy surface. The night sky so dark beyond it. A whisper of cloud here and there.

It had felt uncomfortable lying there in bed, with her thoughts and her grumbling abdomen. Joe was fast asleep, she could tell by his breathing. She hadn't want to disturb him with her tossing and turning, so got up and made a cup of camomile-honey tea. She realized she was still hugging the mug. Tomorrow, no today now, she'd know for sure. But her body was already telling her.

She thought these thing happened to other people. Everyone had heard of miscarriage. It wasn't that uncommon. But she hadn't *felt* it, *known* it until now. Hadn't known how dark and lonely it could be.

Keep positive, pet, a voice in her mind spoke up. *If it is the worst, I know you can deal with it. Life knocks you sometimes, Ellie pet. But you can come back stronger. You will.* And the voice sounded just like her Nanna's.

And then she felt two arms, firm but gentle, slide around her. 'Having trouble sleeping?'

'Uh-huh.'

She let herself lean back against him. He would be hurting too, of course he would.

His chin rested gently against the top of her head, then she felt the brush of a kiss in her hair.

'Feel like coming back to bed?'

'Yeah, think that might be a good idea. It could be a long day tomorrow, too.'

'Whatever we face, we face together, yeah.'

'Yeah.'

21

An early start, shower, tea and toast. Ellie had drifted back to an uneasy sleep after their 3 a.m. vigil.

They were heading out to the car, 7.45 a.m., to get on their journey back down to the hospital, being out in rural Northumberland it would take around fifty minutes to get there. Lord Henry caught up with them in the stone-cobbled courtyard of the castle. He was still in his long, maroon velvet dressing gown that looked rather like a smoking jacket. It reminded Ellie of one of the meerkat characters on the television adverts lately. In an odd way, in the depths of her pain, that made her smile.

'Ellen, I'm so, so sorry to hear about what's happened,' he said. Joe had phoned him from the hospital last night, to let him know where they were. 'What a terrible misfortune.'

And then he held his arms open for her. Lord Henry

was never one for displays of affection – a polite kiss on the cheek at Christmas or birthdays, and that was about it. She hesitated for a second, just because it was so unusual, but then accepted his embrace. His arms were solid, reassuring, fatherly. It brought a fresh tear to her eye.

'There, there,' he soothed, then he pulled gently away. 'Look after her, Joe.'

'I will, of course.'

The men nodded sombrely at each other.

It was a morning of waiting, then the scan, and the disappointing news that Ellie had in a way been expecting and dreading all at once. That was it, no more baby.

The doctor recommended non-intervention. The miscarriage appeared to be clearing everything away naturally. Ellie was advised to keep an eye on things, take it slightly easier for a week or so, but she was told everything would be back to normal soon. Well, physically at least. For now, her emotions felt like they were on a rollercoaster. And so, they were back on the road heading up the A1.

The next day, the castle support network stepped into action; Doris popped to see her with a hug and lovely scented candle, Deana brought her some gorgeous bubble bath and stayed and chatted for an hour, Irene baked her a Victoria sponge and a lemon drizzle for Joe, Malcolm and Derek surprised her with a beautiful bouquet of flowers and chocolate truffles. All of them were ready with some chat and friendly advice, or in Malcolm's case a bit of banter which was in fact great (it was nice to think about something else completely, and to find herself smiling again, however briefly).

She appreciated that so much. They weren't just work colleagues, they were her friends.

She received phone calls from her mum and dad, who Joe had phoned to advise of the sad news, and Gemma her best friend from the insurance office (from the years before Ellie moved up to the castle). She'd seen Ellie's mum on the street and had heard. Gemma was married herself now, and still living down in Newcastle-upon-Tyne. Also, Joe's mam Sue rang and was so lovely and supportive, it felt like she was giving Ellie a big hug down the phone.

Everything felt a little surreal for Ellie over the next few days. Instead of announcing a lovely new baby, there were tears, and the sharing of altogether sadder news.

'I'm thinking of coming up for a day. We could do lunch, or something.'

It was Sarah, Ellie's mum. Sarah, wasn't the kind of lady who 'did lunch'. She worked hard as a cleaner at the doctor's surgery, kept a tidy house, made good wholesome home-cooked food for her family, but was in no way extravagant with either her emotions or her hard-earned cash.

Ellie had a feeling this was her mum's way of trying to look after her after the miscarriage. 'Well, yes, that would be nice. When are you thinking?'

'Tomorrow, if you're free. Dad's busy working, Jason will be doing his own thing, so I thought I'd pop up to see you.'

In the past five years, Mum had never come up on her own without Dad. She didn't really like driving outside of her comfort zone of the Newcastle city streets she knew.

'Okay, that sounds good.'

'I thought I'd see how you are getting on . . . you know.'

'I'm all right. Well, I'm getting there . . .' They both seemed to be skirting the 'M' word; Ellie picking up on her mum's awkwardness. Sarah had never been the most open with her emotions, but Ellie knew it was never through lack of love.

'Right, well then, I'll see you tomorrow then, Ellie. Take care, pet. I'll leave at about nine in the morning. So I'll be there by tenish, I suppose.'

'Thanks, Mum.'

Ellie put down the phone, feeling strangely emotional.

It was lovely to have a bit of time out. A change of scene. Irene and Doris had insisted Ellie take a few days off from the teashop.

A frosty start had led to a stunning October-blue sky. The damp sands of the bay swirled in dark-blonde ripples, the sea a choppy blue-grey. Ellie and her mum had decided to have a short walk on the beach at Embleton, before driving down to the harbour village of Craster for lunch.

'We used to come here when you were little.' Sarah looked around her. 'I can just picture you and Jay making sandcastles on the beach, and you used to spend ages looks for tiny fish and crabs in the rock pools just over there.' She pointed at the dark craggy masses at the far end of the bay, which curved like a half moon ahead of them. The striking outline of the ruined Dunstanburgh Castle was dramatic on the headland in the distance.

Sarah stopped walking, 'I'm very proud of you and Jason.'

Ellie looked across at her, surprised; Mum never came out with slushy stuff like this. She almost felt like saying, 'Are you okay?' but then thought better of it. Actually, she hoped she really was okay, what if her Mum was ill or something, had come up to try and tell her? Ellie felt a horrid chill through her.

'Thanks,' she answered.

There was a second or two of silence as they walked along the shore once more. Ellie looked out to sea, watching a tern bobbing on the waves.

Sarah took a slow breath, 'I've got you and Jason, your

dad, and life worked out for us, really well . . . But before that. Well, I had what you had . . . what you have just gone through.' She sounded awkward, as though the words were costing her.

'A miscarriage.' There, it was said.

'Yes . . . I was four months gone.'

Ellie had never known.

'And I remember feeling so devastated at the time,' she continued.

'Oh, Mum. You never said.'

'Well, it had been a long time before, and then you were there, a little girl. And, as you and Jay grew up, well it isn't the sort of thing you just come out with, is it?'

'No, I suppose not.'

'And anyway, what I'm trying to say, is that it was all all right in the end. I had, have two beautiful children.'

'Well, I can see that about one of them,' Ellie smiled. 'Not so sure about Jay.'

They both laughed.

'Sorry, couldn't resist that.' Ellie didn't want to sound too flippant.

'It *can* all work out in the end, Ellie. I know you'll be feeling terribly sad, and it'll be hard for you and Joe for a while. But it doesn't mean you won't get your own lovely family soon . . . Well, hopefully.' With that, she patted Ellie's shoulder.

Sarah looked more relaxed, now she'd said what she'd

needed to. Ellie sensed that this had been quite hard for her, having to peel away a layer of her reserve.

'Thanks, Mum. Shall we head for some lunch?'

They wandered back to the car that Ellie had parked up in the lane by the golf course, the conversation returning to Dad's work being so busy, how the castle was doing, the latest gripping crime novel Sarah was reading, and the state of the roads these days. Sarah had apparently struggled, avoiding potholes and pheasants who were trying to commit hari-kiri in front of her, all through the lanes from the A1.

They sat at a corner table, warming up from the chill of the walk by a real fire, with logs crackling and glowing next to them. Ellie chose local crab sandwiches with some homemade chips, her mum went for the salmon fishcakes. It was lovely to sit and chat some more, how Jay was finding the plumbing business, the Christmas Fayre, about Lucy and Dan.

Ellie's mum mentioned her cousin Lynn's baby who was now a few months old, and smiling, loving being played with, then she paused looking at Ellie a little concerned, afraid she might have said too much, had veered too near the subject. But Ellie realized it was okay, talking about babies and life, and family – that was nice. 'It's fine, Mum. It's nice to know how they are doing.'

The food came and was delicious. The wholemeal sandwiches were fresh and tasty, with lots of flavoursome crab meat. The chips all crispy and salty. It was nice to be served by someone else for a change, and to be pampered a little.

Sarah insisted on paying, though Ellie offered. She said she wanted to treat her.

Ellie suggested they head back to the castle, they could relax and have some tea and cake later. Ellie had been trying out some new recipes, and had a nice coconut and lime cake ready that she'd made this morning. The closed season was the ideal time to try out new bakes, and see what might work to shake up the cake selection when they reopened the castle and the teashop in the spring. She liked having the time to experiment with new flavours and ingredients.

'Well, I have brought something up to help with supper tonight, too. I have the cool box in my car, back at the castle. Oops, I forgot to take it out. It should be fine though, I did pop an ice pack in.'

'Yeah, it'll be like a fridge in there, anyhow,' Ellie smiled. 'I don't think you'd need a cool box, it's never got above four degrees today, for sure.'

There was a large cottage pie and a crumble, rhubarb and ginger, which sounded delightful.

Later on, they ate in the apartment with Joe, who'd been working through the day – there was still plenty going on with the estate side of things, the farm to keep an eye on, woodland to manage, the grounds to keep up.

The fruit crumble was definitely comfort food at its best. 'This is gorgeous, Mum. I love the ginger flavour through it too.' The rhubarb was soft and tangy, the little pieces of ginger, fragrant and warming and then the melt-in-the-mouth crumble with its crispy sugary top. Scrummy. 'I'm going to have to get this recipe for the teashop.'

'I didn't quite get the baking gene, did I? But I must admit I do make a good crumble. The ginger is actually one of your Nanna's tips. This was Nanna's recipe. You use stem ginger finely chopped, and a little of the syrup from the jar. Makes it really warming, doesn't it.'

'It's just delicious, Sarah. Really good,' Joe added, pouring a little more custard over.

Ellie's mum seemed to glow a little, and a smile spread over her face.

Ellie felt a warm glow too. She'd had a really lovely day with her mum. She couldn't remember the last time when it had been just the two of them together like that. For years, probably since Ellie had been a teenager, there had been a slight distance. It was hard to pin it down, she knew she was loved, and that her mum would be there for her no matter what, perhaps it was just that they were different personalities. But something had shifted between them today; Ellie felt a little bit closer.

They finished the meal, and had a quick cup of tea. It was coming up to seven thirty.

'Well, I suppose I'd better be getting on my way. Never did like driving in the dark much,' Sarah said.

'It'll be pitch-black out there now, so take it steady, Mum.' Her day trip really had taken her out of her comfort zone; Ellie really appreciated that.

Joe and Ellie walked Sarah down to her car, which was parked in the semicircle of gravel driveway that came right up to the main castle steps.

'You take care now, Ellie. No overdoing it. I know what you're like.'

'I won't, I promise.'

'Not sure when we'll see you next, but Dad says he'll pop up soon. He's just had so much work on just now.'

'Oh, I meant to mention, it's not that long now really, would you like to come up for Christmas again this year, spend it here at the castle? Come for a few days. I'll do dinner, the works, make it special.'

'That sounds lovely, but on one condition, you let me help. And I'll bring some food to contribute. I could do one of my boiled hams and a trifle or something.'

'Yes, okay, that's a deal . . . And Jay can bring Carmel too, if he wants. More the merrier. We've got plenty of room.' She smiled, looking over her shoulder at the huge stone castle that was now home; what a contrast to their terraced redbrick house in the Newcastle suburbs. And yet, both places were warm, filled with love and caring. It was all bricks (well, stone) and mortar at the end of the day. What really mattered were the people inside it.

'Have a safe journey.'

'Lovely to see you, Sarah, and thanks for bringing up that gorgeous supper.'

'You're very welcome.'

'And you take care of yourself, Ellie, pet. No doing too much, like you usually do.'

'I'll be keeping a very close eye on her.' Joe answered, as he placed a caring hand on Ellie's shoulder.

And off Sarah drove, into the dark, with a quick wave out the window.

22

'Are you sure you still want to go ahead with this, Ellie? We could cancel or make it smaller scale. We don't have to open the teashop, just keep it to the craft stalls in the hall.'

There was only one week to go until the first ever Claverham Castle Christmas Craft Fayre, and Joe was concerned.

'No, I'll be okay. I've done lots of the baking for it already. It can't go to waste. And I have my team to help me. And you know, I think it'll give me something to focus on. I can't just sit about and mope anymore.'

'You'd have every right to. And you should be taking it a bit easier, at least.'

'I know. But that's *so* not my style. And we're so close to this event, all the posters are out, it's in the papers and everything. Let's make it a success. We've all put so much effort in already. I'm more than ready to go back to work.'

'Well, just promise me you won't overdo it, okay?'

'Okay.'

There was a sense of tension and anticipation about the Christmas Craft Fayre through the castle staff. If this went well, then it could become an annual event, and draw people (and income) to the castle at what was usually a quiet time of the year. Joe had been busy with advertising – there were features in the local press, notices in the Tourist Information centres, and posters around the area including Kirkton, Bamburgh and Seahouses on the coast.

Deana and Doris had co ordinated all the stallholders, and they had a grand total of sixteen different crafts with everything from cakes to candles, knitted toys and teddies, embroidery, wood turning. There was going to be a hands-on pots-and-paints table for the children to really get stuck in to. This had displeased Lord Henry no end, but he had been unanimously outvoted. They'd definitely need the oilcloths out to cover the tables for that though.

Malcolm and Derek had secured a Santa and a sleigh. Doris's husband, Clifford, had been taken up on his offer to appear as Father Christmas. Malcolm had procured a horse and cart for the afternoon, not Patrick the pony – though that might have been highly entertaining – but a fab little Shetland who could take the children on a trip up and down the drive, *and* was happy to wear antlers apparently. A local carpenter was going to make some fake sides for the cart out of MDF wood and paint them to look like a sleigh. With a touch of tinsel here and there, it would look the part and very festive. The only downside *(why was there always a downside with Malcolm's plans?)* was that being a small Shetland, the pony couldn't manage to pull an adult, so Father Christmas would be following on a quad bike. Well, it was the countryside after all.

Ellie kept baking like a mad thing; it kept her busy and her mind off things. She managed the day-to-day teashop activities, whilst making as much shortbread, gingerbread, brownies and fudge as she could in between times. She was just taking a batch of vanilla cupcakes out of the oven ready to ice with coconut snow, then she was going to decorate them with ready-made sugar figures of Christmas penguins, snowmen, trees and polar bears. She was tired of an evening, and Joe kept telling her to ease off a bit. But she didn't want to sit and dwell. She was better kept busy.

Friday, one day to go, and full preparations were underway. Christmas had come early to Claverham Castle! Colin was out in the estate woods with James, who was now a strapping lad of twenty-two, looking for a suitable fir tree they could chop down, and bring back to display and decorate. They couldn't access the Great Hall until after 4 p.m. when they closed it off to day visitors. So, it was going to be a long evening and busy morning, getting everything ready.

The teashop kitchens were all hands on deck. Irene, Ellie and Doris were busy mixing, baking and icing, in between serving the regular teashop customers. Wendy had come in to help decorate the teashop with festive florals; she'd then concentrate on the Hall tomorrow. Holly, ivy and red and white carnations gave a splash of festive colour, gracing window ledges and the counter. She'd also made gorgeous table decorations with a very real-looking battery operated candle in each (for safety reasons). She would be selling them in the Great Hall too, along with Christmas wreaths. Having reserved a table for her florist's stall – her mother was going to mind the shop, and a friend was going to help her here on the day. She'd seen it as a great opportunity, and was going to take Christmas orders too, for items that would need to be made up nearer Christmas time.

It was lovely when the whole team came together, like they did with the wedding events; it was hectic but there was a real sense of the castle community, the staff, working as a team. Yes, there were always the odd hiccups, and someone would definitely have a minor strop at some point, but hey, it all worked out in the end. And they managed somehow to remain friends as well as colleagues. And whatever ups and downs they faced, and the sadness of the past ten days for Ellie, it made her see how much she had grown to love this place and the very special people in it.

Saturday morning, 10.30 a.m. There was already one major strop going on, but luckily it wasn't any of the castle staff. Little had they known that there was a pecking order for stallholders, and prime positions for stalls. Mrs Jam Lady was having battle of the stands with Miss Sewing Delights. Joe had tried his best to calm the situation as it was evident both of them couldn't occupy the first stand by the main entrance doors where the customers would all (hopefully) flood in, by suggesting a toss of a coin, which they had agreed to, but then carried on arguing once Mrs Jam Lady realized she had lost, and would be banished an alternative spot mid-room by the fireplace. It took Doris to manhandle her and her goods across to the empty table, offering her the £20 stallholder fee back if she wished to leave. Mrs Jam Lady realized that she had met her match, and backed down grudgingly, with the odd black look fired across at Sewing Delights.

Ellie settled the stallholders by offering to make a big pot of tea, and she warmed some mince pies to bring up to them all. That seemed to work well, and most were smiling as they were setting up their stalls, bar Jam Lady who persevered with a straight line for a mouth. Ellie guessed her marmalades might be a touch bitter.

Malcolm was now teetering up a stepladder – Colin

had chosen a ten-foot tall monster of a tree, which was fantastic to look at, but pretty difficult to decorate. He'd just draped round the third lot of fairy lights, with Derek supervising positioning from down below. Then, there was the big light-up moment, Malcolm still up the ladder, in case any tweaking was needed. Colin went to turn the electric switch on. A second of glory and sparkly glow, and then boomph, the whole hall was plunged into a dim half-light.

'Shite,' came a mutter from the back of the tree.

'Bollocks,' came Malcolm's groan from the top of the ladder.

A general mumbling, grumbling and 'Oh, nos' spreading around the stallholders who were busy setting up.

'It's okay, just hold fire everyone. I'll go and check the fuse box. We'll see if anything's tripped. Might be as simple as that.' Joe called out.

Well, that was great. Only two hours to go, with hopefully hundreds of people attending, and no electric. Joe hoped it hadn't affected the whole castle, imagining the chaos if the teashop was down too. He tried to remain calm, found a torch in Deana's office and headed for the main fuse box, uttering a silent prayer.

Lord Henry caught up with him at the electric box.

'What the devil's going on now? I've got no damn electric in my rooms. I was just enjoying the snooker at the Crucible on the television. Bloody bad timing.

O'Sullivan was about to get a one-four-seven, I'll never know if he did it now.'

'Don't worry about your bloody snooker. I've got a hall full of angry stallholders and a Christmas Craft Fayre about to happen.' Joe very rarely lost his temper, but this was one of those times when his nerves were frayed.

'Right, yes, it had slipped my mind . . . I suppose I should be helping somehow.'

'Yes, well that might be good. Hold the torch could you, that'd be a start.'

Even in the daytime the castle was a gloomy place if there was no lighting. Designed with heavy stone walls and tiny windows to keep raiders out, it unfortunately let little light in.

'Right, hold it steady. Hmm, I can see the trip is down for the Great Hall circuit and it seems to have tripped the whole of the west wing of the castle too. That's why your rooms are out. Right, I'll put them all off and then back on again, reset the lot.'

He'd had to do this on several occasions over the years, to be fair. The electrics for the castle had been updated, but the whole system was made up of add-ons, and could be quite sensitive at times.

'Right, I'm going to dash back and tell Colin *not* to try the Christmas tree lights again, as one set's probably out. Malcolm will have to take them all down again and test them – ideally elsewhere, back in his cottage or something, where he can't set off the castle again. I'd have thought he'd have tested them in the first place. That would have helped.'

'Well then, shall I come across to see if there's anything I can do? My snooker's scuppered now anyhow.'

'Yes, you may as well. It's going to be a busy day, so the more help we have the better.'

'Just don't get me mixed up with a load of kids. I'll call the raffle or something, that'll do.'

Lights tested – back at Derek and Malcolm's cottage, tripping their switches too, with one dodgy set having to be discarded – they were left with a slightly less twinkly display of two strands. With plenty of tinsel and baubles from previous Christmas's dragged out from storage – some of it looking distinctly Victorian – the tree still looked really pretty.

The stallholders had set up. The hall was looking fabulous. Wendy had woven her magic with festive florals and greenery, and the smells from the room were wonderful, of pine and cinnamon, scented candles, spiced cookies. Ellie had organized her table of teashop goodies and Lauren, one of her waitresses, was going to mind it for her; they were also taking orders for Christmas cakes and hampers. Ellie herself would have to stay down at the teashop to help keep up with the steady flow of customers they were hoping for. With her last batch of mince pies still warm out of the oven, she made up a pot of tea for herself, Doris and Irene, before it all got too busy and they never had chance. Ellie bit into a crumbly mince pie – well, someone had to check they were all right – spicy, fruity and warm, delicious.

Doris's mobile phone rang, interrupting their break.

'What do you mean you can't get out of bed? You're meant to be here by 11 o'clock.' They listened in to one side of the conversation. 'Ooh, I see . . . So you've been sick too. Oh dear . . .' Doris was shaking her head at them dramatically, a frown forming across her brow.

She switched off her phone. 'Father Christmas is poorly. He can't make it.'

'Oh dear,' said Irene, 'The children will be so disappointed. We had the bran tubs of gifts ready and everything. And he was going to make a grand entrance down the driveway.'

'What a shame, it won't be the same without a real Father Christmas.' Ellie was racking her brains for an alternative, but everyone else who was involved in the event was already so busy.

'Oh well, I'd better go up and tell Joe the bad news, hadn't I,' Doris said.

'Such a shame.'

Doris found Joe, soon after he had sorted out the lighting problems, just as he thought he'd got everything settled.

Malcolm came dashing in at the same time, 'The sleigh and pony are here, but no Father Christmas as yet.'

'I'm sorry, I've just heard, it's my Clifford, he's been right poorly. I hoped he might rally, but he's just phoned in. Thinks it's the flu. He daren't come and spread all his germs to the children. He can hardly get out of bed anyhow, by the sounds of it.'

Just then Lord Henry wandered across, 'Some decent prizes there. What's the raffle for then, Joe? Some charity, I presume.'

'Yes, the air ambulance.' It had been chosen especially, bearing in mind how it had helped Daniel during his motorcycle accident.

Suddenly, three sets off of eyes landed on Lord Henry, the same thought flashing across three faces.

Doris strode in where the other two dare not, 'Lord Henry, I need a *really* special favour. You couldn't just try something on for me, could you?' And with that, she whisked him away.

From her office window, Deana could see people beginning to queue outside the main entrance; it was nearly ten to eleven – that looked promising. Derek telephoned through to say they were ready for the off up in the Great Hall, and that he and Malcolm would be down at the front steps in ten minutes to organize the arrival of Father Christmas and the 'reindeer' pony and sleigh, so could she could let the visitors know, especially those with children.

'Ho, ho, and bloody ho. That good enough, Deana?'

In walked a very grumpy Father Christmas, followed by Doris with a red face, saying, 'Sorry, but I've got to hand him over. I'm needed at the teashop, sharp. Just make sure he doesn't bail out.'

'Lord Henry, how the hell are you going to be nice to children for a whole hour or two?'

'I haven't the faintest bloody idea. The beard's scratchy already. And the suit's snug to say the least. Evidently not designed for a six foot two man.'

Deana tried to suppress a grin, but failed miserably; it spilled out over her trembling lips. 'They should have had you lined up as Scrooge, might have been an easier part for you to play.'

'Hah, bloody, hah. I'm only doing this to stop the bloody children crying 'cos there's no Father Christmas. He can't very well be ill can he?'

'Is that what's happened? It was meant to be Clifford, last I heard.'

'Yes, indeed. He's now been struck down with flu. I'm the last resort.'

'Well, I kind of guessed that.' Deana held back a wry grin.

He decided to ignore that comment. 'I have to drive in on a quad . . . a quad I tell you. Greet the masses, go up to the Hall and sit and dish out gifts, thinking of sickly sweet things to say to all the little buggers who'll want to sit on my knee.'

'Ah, you'll be fine . . . Just don't swear, or say anything to frighten them.' Was this *really* a good idea? What was Doris thinking? No Father Christmas at all, might actually have been safer than a crotchety, swearing one.

'It's all right, I know what you're thinking. I can act, I'll just pretend I like children for the hour. Just be ready to hand me a stiff gin and tonic afterwards.'

It was well known that Deana had a little supply of gin and cans of tonic in her bottom drawer. Handy for the odd occasion. 'Deal. I might be needing one too, by then.' She winked at him.

Derek came past to unlock the gates, there was no admission fee today. They'd decided that might help encourage more people to come along; they hoped they'd spend their money inside.

'Right, you'd better hide in the back room with the filing cabinets, 'til they're ready for you. Don't want to be giving the game away too soon.'

'Fine. I know my place. Lord of the bloody Manor dressed up like an idiot and hiding in a broom cupboard. I could have been back in my rooms, minding my own business, watching the snooker, if I'd had any sense . . .' he grumbled on.

23

Up in the Great Hall, visitors started filing in. There was soon a lovely buzz about the place, as they chatted amongst themselves, picking up the festive items with lots of oohs and aahs, and talking with the stallholders. There was a sign for the teashop too, letting them know they were open for tea and coffee, fresh mince pies, cakes, hot chocolate and more.

Malcolm came in a short while later, raising his voice splendidly to announce that Father Christmas was about to arrive down the main driveway, and if anyone wanted to see him or to have a reindeer sleigh ride they needed to go down to the front steps immediately.

Joe felt a sense of dread. The grotto area, a garden shed they'd relocated from one of the empty cottages on the estate, was all set up with an antique wooden chair and the bran tubs of gifts and sawdust shavings, each side. Colin had even brought in some potted shrubs from the garden and twined them with delicate white fairy lights, so it looked rather magical. But Joe really didn't know how his father was going to cope with it all. It was *so* not his thing. Joe had never even seen him interacting with a child. He preferred to avoid them as a general rule.

Joe had to stay put to oversee the hall and what was going on. The only thing he knew was that 'Christmas' Lord Henry was arriving by quad at any moment.

There was quite a gathering on the steps as an antlered pony appeared, being led by his owner, local farmer's wife, Mary.

'Aw, look he's so sweet.' 'And look at the sleigh!' 'Mu-um, I want a go, can I have a ride?'

A short distance behind was a figure in red, revving up a quad erratically, managing to wave with one hand.

'Can't wait to see this,' Malcolm whispered to Derek. 'What a turn-up for the books. I never thought he'd do it myself.'

'That's the Doris effect, makes you say yes to all sorts of thing you wish you hadn't,' Derek replied.

'Right,' Malcolm shouted out. 'At the ready children. We need a big cheer and lots of waving for Father Christmas.'

'Ho, ho, ho!' Lord Henry managed from the back of

the quad, as he turned the vehicle to a halt with a crunch of gravel. The lads in the crowd were very impressed.

He swung a big red sack over his shoulder, which he poised for dramatic effect, as he got off of the vehicle. Then the crowd of children and parents parted to let him through. 'I hope you're being good girls and boys,' he boomed as he passed.

'So do I,' muttered Malcom under his breath, 'Or they'll be in for it at the grotto.'

Derek called out to the audience. 'Santa's grotto is in the Great Hall. And, we are taking sleigh rides out here with the reindeer and cart. Only £2.50 a go, max two children at a time.'

'Have a wonderful time!' called Malcolm. 'Christmas at the Castle is here.'

The teashop was on full throttle, rather like 'Christmas' Henry's quad. Mince pies were flying out fast along with orders for tea/coffee and frothy hot chocolates with marshmallow tops. Ellie's chocolate-orange brownies were proving popular, plus her gingerbread snowmen for the children. She'd kept lunch options to a minimum knowing it would be a hectic day, but the homemade vegetable soup with a bread roll was going out well too.

Clusters of people were coming in to warm up from the chill of a November afternoon, they enjoyed the crackling fire, and some good home baking. Hopefully, some new customers from the locality might have found out about the teashop now, and would come back and recommend them for next season too. Ellie had put a selection of her festive gift bags of shortbread, ginger-bread stars and fudge on the counter too, and they were getting snapped up as well. It was going to be well worth all the planning, hard work and effort, and hopefully the takings would be good. She was so glad she hadn't let Joe persuade her to cancel. Though, she realized she was aching a bit now, and the small of her back had begun to nag. She sat herself down for a minute on a stool in the teashop kitchen.

Doris found her.

'You feeling all right, pet? I thought this might all be a bit much for you. So soon after . . .' the words trailed.

'I'm fine Doris, honestly.'

'Well, you look a bit peaky to me. I'm making you a cup of tea, and you're not to move. It's started to ease off in the teashop now, so we'll be fine.'

Irene popped through soon after, to get a new can of spray cream for the hot chocolate toppings.

'Overdone it a bit,' Doris explained.

'Oh Ellie, lovey. Take a few minutes rest. We're fine in the teashop, aren't we Doris. It's all in good hands.'

'I know . . . and thank you.' And the tears she'd kept back for the past few days started to flow. 'Sorry.'

'No need to be sorry, lovey. Here now.' Irene handed

her a crisp white old-fashioned embroidered hankie. 'Let it all out.'

Doris passed her a warm mug of sweetened tea. And then rather surprisingly gave her a very bosomy, motherly hug.

Actually, after having a good cry, a nose blow and the cup of tea, Ellie began to feel a little better. Doris made her sit quietly for another fifteen minutes, checking that she didn't feel faint or anything as she stood up, then finally let her go with a word of warning to take a seat straight away if she felt giddy at all.

Ellie glanced at her watch, ten past two. Blimey, those three hours had flown. She wanted to nip up to The Great Hall, and see how Lauren was getting on with her gift bags, and the hamper and cake orders. Ellie filled a small box with a selection of her homemade biscuit and fudge packs to take up with her too, just in case.

'I'll be back in a short while, ladies,' she told Doris and Irene. 'I just want to check how things are going up in the Hall.'

'Okay, now you take care of yourself. We can manage fine, so if you need to take a proper break, just go and have a lie down in the apartment.' Doris was firm.

'Thank you, but I think I'll be all right now.' If she lay down now, Ellie had the feeling she might just fall asleep and miss the whole afternoon.

* * *

Ellie waved across to Joe who was talking to a couple of old ladies, whilst selling them raffle tickets. He winked back at her, with a smile. She hoped that meant it was all going well.

She spotted Lauren's 'Teashop' table, decorated with festive bunting that Deana had made for her, and headed there.

'Oh great, thank goodness you're here, Ellie. I'm nearly out of the fudge bags and the choc-chip shortbread.'

Ellie lifted the box she'd brought up with her, filled with goodies. 'Good timing then.'

She and Lauren restocked the stall, which caused a new flurry of interest. A little boy barged to the front, shouting, 'Mam, the fudge is back. Which flavour for Gran?' At first he seemed somewhat rude, pushing in, but Ellie melted when she saw him holding out his two pound coins eagerly. As she took the coins, she felt they were still warm; they must have been held in his clutched fist for the past hour, waiting for just the right gift.

'Thanks,' he grinned.

It was then that Santa's Grotto caught her eye; beside it was a small queue. Blimey, was Henry still there? He'd started at eleven. And yes, a long-legged, slim, Father Christmas was still on duty. Ellie zoned in. Crikey, he actually had a child on his knee. She was drawn towards the scene, curious to get a better look.

'Now then, and what are you wanting for Christmas, young lady?'

Wow, he *really* had warmed to the role. Ellie recognized the little girl, Katie, from Wilmington village, just down the road. She was four years old and had Down's Syndrome, and often came in to the Teashop, with her mum and dad for tea, juice and cake. Her favourite was chocolate cake, always the same, and she liked to have it with rainbow-coloured sugar strands on the top of the whipped cream that Ellie had to place at the side.

'A star,' was the answer, bold and clear.

'A star. How lovely.' Henry's gaze went searchingly to the parents. He wondered how on earth they were going to sort that one out. They smiled on happily, so he continued, 'Right, well, I'll try my very best with that for you . . . And what's your name?'

'Katie.'

'Well, Katie, you have a very lovely Christmas.'

Ellie noted that Henry was even putting on a deeper, gentler voice. She was impressed, and her heart lifted and sank all at the same time. He might just make a lovely grandad after all.

'And if you have a little dig in that tub there,' he pointed at the bran tub marked for Girls with a pink sign – Doris's idea, so the lads didn't end up with dressing up shoes or fairy wings or such like. (Malcolm had called her a spoil sport.) 'There's a little gift for you to have now.'

''Fank you.' And she gave him the biggest hug and planted a kiss smack on his white-bearded lips.

He looked a bit taken aback, but then smiled.

Well then, that was a turn up for the books.

The little girl bounced off his lap and dug straight into the boy's blue tub.

'Ah . . .' Henry tried to stop her, but she was already unwrapping a small parcel.

'It's fine.' Her parents had seen what had happened.

Katie had unwrapped a toy car by the looks of it. As her parents helped her get it out of the box, Ellie could see out that it was actually a miniature toy quad bike. The little girl pointed to it giggling, and then pointed at Lord Henry 'Christmas'. 'You,' was all she said, with a huge grin on her face.

Joe caught Ellie's eye then, and they shared a poignant smile. Little Katie was so sweet . . . And one day, please dear God that it might really happen, one day Grandpa Henry was going to be absolutely fine.

Out on the main driveway, the 'reindeer' was having a few issues. Malcolm had come up with the great idea of making up paper bags of pony nuts and selling them as 'reindeer food' for an extra 50p – ever the entrepreneur. The pony's owner said that would be fine, but they hadn't realized quite how popular that would prove; they'd done a roaring trade. Subsequently, Douglas, the pony was now full to the brim and was looking forward to a little lie down and rest. The last two sleigh rides had hardly moved anywhere. And the parent of the last child, who's 'ride' had moved no more than two metres, had asked for a refund.

There was still a queue of five or six children to go; it looked likely were going to be sorely disappointed.

'Sorry children, we really need to give Dasher (his new stage name) a rest for now,' Mary, his owner, explained. 'You could try again in maybe fifteen minutes, but I think he might well have had enough for the day.' Literally – no extra tea for Douglas tonight.

'But that's not fair. Mu-um.' 'Oooh.' One little girl was nearly crying.

'Never work with animals and children,' Derek whispered in Malcolm's ear.

'Come with me kids,' Malcolm rallied out. 'Who hasn't visited Santa's grotto yet? There may be a few gifts left, let's go take a look, shall we? *Diversion tactics*,' he quipped back to Derek with a wink. And off he went looking like the Pied Piper, with a trail of children and adults behind him.

Ellie worked for a further hour down at the Teashop. The stream of customers began to thin out, which was probably as well, as so was the supply of cakes and cookies. All the mince pies – 120 of them – had gone by 3.30 p.m., there was one slice of Victoria sponge left, a couple of brownies and three fruit scones. All her gifts bags had sold – she was definitely on to a winner there. She might see if one of the local stores in Kirkton might stock them over the winter months too, especially in the run-up to Christmas, with the castle closed for the quieter season except for wedding bookings, it could give her winter income a much needed boost.

Doris had started clearing up, and they were down to just three tables still occupied by a quarter to four. Ellie knew Joe was thinking of wrapping the event up at about fourish. This time of year with the light fading fast, people were often keen to get away before dusk started to fall. She thought she'd nip back upstairs to the Great Hall and see how Lauren and the others were getting on, help clear the teashop stall, and see if she might be needed for anything else.

As she got to the Hall, Joe was just about to start the raffle draw. Lord Henry, now back in his usual tweeds, was next to him, ready to select the winning tickets by the looks of it.

'Ladies and gentlemen,' Joe knocked on the table to get the crowd's attention. 'Thank you all so much for coming along to our inaugural Christmas at the Castle Craft Fayre. I think you'll all agree it's been a great success.'

The stallholders were nodding their heads vigorously,

so that looked positive. And the crowd were generally smiling too.

'We are just about to draw the raffle. So, whilst you find your tickets a moment. I'd just like to tell you about our chosen charity. All proceeds from the raffle will be going to the Great North Air Ambulance, who do an absolutely amazing job. They are totally charity funded. It's not NHS funded at all, and needs ongoing support to survive. Being out it in a rural community like this, in times of emergency, we appreciate how very special and invaluable this service really is.'

There were lots of heads nodding in agreement, and a round of applause.

'On a more personal note, we had a wedding booked here at Claverham Castle for this summer past. Unfortunately, the groom was involved in a very nasty, road traffic accident just before that was due to take place. The air ambulance was at the scene quickly and without their intervention and the skills of the paramedics on board, who knows what the outcome might have been. So, I'm sure Daniel and his fiancée Lucy would be extremely grateful for your support of this charity. Hopefully none of us here will be needing it anytime soon, but if any of us ever do, we'll be so glad the service is there. So, thank you for your generosity. Any last tickets, Lauren here has the book, only £1 a strip. So we'll just wait one minute . . .'

There were a few more takers, and then they were ready for the draw. A sense of anticipation filled the room as there were some great prizes lined up: a meal out for two at The Swan Inn, a meat voucher for £25 from the local butcher, bottles of whisky (Henry had kindly donated one of his twenty-year-old malts), wine and champagne, a voucher for afternoon tea for two at the castle teashop. Ellie had also donated a hamper, there was a gorgeous cuddly reindeer (from Deana), board games and more.

Lord Henry, after again thanking everyone for coming along to Claverham Castle, dug out the first couple of tickets and read out the winners. There was a flurry of excitement, as the prizewinners came forward. Then, various members of the audience drew tickets too, until the prize table was emptied.

There was a big round of applause, and the event was drawn to a close. Ellie heard snippets of conversations as the visitors started to filter out, 'That was really good.' 'Can't believe I've won a bottle of champagne.' 'Can't wait to try that fudge.' And Ellie felt a little tear form in her eye. All the hard work and the planning had paid off, despite their recent personal tragedy. She couldn't wait to tell Joe about the takings in the teashop – best ever. Even better than the Saturday this summer when she had three coachloads in. Result!

Ooh, she found herself feeling a bit weepy. Hormones

still all over the place, no doubt. She'd just about held it together through the day, thank goodness. The show had gone on!

'Well, that was some day.' Joe passed her a cup of tea he'd just made. 'You okay? I know it was a lot for you to have to do.'

'Yeah. I'm just so glad it went well. *Really* well, in fact.'

'Think we may be doing "Christmas at the Castle" Round Two next year.'

'Absolutely.'

'Hey, never in a million years did I think Henry would make such a great Father Christmas.' Joe smiled.

'No, I know, that was a real turn-up for the books.'

'Mind you, just before little Katie appeared, I heard him telling off two little boys for being greedy, as they tried to dip in for second gifts each.'

'Hah, I missed that one. That sounds more like him. Bet they got a shock.' Ellie smiled.

'Yeah, they certainly put the extra ones back pretty swiftly. Their parents looked a bit surprised by the grumpy Santa Claus, mind.'

'It was really lovely to see him there with Katie.' Ellie pictured the little girl there in his lap, and then had to bite back tears, but Joe spotted them. She was never much good at hiding her emotions.

'Hey, it's been a long day. Come here you . . .' He

sheltered her in his arms. 'And you are not to do anything else tonight. I'm going to fetch us a Chinese takeaway from Kirkton, okay. Sweet and sour chicken and prawn crackers for you.'

He knew her favourites.

'Okay. Thanks.' She was actually feeling a little sick, but she tried to smile through her tears.

24

Monday by noon, despite being told by Joe to stay in the apartment and rest up, Ellie had had enough of daytime television and sitting about, she headed down to the teashop kitchen and started making some more Christmas cakes and fudge for their hamper orders. She had just poured out a batch of sugar-sweet rum-and-raisin fudge to set in a large tray. She'd cut it into squares once it had cooled.

'Hey, Ellie, hope it's okay just to call in?' The voice startled her, she hadn't heard the door go at all. 'I was working up this way today, and was literally coming past your turning on the A1.'

'Lucy, hi.'

They gave each other a friendly hug. Lucy pulled away with a compassionate smile. 'Deana let me come on through. She found me lurking at the main gates on her way in. She's just told me about the miscarriage . . . I'm so sorry to hear that, hun. What a bloody shame.'

'Yeah.'

'I *do* know how you feel. Well, my version of it, anyhow.'

'It happened to you?'

'Yes . . . over a year ago now. We'd only been together a few months by then, me and Dan.'

This called for a cup of tea, and a slice of chocolate cake.

'Kettle-on time?' Ellie managed a smile.

'Yes, thanks, Ellie. Some tea would be lovely . . . Well, I wasn't even trying to get pregnant,' Lucy continued, 'and it was like whoops! Well, okay then. I guess it's go time.' She paused, 'But then things took a bit of a turn . . . Ah jeez, it was horrendous . . .'

Ellie popped two tea bags in a pot and stirred before closing the lid. She let Lucy gather her thoughts. It wasn't going to be an easy tale to tell, she knew that well enough herself.

'It felt like I had extreme food poisoning or something, like the worst period I've ever had.'

'Yeah, my cramps got pretty bad too.'

'Ah, I'm so sorry for you hun, I know how it's such a sad time. I hadn't even planned the baby, but me and Daniel we were right together, you know. And we got all excited . . . and then it was all taken away again.'

Ellie was nodding. A tear forming on her eye.

'You feel kind of lost for a while,' Lucy carried on. 'I remember that so well.'

'Yeah, definitely.'

They sat on the kitchen stools, the tea poured out now. Ellie served out a couple of slices of cake and some homemade shortbread biscuits.

'I don't know about you, Ellie, but the really hard part was not knowing why, and then thinking if we did ever try again – not that we are trying at the moment obviously, far too much on our plates as it is. But could it all happen again?'

'Yes, I feel like that now. I wish I'd asked at the hospital when we could start trying again. But I'm scared now, too. I've looked online, some sites say with an early first miscarriage that you can just try again straight away, and I'm sure the doctor at the hospital said that too, but then I've also read that they suggest leaving it three months.'

'Maybe, physically you could try straight away, but I think emotionally, you might need to give yourself the time to get your head around everything. Have time to grieve.'

'That makes sense I suppose, yes. But I *so* want to try again. I don't want to have to wait.'

'No, I can understand that.' Lucy placed a hand on Ellie's shoulder.

'Thanks for coming here, and for speaking so honestly.

It's nice to know I'm not the only one that's gone through this.'

'It's really quite common. But, no one seems to speak about it much. We keep it guarded, like some secret sadness. But then, once people knew I'd had a miscarriage, they started to open up, to talk about it.'

'I suppose it is hard to just launch in to, "*Oh, I've just had a miscarriage*," if someone asks how you are, especially when it's so early and no one actually knows you are pregnant . . . I'd been so excited just before, too, looking forward to telling my mum and dad, Joe's mam . . . and then it was so awful that instead of the news I thought we'd be giving, what we then had to tell them was that we'd had a miscarriage. What kind of news is that? I can see how people don't say much. If we hadn't had to tell Henry when we'd dashed off to the hospital, I'm not sure I'd have wanted people to know either. It's so personal. And you're just trying to deal with it yourself at the time.'

'Yes.' Lucy got off her stool and went and gave Ellie a hug. 'You'll be okay, hun.'

'I know. I am feeling a little better today.'

'One day at a time.'

'Yep . . . and hey, what about you and Daniel? My worries are small compared to what you guys are going through. How's he getting on?'

'He's getting there, slowly. He's had yet another op, and all the metal external metal rods are out. But he's just frustrated that he still can't walk yet. He just can't take that pressure on his legs. He's doing loads of physio, they're trying to build up the strength, but it's going to be a long job . . . It's hard on him. To be honest, I think he's frightened that he'll never get that back. That he'll always have to rely on a wheelchair.'

'Aw, that's so tough.'

There was a short silence, then Lucy helped herself to a shortbread. 'This is delish.'

'I'll give you a couple of bags to take away home, if you like. I'm making up lots of Christmas goodie packs.'

'Oh wow, yeah . . . gosh, Christmas.' Lucy looked thoughtful. 'To be truthful, I've hardly thought about that. I suppose it'll be here before we know it. I usually *love* Christmas, one of my favourite times of the year. But this year . . . well . . .'

'Hey, no wonder. You have had *so* much to deal with.'

'Yeah, it'll be a quiet one for us, whatever.'

'I don't think I'll get away with a quiet one, I've just invited the family up. Actually, it was lovely here at Christmas last year, if a bit chaotic. Mum, Dad, Jay – that's my brother, were here plus his girlfriend. Then Henry came across for his Christmas dinner with us too, all very traditional, turkey, the trimmings, the lot. Yeah, it's always really noisy when my lot are up. They all chat at once.'

The two girls talked some more about everyday life.

Lucy loved hearing about all the antics in the castle, and wanted the full rundown on the Christmas Fayre.

'Lord Henry as Santa on a quad bike – that's just a classic.'

And then it was time for Lucy to get going and head for home herself.

'Thanks for coming out of your way, Lucy. It was really good to see you.'

'Yeah, well I'd decided to call in anyhow . . . and then when I heard what you've been through, I was so glad I had come to see you.'

'It's been good, having someone to talk to. Someone who's been through it themselves. I don't want to keep going over it with Joe, really. We're just trying to move on somehow. But today's really helped . . . Thank you. And, onwards and upward for Daniel and his recovery. Send him our love. We want to see him up and dancing very soon at this wedding of yours.'

Lucy gave a brave smile, but both of them knew that was a long way off yet. The dancing *and* the wedding.

As she spoke, she hoped she hadn't upset Lucy. She hadn't meant it to sound thoughtless. 'Sorry, Luce . . . I just meant that I'd love for that to happen soon.'

'I know, me too.'

'And, *when* the time is right, we'd so love to hold the wedding here as planned. To make it really special for you both. Anytime . . . you just say.'

'I know, I'm holding on to that dream . . . But I think Dan just needs more time. He wants to be more like his old self before we can even think about wedding plans again.'

'Yeah, I can understand that.'

'What he really wants I'm sure, is to be able to walk down that aisle, like that's his goal . . . But Ellie, what if he can't? What if that just isn't going to happen? I don't mind. Well, only for him. I hate to see him so sad, so frustrated, but if he'll have to use a wheelchair from now on, or even if he had no bloody legs, I'd still want to marry him. I'm just so thankful he got out of that accident alive.' A tear rolled down Lucy's cheek.

Ellie got off her stool. It was her turn to give Lucy a hug. There was such raw honesty between them today; their friendship blossoming into something so supportive.

'Thanks . . . I'll be all right in a mo.' Lucy wiped a tear from her cheek. 'Phew, I think I've been keeping all that to myself . . . What a pair we are, I was meant to be here cheering *you* up. Now, look at us.'

Yet, they were smiling through their tears.

25

'Do you fancy heading off to the hills for a walk?'

Now the Christmas Fayre was over, and with the teashop now closed for the winter season, it was lovely that Joe and Ellie finally got some time together, especially after all they had just been through. Though Joe still had plenty to do on the estate all year, Henry could help keep an eye in things, and they could take a few days out, go for some walks, have some pub lunches, and just make the most of the local countryside.

'There's this great waterfall, set high in the hills at Linhope. I haven't been there for ages,' Joe added.

'Okay, it looks like it's going to be a lovely, clear day. That sounds nice.'

Time to don a pair of walking boots, pack up a rucksack with a few goodies, and take the car the twenty-minute drive to park up in the foothills of the Cheviots.

Apparently, Joe told her on the way, he had found this place on his countryside treks when he'd first started working at Claverham Castle. He'd only been back there once since, but remembered it as a beautiful place, nestled high up on the hillside, in a hidden moorland valley. He wanted to share it with Ellie.

It was a crisp, clear November day. The sky an autumnal azure, with just the odd puff of white cloud. They parked up at the very end of a narrow road. From here there was just a farm track to follow. Their walking boots crunched over frosty ground. Little patches of ice having formed in the shallow puddles of the rough track. The hills rose ahead, their peaks of short moorland grass were scattered with woolly horned sheep. Fronds of bracken that were lush and green in the summer, now bent and tumbled into bronzed heaps at each side of Ellie and Joe's path.

Off the farm track now, climbing the sides of the hills, following the sheep tracks and the odd wooden marker to show they were on the right trail.

'Everything okay? You all right?' Joe asked, turning his gaze to Ellie.

They were holding hands. Hers were in gloves, yet she could still feel his warmth.

'Yes, I'm fine.' She'd felt a bit tired climbing this steep rise to be fair, and it was no wonder after the hectic weekend she'd just had with the Craft Fayre. She was also aware that the impact of the miscarriage was still with her. She still felt like it had knocked the wind out of her sails.

Ellie felt that he was asking more than how she was handling this walk, but wasn't sure where to begin. There had been so many emotions going on within her in the last couple of weeks, and she'd had to keep them cornered in order to keep going; keep herself focussed and get everything done she needed to in time for the Fayre.

'We've been so busy, haven't we,' she followed up.

'Yes, and I know it's been a really tough time for you.' He gave her hand a squeeze.

'I'm okay.' She batted off his sympathy.

'Are you sure?'

She stayed quiet, concentrating on the uneven ground underfoot, taking care over the rocky outcrops, and the squish of peaty mud. 'Uh-huh.' She found she didn't want to talk about it.

They rounded the side of the hill, and after another climb, found the valley they were looking for. Ancient hawthorn trees, now bare of leaves, sheltered by the riverside, rocks formed shallow rapids in the stream that tumbled away down the valley. They could hear the rush, the flow of the running water ahead, couldn't yet see the fall itself.

They walked on along a narrow moorland trail, with

patches of mud and clumps of marsh reeds to watch out for, they had to mind where they were stepping. And then ahead of them it was there, the waterfall of Linhope Spout cascading down the high moorland crag – a bold rush of white water, shafting down into a frothy pool. The water that flowed from the fall out into the stream below was dark, rich in minerals and mud, and as brown as Marmite. The waterfall was quite stunning. They stood and watched for several seconds.

'Wow.'

'It's great, isn't it?'

'Worth the walk.' She could imagine having a picnic up there in the summer months. They might have to come back. The summer . . . might she be pregnant again by then? She wanted that so much. She didn't mention her hopes to Joe, just stood watching the wild flow of the fall.

Joe sat down on a large rock, and patted the space beside him. Ellie joined him; she could feel the cold damp of the stone through the cotton of her trousers.

'It's beautiful, isn't it,' Ellie commented.

'Yeah. I bet you could swim in that pool at the bottom in the summer.'

'Maybe, but I'd bet it'd be freezing even then. Might be deep too.'

'Yeah, suppose so.' Joe turned to look at her seriously. 'Ellie, I've been thinking, I was wondering if maybe we should just leave it for a while . . . You know stop trying for a baby. Just to give you a bit of space . . .'

Whoa, had he been reading her thoughts from before?

She suddenly felt angry, like a flare sparked in her mind. 'It's not space I need, Joe.' She frowned. 'The doctor said it was fine to try straight away again, remember.' No, it wasn't *space* she yearned for. It was a child. *Their child.*

'I know, but maybe you just need a bit of timeout. From all the emotions and everything. I can see how much it's affecting you.'

'Yes, I'm upset. Anyone would be. But I'm okay . . . What is it, Joe?' She paused, feeling hurt, confused. 'Do you not really want a child any more, then? Have you just been playing along all this time for my sake?'

'No . . . of course not. But it doesn't *have* to be right now, does it, not necessarily this year?'

She couldn't believe what she was hearing. And from Joe? She thought he was in her side. She'd thought he'd wanted to be a dad as much as she had yearned to be a mother. But it didn't seem like it now, did it?

'Oh.' How could she expect him to understand everything she'd been feeling inside in the past few weeks? He wasn't a woman, he hadn't carried that tiny child within him, had he? How could he possibly now ask her to wait?

'You might be physically okay, Ellie, but maybe not emotionally, not yet.'

257

'What are you saying, Joe? That I'm some kind of neurotic, now? I just want to be a mother, is that so bad?'

'No, of course not. But, it's what, eight or so months we've been trying now, and with the miscarriage and everything, I can see it's getting you down. I don't want you to get even more hurt. You're just putting yourself under even more pressure. There's still plenty to do at the castle, with the wedding events, and all the Christmas hampers and cakes to do now, it won't be that long before the teashop will be reopening for the spring. Let's get more established with all of that. We can try again next year, or something.'

'You just don't understand.' Not trying would be so much harder for her than trying.

'No . . . well maybe I don't. But, someone needs to look out for you. I just don't want you to keep getting hurt.'

Ellie jumped up off the stone; they hadn't even had time to have the small picnic she'd brought for them. She marched back off along the track ahead of him. Her emotions felt so bloody raw, like he'd stirred up some maternal hornet's nest. She couldn't bring herself to talk to him just then, her frustrations were buzzing away so angrily inside her.

He followed her, of course. Tracing her footsteps, drawing parallel with her half way down the hill.

'Ellie wait. I'm only trying to help.'

'Well, it's not helping. Okay.'

There were some stonily quiet moments on the walk back down to the car.

And she felt frustrated with herself, too. This was meant to be a lovely, relaxing walk in the countryside. Some time out together. They were in such a beautiful place. But tension now sparked like static between them. Agh, it was just so hard to even voice all those emotions going on inside her. So hard to try to get him to understand. What was meant to be a wonderful, exciting family time, a new happy stage in their lives together, was turning into a battleground.

26

Joe appeared in the teashop kitchens where Ellie was 'feeding' her lineup of Christmas cakes with brandy. A week had passed since the waterfall walk. Ellie had forced herself to focus on work, and get on with her Christmas Hamper orders. There was still tension hanging between them, and so much more to say, but Ellie really didn't know where to start. Joe even seemed to be avoiding sex, unheard of for Joe. Perhaps, he just wanted to make sure she wasn't going to rush into anything, and that was the only way he knew how. But that distance, and lack of physical contact, made Ellie feel even more lonely and confused.

'On the booze already?' he said jokingly, seeing the bottle in her hand at 10 a.m. in the morning. He was trying to make light conversation, but obviously well aware what she was really doing. 'Hey, guess what, I've just had a call from Daniel.'

'Uh-huh. *And?*'

'He wants to rebook the wedding.'

'Aw, how lovely. That's such great news. Lucy will be thrilled. He must be feeling a lot better then.'

'Sounds like it, yes.'

'The thing is . . .' Joe paused. 'He wants to have it on the day before Christmas Eve. Says Lucy loves Christmas, and it will make it all the more special.'

'Whoa, okay . . . Well yes, that'll be all right . . . Won't it?'

'Well, are you sure? It's a hell of a lot to for you take on just before Christmas. You've asked your parents and family to come up then, too. Might it be too much for you?'

He was obviously thinking of the miscarriage again. But hey, she was getting there, physically she was okay now, and despite the friction of the past couple of weeks, this wedding would give her something positive to focus on. And, because of who it was, and what they had been through, she *really* wanted to do this. To make it the most wonderful Christmas wedding for Lucy and Dan – the kind of wedding they deserved.

'No, honestly, I'll be fine. We had all the original arrangements in place. I have all the notes and contacts. We can soon get up and running with it all. It'll give me something else to think about,' she said pointedly. 'They deserve their special day *so much*. Let's say yes, and make it fabulous for them.'

'Right, great. Well, I'd better ring him back, then.'

'Yes, yes, go. Don't keep him in suspense.'

'Oh, talking about suspense, don't say a word to Lucy. She doesn't know.'

'Wow, honestly? When's he intending to tell her? It's only just over a month away, as it is. How will she know to get herself ready, and organize the bridesmaids, the dress and everything?'

'He said he *will* tell her, but just two weeks before. He thought that'd be enough time to surprise her, but some time left so she doesn't go ballistic with panic.'

'Aw, she will love it! But yeah, I'm glad he's going to give her a bit of notice. I think I'd want that too.'

'So, only his parents and the best man know about it for now, so shush.' He placed a finger over his lips.

Ellie suddenly had the urge to kiss the finger and his lips right then. So, without thinking, she stepped across, and did just that. She felt such a buzz of excitement about the wedding plans. Joe looked surprised, then smiled.

'Come back down and we'll have a cup of coffee, when you've made the call,' Ellie said, feeling more positive than she had in weeks.

He was still standing there just looking at her.

Ellie smiled, and shook her head. 'Go. Go and make the call. Go make someone's day.'

Her head was then spinning with the practicalities of arranging a wedding function in less than five weeks. Most of the plans had already been discussed with Lucy and Daniel, but she knew some things might have to alter. She'd have to check if the caterers would be available and so near to Christmas that wasn't guaranteed, also she'd have to speak with Wendy the florist, plus try and reorganize the band who'd been booked originally.

On top of that, she still had to put the final touches to and coordinate a smaller wedding event for an elderly couple, for the following Saturday, just over a week away. Boy, all of a sudden, she was going to be busy.

A while later, Joe came back down for his cup of coffee. He perched on one of the kitchen stools.

'Thanks for that, Ellie . . . for agreeing to take all that on just before Christmas. Dan sounded really chuffed.'

'Did he say how he was getting on? How he's recovering?' Ellie remembered Lucy being so worried about him, and the fact he wasn't yet able to walk.

'Says it's slow. I don't think he's really mobile as yet, but he says he's doing loads of physio. He was joking on the phone just then, about trying to do wheelies and doughnuts in the hospital corridor in his electric wheelchair apparently, much to the nurses' annoyance.

But he's adamant he doesn't want to wait any longer to hold off the wedding. Says Lucy's waited long enough. He sounded in pretty good spirits, to be fair.'

'Aw, that's good. Well, we'll have to make sure everything goes smoothly for them with all the arrangements here, anyhow.'

'Yeah.'

They chatted for a while about the replanning they now needed to do for Dan and Lucy, and also about the wedding lunch they were holding soon, for the older couple in their seventies. They were to be married at the church in Kirkton and then were coming across for a special lunch at the castle with their close family. Ellie was to do the catering, but as it was for twenty-four people and not too complicated a menu, she felt fairly confident with this. The story was that the couple had been childhood sweethearts in Kirkton and the groom Stan had delighted in telling her all about their past. They had grown up and gone their separate ways. Both had been married, Stan who'd stayed locally had divorced many years before, and more recently, when Janet's first husband died, she decided to move back to the area. They met by chance at a coffee morning in the church hall, remembered each other from all those years ago, the spark was relit and that was that. It just went to show you were never too old to fall in love.

'Well, I suppose we'd better both be getting back to

work, Joe. Especially now I've suddenly got loads to do. A whole new wedding to plan, in fact,' Ellie said.

'See you later.'

'Alligator.'

'No need to get snappy.' He winked and was joking, but it jarred just a little with her.

Did he really think she was being snappy lately? She so wished they could somehow move on from this awkwardness between them. Yes, they could chat about work, and the day-to-day stuff. They could pretend all was fine. But neither now dare mention the baby issue, and what was really bothering them, for fear of upsetting the other.

Ellie managed a brief smile as her husband stood to leave. Surely, they would be all right, wouldn't they? Didn't every couple have their ups and downs?

So, it was all systems go for the 'Surprise Christmas Wedding'.

Ellie couldn't wait until Lucy found out and could share in all the excitement, and the last minute planning. But for now, it was all steam ahead for Ellie, making sure she had as much organized in advance as she could.

Ellie phoned Wendy to let her know the exciting news, then popped to Kirkton to have a chat with her in person, and discuss which flowers might now suit a Christmastime wedding. She remembered that the flowers Lucy had originally ordered for her bouquet, the bridesmaids, and the table decorations, had included peonies and summer roses, which might well be impossible to source at this time of year. If she and Wendy could come up with a floral masterplan, then they could present their ideas to Lucy once she found out and hopefully she'd like them, or they could at least tweak them to her preference. It would be one less thing for Lucy to think about in her two-week pre-wedding frenzy.

Wendy made them both a large mug of instant coffee and they sat at a little wooden table in the back of the shop, where she made up her bouquets. The shop smelt lovely, fragrant and floral-scented. Big white lilies, huge red and pink blooms of amaryllis, carnations, roses and delicate white sprigs of gypsophila surrounded them in green tubs, ready to restock the front displays or go straight into arrangements.

'Right, so we have a Christmas wedding on our hands,' Wendy started. 'I have looked up the original order. I know Lucy wanted big blousy ivory roses, I can probably still manage those, unfortunately the peonies are total non-goers at this time of year, but we could maybe substitute them for some anemones in her bouquet. The best I can do with the roses are David Austins in a pretty ivory shade, and they will have a really lovely scent. Then, a little different, and I used these last year in a winter wedding, are the eryngiums, they are delicate purple-blue thistles, "Scottish thistles" some call them. Really pretty, and with the roses, anemones and some sprigs of greenery, perhaps with some sprayed with just a touch of silver, or eucalyptus leaves. They work well in winter bouquets. You can get a really stunning, slightly frosty effect.'

'Sounds gorgeous.'

'Here, take a look. We took some photos of a winter wedding we did last year.'

Wendy passed her an album. The bouquets looked wonderful, elegant and wintery but not too blatantly festive. 'Yes, I think she'll love this look. What about table decorations?'

'Hmm, let's keep to a similar theme and colour, but we can raise them up on log circles, and we'll need lots of candlelight, it'll really lift the room as it'll get dark quite early on the day. So, imagine you have a tall storm candle to the centre of the log base, your floral display around that, with the ivory and purple-blue flowers similar to the bridal bouquet.'

'Love it. You're a gem, Wendy.'

'Oh, and don't forget we can decorate the windowsills, and the balustrades coming down from the Great Hall into the courtyard. We could get a load of holly and ivy and twine it along.'

'Yes, that sounds fab. And, you won't need to buy any, the estate grounds will be full of it, just come along and help yourself nearer the time.'

'Thanks, that'll be perfect. I might find some other greenery there too, if that's okay. Sometimes sprigs of pine work really well.'

'Yes, you go ahead and work your magic, Wendy. And take as much as you like from the castle grounds.'

'That'll probably keep the costs down a bit for me and for them too.'

'Yeah, I know they had quite a generous budget originally, but with Daniel being off ill for so long, I'm not sure if they'll be able to be quite so lavish this time around. We can all do what we can to help, I'm sure . . . So, you're all sorted for this wedding on Saturday for me, too?'

'Oh yes, Janet and Stan, they're such a sweet couple, aren't they. The flower order will come in on Friday and I'll make it all up first thing Saturday morning. She's collecting her bouquet from here and the buttonholes, before going along to the church. And then, I'm to pop along to the castle by noon, with the four table decorations. White calla lilies with sprigs of lily of the valley, simple but really effective.'

'That sounds great. Thanks Wendy, you're a star. And I can really picture those flowers working so well for Lucy and Daniel. All winter-wonderland with a touch of frosty sparkle. Perfect. Can't wait to show Lucy the images and our ideas. Can I take a couple of those winter wedding photos with me?'

'Of course. Take the album. If I need it back, I'll give you a shout.'

'Thank you, that's fab.' Ellie just hoped Lucy would like all the new plans they were making.

27

So, Ellie, wedding coordinator extraordinaire, had kicked into action. She felt happier now that she had lots to do, it was certainly helping to keep her mind off all the other stuff.

The flowers were sorted, as long as Lucy liked them, fingers crossed. Now she needed to phone the original catering company that had been booked, to see if there was any chance they might take on the new wedding date, and they also needed to see if the original band were still available (Joe had said he'd look into that for her). Ellie had spoken with Daniel yesterday, and offered to reorganize the main wedding arrangements for him, having kept all the original contacts and details. She'd insisted, telling Dan he had enough to do with reinviting all their guests, whilst still trying to keep it quiet from

Lucy, not to mention coping with his own health issues and the physio sessions he needed to attend.

She dialled the catering company. She knew it was a big ask so near to Christmas, but, here goes . . . she held her fingers crossed behind her back as she listened to the dial tone.

'Good morning, The Glendale Catering Company. How can I help?'

'Oh hello, my name is Ellie Ward. I'm the wedding coordinator at Claverham Castle.'

'Oh hi, Ellie. Yes, I remember you.'

'We had a booking made with you for a wedding back in August. That had to be cancelled sadly, as the groom had a terrible road accident.'

'Yeah, I remember. That was such a shame.'

'Well, the thing is they've rebooked for this December 23. I'm just wondering if there's any way you might be able to do the catering for this new date?'

'Ooh, right, well it is *very* close to Christmas. I'll have to check in the diary and then with our manager, John, to see if we have any bookings, or if it's possible to arrange the necessary staff we'd need that near to Christmas. Can I give you a call back?'

'Yes, of course, use this same number.'

'Okay, well I've got the details on the original booking here, Lucy Coates and Daniel Edwards, for sixty-five people, right?'

'Yep, that's it.'

'Right, well just let me look into it. I'll get back to you soon.'

Two days later.

'Morning, Ellie. You seem a world away there.' Doris marched in to the kitchens, ready to help prepare the vegetables for the wedding meal Ellie was catering for, for *tomorrow*. It was going to be a busy couple of days.

'Hmm, I was just thinking . . . about the *next* wedding event, actually. In fact, I need to ask you and Irene about it too.'

'Right. So, have we got a new booking then?'

'Not really, more of a rebooking. The thing is, it's for the day before Christmas Eve.'

'Oh, crikey.' Doris's face dropped; she looked as if she was about to launch into a rant about selfish people wanting Christmas weddings at the expense of everybody else's festivities.

Ellie cut in quickly, 'I wouldn't normally have said yes, considering how close it is to Christmas, but it's for Lucy and Daniel. The chap who had the accident.'

'Oh . . . I see.'

'It's okay, if you have other plans and things arranged for Christmastime, I'll try and source some other staff. It's just that Dan wanted to surprise Lucy, and after all they've been through . . . well.'

'It's fine. Yes, of course I'll help. Can't leave you to do it all on your own now, can I. And I liked the couple.'

'Thank you, I really appreciate that.' Ellie smiled.

'Right, well, we'd better set to work on this other wedding, now then.'

And they were off, Doris peeling and chopping potatoes, Ellie whipping egg whites ready to make the meringues for the dessert.

Joe called in later. 'The band can't make it. The one for Dan and Lucy's do. They have a gig down in Newcastle that evening.'

'Damn. Oh well, we'll have to put our thinking caps on. We'll need some music for sure, and a live band is so much better . . . Dan's into rock stuff, I think, isn't he? Aerosmith, that type of thing?'

'Yeah, he loves Nickelback, and Bon Jovi too. He mentioned that was playing on his iPod in the hospital, when we went in that day. Said it was keeping him sane.'

'Isn't there some tribute band does that type of stuff, around the local pubs up here? Ah, what were they called now? They were quite good back at the BBQ in The Swan in the summer, when they had that real ale festival on. Do you remember?'

'Yeah, they got us all up dancing, or that might have been the ale, but yeah, they were really good. I'll get on to Alan at the pub. See if he has a contact number for them. Good thinking, Robin.'

'Hmm, I have my moments. So, go Batman, go get something booked.'

28

It was Saturday morning, the third weekend in November, and Ellie's last but one wedding of the year. She was up to her ears in salmon starters, and wrapping chicken fillets in bacon ready to cook for the main course. She'd also made some gorgeous chocolate truffles and fudge yesterday, as petit fours to go with the after-dinner coffee. Doris was preparing broccoli and chantenay carrots for the side dishes, with Irene whipping cream to go with the meringues, raspberries and blueberries for dessert.

As Ellie was arranging sprigs of dill on the side of the starter plates, the phone went. It was the call back from the Glendale Catering Company. They said they were very sorry but they couldn't do the December 23 wedding. Some of their staff were booked off on holiday, and they had a big event to cater for the day before, so they couldn't possibly take it on.

Nooo, she *so* wanted to make this wedding day special for Lucy and Dan, and she didn't now want to risk having to put it out to some catering company who she'd never heard of. There was only one thing for it, they'd have to do it themselves here at the castle. She would, she could. There would probably be no more than sixty or so people to cater for, if the numbers stayed the same as before. She'd just have to set her mind to it, and come up with a gorgeous (but not overly complicated – she was a cook, not a chef after all!) menu.

But here she was today, November 19, and there was another couple and their family and friends, who needed their special day too. They had had their wedding this morning in the church at Kirkton, and were coming along to the castle for their Reception meal. Ellie reset her mind to the task in hand, and concentrated on making the smoked salmon starters look pretty with the dill, a drizzle of dressing, and a caper on each. There were homemade crusty white and wholemeal rolls to go with it, which Irene was finishing baking just now. They were smelling gorgeous. The first course was ato be ready to be served in fifteen minutes. Deana, Joe and Malcolm would be welcoming the wedding guests in to the Great Hall right now, with Derek as runner between the Hall and kitchens. Ellie was about to join them in five minutes, when the waitressing team of Doris, Irene and Lauren would take over.

* * *

Seven-ten p.m. and they waved off the bride and groom, plus a few merry stragglers, at the front steps of the castle. It had all gone well, the happy couple seemed delighted with their meal and event. And, being a local family, they hadn't needed to book out any of the guest rooms for this wedding, so it was an early finish.

The castle staff had an 'all hands on deck' pick-up, wash-up and Great Hall tidy-up. Ellie felt pretty shattered, but so pleased that it had been a success.

Joe found her in the kitchens loading the last tray for the dishwasher. The other staff had just left. 'You okay?'

'Yep, bit tired, but fine. Went off well, didn't it.'

'Yeah, you did a great job with the food today. It looked amazing what was coming out. And they all seemed really pleased with each course.'

'Thank you.'

For her lack of catering training – basically, she'd taught herself, with a little help in the past from her Nanna, and she'd learnt on her feet over the past five years working at the castle – she felt she'd done well, first in the teashop and now, moving into the catering side with some of the less complicated wedding functions. It was just the best feeling when her customers enjoyed her food. She'd kept all the thank-you cards from wedding and teashop customers since she'd started here, and put them on a pinboard in the kitchens (there had even got too many, and some were now stored in a file in the apartment). It reminded her of how far she'd come.

'Well then . . . it's pretty late, and I think we need something to eat ourselves.'

'Agh . . .' The last thing she could think of was starting to cook again.

'So, I suggest we go along to the pub in the village.'

'The pub, yes, that sounds like a damned good idea. Better get there soon though, before I fall asleep.'

'Thanks, and I was so looking forward to your company . . . actually, hmm, what exactly does that say about mine?'

It was warm and cosy in the Swan Inn. They were sat at a table next to a roaring log fire. Ellie had a glass of cider before her, and Joe a glass of red wine. He had ordered steak pie, and Ellie some local sea bass. This was so much better than having to forage in the freezer back at the apartment, especially after having cooked for two days solid now.

Landlord Alan came across to let them know the food would just be a few minutes.

'Oh, Al, I need a word actually,' Joe said. 'Did you get my call earlier?'

'Nah, sorry mate, my phone's been out of battery. Just recharging it now.'

'Right, well, I was after the number for that band you

had playing here back in the summer. They did the rock tribute stuff.'

'Yeah, I know the ones. Rock Revival, I'm pretty sure that was their name. I'll look them up for you and let you know.'

'Thanks.'

'Be good if we can get something organized for Dan and Lucy sooner rather than later,' he added to Ellie, hopefully.

'Yes. We'll need some kind of music for the evening, and a band is so much better than just a disco. Going to be a challenge getting something decent just before Christmas mind. A lot of the better-known groups will be booked up already, I'm sure.'

'Yeah, possibly, we'll have to see. Let's not worry just yet. Anyway, you did a great job today, Ellie, and we had so many positive comments from the guests. I think they'll be spreading the word about the castle,' Joe said.

'That's fab. It'll be good if we can get some more regular events throughout the closed season. It needn't just be weddings either, special birthdays, anniversaries . . . there are lots of things we could promote, now I'm getting more confident with the catering.'

'Yeah, you did such a good job . . . Onwards and upwards, hey.'

Yes, she really hoped it would be. Not just for the castle events, but for them personally too.

They were sat side by side on a wooden bench seat, with the chatter and bustle of the pub around them. She slid her hand over his, felt his warmth, his quiet strength. She so needed to feel close to him again.

29

'Whaaaaayyyyy!'

Who on earth was this at the end of the line?

'I'm getting married . . . and I'm going to have a Christmas wedding!'

'Lucy? Hi!'

'Yay – he's just told me. We're at the top of the Baltic Gallery looking out over the River Tyne. We've just had a lovely lunch and he's re-proposed.'

'Aw, that's just brilliant.'

'I can't quite believe it, after everything that's happened. We're finally getting our wedding day.'

'Well, we've already been getting organized and making plans for you both.'

'Yes, I've heard. You sneaky lot! Scheming behind my back . . . fancy that. But I love you guys for it too, though.'

'Well, I've had a lovely chat with Wendy about winter

blooms and displays, Joe is sorting a band out for you as your others were booked out, and *I'm* now officially head of catering.'

'You are? Oh, that's fab, Ellie, thank you so much. I was getting a bit panicky thinking I had so much to do in two weeks, but this all sounds brilliant.'

'Great. We'll chat some more about all the details soon. You get back to your lovely fiancé and enjoy your day.'

'I will. I'm *sooo* happy. Dan knows how much I love Christmas time, so this will be extra special now. It'll just be perfect . . . I hope it'll be perfect for him, too. He's been through so much, and I know he wanted to be more like his old self, but that will come in time. We'll get there.'

'You will. Okay, so we'll have a meet-up soon, call me later and we'll sort a time? I'd just like to check everything we've thought of so far suits you, and you'll be happy with it.'

'I'm sure I will be happy with it *all*, but yes, I'm planning on coming up. Tomorrow, if that's okay with you? Got a half day off work, as I know my mind will be in full spin 'til I can chat about the plans. And next, I need to try and rebook the hairdresser for me and the bridesmaids.'

'It'll all work out fine. We'll make sure it's special for you both . . . Aw, has it been a really romantic day? Where did you say you are?'

'Well, this morning, two of his mates turned up on their motorbikes with sidecars on – hilarious. So we both got in, one of us in each, and his dad came along to meet us with Dan's wheelchair. We were taken to the quayside. It's been one of our special places. And the view from the gallery and the restaurant at the Baltic is just amazing. Wow, even more special now. It's a gorgeous clear day here, blue skies, we've had lunch sat at a table that looks out along the river, so it's been lovely. He couldn't really get down on one knee again, bless him, but it's been like a second proposal. The waiter came over with a bottle of champagne. Oh, and Dan was very formal, and asked if I would do him the honour of marrying him on December 23. I thought he meant next year. Then, when he said *this* December, I nearly exploded along with the champagne cork.'

'Hah, that's so lovely. I'm so pleased for you both.'

'The lads are picking us up in fifteen minutes, so I'll have to get away for now. But I'll see you tomorrow.'

'Yes that's great. What time are you thinking?'

'I'm working 'til 12.30, so maybe 1.30, or soon after.'

'Right, well, I'll do us a late lunch. We can chat over a sandwich or something.'

'Aw, that sounds lovely. You sure?'

''Course I am. Planning over paninis, sounds a good idea.'

'See you tomorrow then, Ellie. I *can't* wait to find out what plans you've all been making. Yay!'

Ellie couldn't help but smile as she put down the phone.

'Why the bloody hell have you agreed to have people traipsing around the castle just two days before Christmas, for heaven's sake?'

Lord Henry caught up with Joe in the corridor on their way to a quickly arranged Monday Meeting; Joe had thought he'd better get the team organized and aware of for the new wedding arrangements. 'And a bloody big wedding do at that, just when we're meant to be relaxing a bit and enjoying the closed season. We can't even get bloody Christmas off now.'

'Morning, Henry.' Joe tried to diffuse the tension, with a hint of sarcasm that his father hadn't even bothered to say hello. He remained calm, 'Henry, this is a couple who we get on really well with. They had a horrendous time with a major road accident earlier in the year, which meant they had to postpone their summer wedding they'd booked with us.'

'Well, why couldn't they have waited 'til after New Year or something?'

'Henry, you don't even like Christmas time particularly.'

'That's not the point.'

'They are friends of ours, and it'll bring in a good income at a time when cash flow gets tight. You know what it's usually like during the winter months.' He didn't want to sound money-grabbing, but they did have to think about the castle being a business, and financial arguments usually won Henry over.

'Peaceful,' Henry answered under his breath.

'Poor,' Joe countered.

'Humph . . . Agh, no, are they staying overnight again, like that awful lot in September?'

'Yes, we have booked out the guest rooms for the night of the wedding, and I think the bride and the bridesmaids are here in three rooms for the night before.'

'Ach, so I'll get all that chatter and noisy giggling again.'

'Well, hopefully, if they're enjoying themselves, yes.'

'I hardly got a wink of sleep with that lot back in the summer. That bloody silly unicorn woman.'

'They were a slightly different kettle of fish. But yes, it'll be nice if there's some laughter and chatter going on. Can't have them coming to a wedding do on a vow of silence, now. And they'll all be away by Christmas Eve lunchtime, I promise. So you'll have your castle back then.'

'Thank heavens for that, at least.'

'Anyhow, talking about Christmas, we've been meaning to ask, would you like to come across and have Christmas dinner with us again this year? In our apartment?'

'Well, yes . . . thank you, that'd be nice. Ellen does make an exceptionally good roast, I have to say.' He seemed to mellow.

Joe didn't like to add that Ellie's boisterous family would also be there too. He'd let Henry find that out a bit later. It'd be good for him to socialize a bit more anyhow. Get him out if his bear's den of rooms in the west wing. Enforced frivolity. He might even find himself enjoying it!

'Right, we'd better get in to this meeting, Henry. There's a lot to get organized now.'

The team were briefed, and more than happy (other than Henry who was still trying to get his head around it) to come along and help with Lucy and Daniel's wedding, knowing the background and the problems the couple had had to face to get this far.

Ellie had met with Lucy a few days ago, and discussed all the plans they had made so far. Lucy had literally jumped up and down, saying she 'Loved it! Loved it! Loved it!' The only change the bride-to-be had suggested was to the proposed dessert menu. Instead of the pavlova and Christmas pudding with brandy sauce options which Ellie had suggested, Lucy had mentioned that she had seen the most wonderful French wedding dessert – all made of profiteroles in a tall stack – and was there any way Ellie might be able to make that? Ellie rose to the challenge, knowing that Irene was a bit of a whizz at choux pastry, and said yes she'd have a go at making it and at least give it her best shot. She'd have to Google how exactly to make the profiterole tower stay standing and not collapse!

30

'Come on, I thought we could pop and take a look at the Dickensian Christmas Market that's on, over at Berwick-upon-Tweed.' Joe wandered into the teashop kitchen. It was just gone 3 p.m., the following day.

'What, right now? I'm still baking. I'm in the middle of another batch of gingerbread stars for the hampers.'

'Yeah, why not. Well, say in fifteen, twenty minutes or so, when you're wrapped up here. What do you think?'

'Hmn, sounds nice . . . And, we might pick up some ideas for next year's Christmas at the Castle Fayre.' This year's festive event had gone down so well, there would definitely have to be a second.

'That was my ulterior motive, too. We can see what kind of stalls they have there. Apparently, the stallholders all dress up in Victorian-style outfits. It sounds like it might be fun.'

'Hah, can you imagine us lot dressed up . . .? There'd be Malcolm and Derek in breeches and cravats.'

'That won't look too far off how they are now,' Joe joked.

'Oh, and Henry, he'd have to be Scrooge.'

'Hah, absolutely! Bah humbug.'

'Okay. It sounds good. Just give me ten minutes here to take the last batch of gingerbread out of the oven. Then, I'll just have to pop it on the cooling racks.'

They drove the half-hour cross country to the market town of Berwick-upon Tweed, that sat right on the Scottish Borders, though was still part of England.

As they reached the town they drove on to a large stone road bridge that crossed the river. It was starting to get dark, being early December, 4 p.m.

'Wow, it's so pretty.'

The bridge's old-fashioned lampposts were strewn with twinkling white lights in the shapes of shooting stars. They spanned the whole of the bridge's length. The River Tweed flowed beneath them, opening out in to the North Sea to their right past the harbour walls. Other lights reflected down from the river sides, shimmering into the water. It looked stunning.

They parked up, and walked down to the High Street, with its imposing stone Town Hall building and its tall clock tower, below it was where many of the stalls were set up. It was chilly, late afternoon, and dusk was already starting to creep in. Ellie was glad of her woollen coat, and hat and scarf. It was a nice cold though, crisp, clear. Ellie smelt a host of festive aromas, cinnamon, orange and pine, roasted chestnuts. There was chatter and laughter; lots of people were gathered, drifting between the stalls. There was a huge decorated Christmas tree at the top of the Town Hall steps, beneath it was a choir singing traditional Christmas carols, and yes, as Ellie looked closer, they were all dressed in long gowns and bonnets, or waistcoats, top hats and breeches. You could almost feel you'd stepped back in time, if you didn't look beyond the market area to the modern-day shopfronts behind.

'This looks great,' Joe said.

'Yeah, there'll be lots of inspiration for us here.'

As they wandered around, testing things, tasting things, looking for gifts and goodies, Joe managed to collect several of the stallholders' business cards on the way. Many were interested in another venue for their Christmas wares. It would be wonderful for the castle to have even more stalls at their own Fayre next year. And these had such lovely things. Ellie picked up some pretty Christmas bath bombs for the two mums and some of her friends, a gorgeously scented candle 'White Winter Spice' as a treat for herself, a bag of marshmallows in Santa and Snowmen shapes that would be perfect for topping hot chocolate, and lots of fabulous stocking fillers.

'You might want to think about setting up a stall here

yourself, at this event, Ellie. The Teashop in the Castle stall. Your fudge, shortbread and gingerbread goodie bags would go down a treat. As well as all the hampers and Christmas cakes. Might be an idea to get some details from the organizers whilst we're here.'

'Yep. Why not? I think that'd be a great idea. I'd have a busy November/December, wouldn't I? But, it's when the teashop's closed, anyhow. Hmm, good thinking, Batman.' She smiled. It was a relief that they seemed to be chatting a little easier today.

They stopped for a warming drink; Joe chose a small spiced gluhwein, and Ellie a mulled cider, which was delicious and warming with flavours of apples, cloves and cinnamon.

This was so nice, being together as a couple. Other than at the pub, the other night, it was the first time in ages she'd felt relaxed in Joe's company, which was such a shame. The miscarriage, and then that row they'd had by the waterfall, had torn at their seams somehow.

They came upon a stall that had the most gorgeous wooden Christmas tree decorations. Ellie spotted the cutest rocking horse and teddy bear. They were made of natural wood, painted delicately; so clever.

'I make them myself. Hand carved from beech.' The man behind the stall commented.

'They are lovely. Such detail.' Ellie answered, handling the teddy bear. The bear fitted in the palm of her hand, he was traditional-looking like a Victorian toy might be, and carved and painted in such a lovely way.

The rocking horse and bear were hung on strings, and seemed the perfect thing for a young child to place on the Christmas tree at home. Ellie gave Joe a meaningful look. She'd love to buy one, but was that just tempting fate?

'Go on,' his voice was gentle. 'Buy them. The teddy and the rocking horse. They can keep.'

And they both knew who they would be meant for . . . if it was ever meant to be.

'Yes,' Ellie smiled. 'I'll take these. Thank you.'

The stallholder wrapped them carefully in bubble wrap and popped them into a navy star-covered paper bag. Ellie took the package from him. It felt like hope, a promise in her hand.

They wandered round a few more stalls, and Ellie bought some red-and-white striped candy canes to take back with them, and a bag of roasted chestnuts to share. Then they stepped out from the crowds, taking a narrow cobbled lane and wound their way along a side street, away from the hustle and bustle. Ellie felt for Joe's hand, her emotions still out of kilter with everything that had gone on recently, but seeking his warmth. They found themselves coming out by the road bridge they had crossed to come into the town, set high above the river.

They walked on to the bridge and paused to look at the view, finishing the last of the chestnuts. Below them to the harbour side was a low stone bridge, that looked extremely old, probably the original crossing to the town. To the opposite side, inland, there was another bridge, an impressive stone viaduct that spanned the River Tweed, its tall Victorian arches were softly lit with a purple hue. It was stunning.

'The Royal Border Bridge,' Joe commented. 'Built by Robert Stephenson, you know. The son of George Stephenson, "The Father of the Railways". Rather beautiful, isn't it. And, what an amazing feat of engineering.'

'Hey, hark at you, Mr Historian. Where do you pick up all these facts?'

'Not quite sure. I just find it interesting. And quite remarkable how they made this kind of stuff back then, with limited resources.'

'I know. Really, how did they do it? Across such a wide river too.'

They both stood, leaning against the solid wall of the road bridge looking up at the vast stone-built viaduct. The star-shaped white Christmas lights that hung from the lamp-posts along the road bridge, twinkling above them.

'Just amazing. Definitely built to last.' Joe put his arm around Ellie's shoulder.

She leaned into him, feeling his warmth and an immense sense of relief.

'Definitely.'

31

It was a week before Christmas. Ellie had her row of twelve Christmas cakes lined up ready to ice for her hamper orders. There were two more of the rich fruit cakes that she was keeping back to make into Lucy and Dan's wedding cake – she already had ideas for that creation.

She'd done the apricot glaze and marzipan layer a couple of days ago. She now wanted to make a snowy icing effect on the top of them, the same as her display cake at the Christmas Fayre. She whizzed up the royal icing, enough for two cakes at a time, so it didn't thicken too soon and be hard to work with. She had Classic FM on the radio and was humming along, in her own merry little baking world. The mix seemed a little stiff, so she carefully added a half-tablespoon of water and whisked again with her electric mixer.

Once it seemed nicely aerated, she knew she had to work with it immediately to get the right effect. So, pallet knife in hand, she set to work making soft peaks on top of the cake. She'd already made a selection of coloured sugar-paste holly leaves, red berries and ivy, and had little silver balls to decorate the top with as well, once the icing had started to set.

It was at times like this when she really loved her job, when she felt relaxed and creative, and could just concentrate on the task in hand. She was so glad she'd taken the plunge those few years ago, to go and do something she loved, setting up her teashop in the castle.

'Someone's happy.' Doris walked in through the swing door of the kitchen. 'Hmm, I can see why, they're looking good.'

Wow, praise indeed from Mrs Super-Critical. Ellie smiled, 'Thanks.'

'Now then, what do you want me to start on?'

'Well, we need to make up all the hampers for delivery over the next few days. I've bought in some wicker crates. I've stacked them just over there. And, there's some red shredded packing paper to line them with. If you could start by filling the bases of those with the paper, that'd be great. Then we need a little production line of the following: a pack of shortbread, the Christmas ginger stars, a fudge pack, meringues, chocolate truffles, a lemon drizzle and one of these Christmas cakes. Of course, the icing on the Christmas cakes still need to set, so we'll leave a space for those and pop them in tomorrow.'

'Right-o.' Doris started lining up the baskets.

Within a few minutes, it was all looking very festive in the kitchen, with the goody bags of biscuits and sweets lined up in rows, all tied prettily with green and red Christmas string.

'I'm feeling like we should have some elves as helpers,' Doris smiled.

'Well, we do have Malcolm and Derek lined up for deliveries, so that's as near as.'

They both chuckled.

By the end of the day, all twelve Christmas cakes were iced and decorated. Ellie was so pleased with the end result. She just had to wait for the icing to totally set by the morning, and then she'd tie a red tartan ribbon around the side of each. The cakes would then be ready to be placed as the centrepiece in each of the Teashop in the Castle Christmas Hampers.

Doris had made a fabulous job of displaying all the other items in the wicker baskets. Her assistant had set off home about an hour ago, after helping to organize some of the crockery and cutlery they'd need for Dan and Lucy's wedding, and ironing a pile of ivory-cotton napkins and table runners. The wedding was in a less than two weeks' time, now.

So that was it, Ellie's Christmas cake orders were met and the first ever hamper delivery was ready for the off tomorrow morning. Ellie gave a sigh of relief and stretched. She'd had to contort in to some weird and wonderful positions to put the finishing touches to the cake decorations, and she was now feeling it in her joints.

The kitchen door swung open.

'Right then, Mrs Ward. Oh wow . . . cakemaker extraordinaire. You have cook and iced all day by the looks of it, so may I suggest a Chinese takeaway this evening. My treat.'

'Perfect.'

'You all done here?'

'Nearly, just a couple of bowls and spoons to put through the dishwasher. And I need to wipe over the surfaces.' She couldn't stop the yawn that escaped her lips.

'Hand me the cloth and disinfectant. I can do that.'

'Thanks.'

'I do have an ulterior motive, mind. My tummy's rumbling, and it means we can get to the takeaway faster.' He flashed a grin at her.

Ellie smiled, shaking her head. Things felt a little easier between them in the past few days, thank goodness. She'd hated that feeling of distance that had crept between them. Thankfully, something seemed to have changed since their evening at the Dickensian market.

Later, after enjoying their takeaway supper and watching a comedy film from the comfort of their sofa, they headed off to bed. Ellie felt more relaxed than she had in ages, and snuggled up against Joe in their king-size bed. She reached up to touch his shoulder, traced her fingers down to feel the rounded firmness of his bicep, then reached across to slowly stroke his chest. He sighed, long and slow, but the sigh soon altered, sounding more sensual. He turned to face her. Ellie felt a tear of relief roll down on her cheek.

'I've missed you,' she whispered.

'Me too.' And he took her into his arms, and kissed her, tenderly yet oh so passionately.

'We're going to be all right, aren't we?' She still felt vulnerable, after all that had happened in the past few weeks.

'Yeah, of course we are.'

It was the first time they had made love in weeks. It was tender and beautiful. It felt like they were coming home.

32

Wednesday, only two days away from Daniel and Lucy's big day, and Ellie's stomach was starting to do somersault flips. She so wanted everything to go well for her friends, for it to be as perfect a day as they might hope for. No one deserved this more. Ellie had been doing as much prep as she could, but there was only so much you were able to in advance. As always, the fresh food would have to be left until later.

She was planning on icing and decorating the wedding cake today. She already had the two fruit cakes she had made earlier; circular cakes, one slightly larger than the other. The top tier was to be a Victoria sponge, which she had yet to bake, so it would be nice and fresh. She thought it would be nice to have an alternative layer for those guests who didn't like fruit cake. She had a design in mind, three tiers, covered in white royal icing, with a delicate trail of sugar paste flowers and ivy that wound around the cake, and cascaded between the tiers. She was going to make icing roses and the 'Scottish thistles' that matched those in the real wedding flowers. It would no doubt take a few hours to create.

Ellie could imagine the colours of the flower trail: soft greens, silver shades, ivory and a touch of purple-blue, with a suggestion of frost-touched sparkle. It would echo the floral theme that Wendy had designed for the Great Hall and Lucy's bouquet (that the bride-to-be had *loved*). Hopefully, the hall and the cake would look every bit as festive and magical as Ellie imagined.

'We have over sixty guests coming for the meal, Doris, so I need you to check that there are enough plates, and bowls for all three courses. That the dinner service is tip-top clean, and the cutlery, with no streaks or marks left from the dishwasher, *and* that the glasses are sparkling.' She realized she was sounding a little bossy. She was probably slightly tense trying to make sure that everything would go off perfectly; she so wanted to do her best for them. 'Thank you.'

'Tomorrow, we can then take it all up to the hall and start setting the tables, so we'll be one step ahead. Wendy's coming in first thing Friday morning, the day of the wedding, to do the table decorations and make her floral displays on the window ledges and the stone mantelpieces of the fireplaces. I think it's all go up in the Great Hall at the moment, so we'll keep the crockery and glasses ready, down here for now.'

Irene was coming in tomorrow, the Thursday, as well, to help make some of the desserts that they had planned. She was a whizz at choux pastry and was going to make several batches of profiteroles, ready for the French-style wedding tower, which could be kept and then filled with fresh cream on the morning of the wedding. Ellie was going to bake two large chocolate fudge cakes, some homemade meringues, and three white chocolate and passion fruit cheesecakes. Although Lucy had only requested the profiteroles, Ellie found she couldn't settle on just one dessert and decided a medley would be perfect. The guests could then go and help themselves, and take a variety of what they fancied.

Lucy wasn't aware, but for a cheese option, that would see them all through into the evening, Ellie was going to make a wedding-cake style stack of large cheese circles, decorated with a trail of fruit, and real ivy leaves. She'd seen it done online and it looked amazing. She'd ordered in the four cheeses from the delicatessen in Kirkton; a cheddar, Stilton, Northumbrian nettle and herb, and a softer goat's cheese for the top. It would be a lovely surprise for the couple, and would hopefully look rather special too.

'Heave. Go on, that's it . . . Left a bit. Bit more. No hang on, drop it back down a bit.' Lord Henry was shouting instructions at Malcolm, Derek and Colin, who were hanging on to ropes and some kind of pulley system, trying to manoeuvre the biggest Christmas tree that Colin could possibly find on the estate, into place in one corner of The Great Hall.

'Who do you think we are, World's Strongest Man or something?' Malcolm shouted through gritted teeth.

The tree from the Christmas Fayre had been looking decidedly ropey, so they had taken that away yesterday, and sent Colin to find another one. He'd deemed it as his mission to find one bigger and better than the last. It seemed everybody wanted to make this wedding something special.

Sue, Joe's Mum, had come up especially to freshen up all the guest rooms and the main reception areas. She had just cleaned the Great Hall right through early that morning. She watched in despair as the room started to fill with pine needles galore. She stood watching the four men and a Christmas tree, shaking her head. The vacuum cleaner was definitely going to have to come back out, but she may as well wait for them to finish now. Lord knows how they were going to decorate the enormous thing; they'd need a cherry picker or scaffolding to reach the top!

Four p.m., Doris had gone home, it was already dark outside. The winter evening stealing the light early.

Ellie was putting the finishing touches to the wedding cake. It had taken her longer than planned to make all the sugar flowers and to paint them the right shades, but she was really happy with the end result. Three circular, white iced cakes were placed on a delicate chrome stand that set them apart in a soft twirl. Then the trail of ivy, and sugar paste flowers, linked them so prettily. She stood back admiring her work, hoping that Lucy would love it.

She hadn't heard Joe come in behind her. Just felt the warmth of his palms as they traced her hips, one hand on each.

'Wow – that's amazing.'

'Do you think Lucy will like it?'

'It's beautiful. She'll love it. Are they made of icing too?' He pointed at the delicate flowers, the trail of sugar-paste ivy linking them all.

'Yes, it's taken a while. Had a few flower rejects along the way.'

'I bet it took you ages. It's stunning, honestly. You need to get yourself on the Bake Off. That's definitely a show-stopper of a cake.'

'Aw, thank you. How did everything go upstairs?'

'Well, we finally have a Christmas tree to match Trafalgar Square's set up in the Great Hall. Mum's had to reclean the whole room for pine needles. And I think Malcolm and Derek are exhausted. Henry seemed to enjoy orchestrating the whole thing, anyhow.'

'Hah, at least he seems to be on board with it all now. He must have warmed to the Winter Wedding idea.'

'Yes, finally. I think he's finally mellowing a bit in his old age.'

'Hah, we might even get him back in the Santa suit, entertaining the children at the reception, at this rate.'

'I don't think so. That's taking it too far.'

They grinned.

'Well then, we've set out the tables in the right places now, so you can carry on tomorrow unhindered.'

'Good. Did you mention to your mum about having supper with us tonight, as she's here setting up the guest rooms? I suppose we ought to ask Henry too. What do you think?'

'Yeah, why not.'

It seemed a little unusual having Joe's parents, who'd been estranged for many years, sitting together eating supper with them, in the apartment. It wasn't your usual family set up, by any stretch of the imagination. But, the awkwardness between Sue and Lord Henry, when Joe had found out the truth of his past, had diminished since Sue had been back working at the castle recently. So many years had passed since their early relationship. There was no longer regret, as they were both so fond of Joe.

Ellie looked around the table; Joe, his father, his mother, chatting about the castle and the up-and-coming wedding.

The world was made up of incongruous, happy families. And time could alter so much; heal hurts and hearts, take you to a whole new situation that you could hardly have imagined, take you past your fears.

'You have really done a splendid job with those guest rooms, Sue,' Henry praised. 'Both in setting them up and keeping them in order. I took a look in some of them the other day. Marvellous.'

'Thank you.' Sue was obviously proud of her work there at the castle.

Sue's bubbly personality kept the conversation flowing over their simple supper of griddled chicken and salad – it had been a busy day cooking for Ellie already. Ellie had also brought up some of her meringues and cream for dessert.

Yes, castle life found a way of moving forward, and this incongruous family were finding their feet once again, with Ellie and Joe's relationship at its core. Ellie found herself instinctively placing her hand across her belly. A twist of sadness hit her. *One day*, hopefully, there might be a new member of the Ward family to come. A new journey. But for now, she'd have to just wait and see. Joe saw her action, smiled softly, understandingly, and took her hand in his under the table.

33

The castle was a hive of activity.

One day left to prepare for the Christmas wedding in the castle – their first ever festive wedding, and one that was extremely special to all involved.

Doris was up in the Great Hall with Joe, setting out all the tables with white linen tablecloths overlaid with a silver-grey shot-silk table runner. Then, she was going to lay out all the cutlery, side plates and glasses. The two large fires of the hall were set with logs and kindling, ready to be lit tomorrow.

Lucy, was coming through late afternoon, for her pre-wedding night with her four bridesmaids. That way, she could see how the reception hall had been prepared so far. She was going to bring up the table plans, the place-names and wedding favour gifts, for Ellie to set out for her. Only one couple couldn't make it from the original guest list apparently, due to a foreign holiday that had already been booked.

Sue had got the bride and bridesmaids guest rooms ready, making sure there was a selection of luxurious bubble baths and body lotions in their bathrooms. Ellie had organized a couple of bottles of prosecco to send up in an ice bucket once the girls got there, as a welcome gift. She had also made mini bags of chocolate truffles and fudge to pop on to the bedside tables.

In the kitchens, Ellie and Irene had been busy making the desserts for tomorrow most of which were now chilling in the fridge, bar the chocolate fudge cakes which were smelling delicious as they cooled on the side, ready to be covered in their rich-chocolate frosting. Next, they had to peel and prepare the vegetables to accompany the main meal; roast potatoes, leeks in a cheese sauce, carrot batons, and broccoli – peeling potatoes and carrots for sixty-plus people was no mean feat. But they chatted away and listened to the radio as they worked.

The windows to the kitchen were small, so it was hard to tell what the weather was doing, especially when they were so busy. It had got chillier over the past two days. The cobbles in the courtyard had been a little icy, slippy under Ellie's feet this morning. But with all the activity in the kitchen and the ovens having been on, it felt pretty warm in there. Ellie would need to get Colin to help stoke up the fire in the teashop tomorrow morning, as they would be in and out and up the stairs to the Great Hall many times; they didn't want to freeze every time they came back down through. The design of the castle meant that food had to be carried up the stone stairwell to be served, or at least kept warm in the hostess-style trolleys they kept for functions out in the castle corridor on the way to the hall – a bit of a nightmare for the waitressing staff.

It was nearly lunchtime before Ellie headed back upstairs to see if Joe, Lord Henry, or anyone else in the team, wanted a bite to eat in the teashop with them. Irene had brought in one of her famous quiches, a large leek, cheese and bacon, what a star – thought they might be glad of it. Doris offered to make a pot of tea, whilst Ellie went to rally the troops.

Through the leaded windows of the teashop, Ellie could see it had turned awfully dark out there, and then yes, little flutters of white were sifting down, settling on the outer window panes. Wow – snow. Maybe Lucy was going to get her wish of a 'white' wedding after all. It would look so pretty if the grounds were covered with a dusting of snow. Ellie wondered if it would last until the wedding day tomorrow. Often they had a few snowy flakes, but then it just melted away as quick as it came.

The castle was often lovely in the winter. If you had a smattering of snow, and then it went all frosty, the shrubs and hedges would be laced with sparkle. It looked magical, when your breath misted the air, you could hear the crunch of frost beneath your feet, and the sky above was a cool bright azure.

After lunch and the rinsing and slicing of thirty leeks, Ellie glanced out of the kitchen window again. It was still snowing. She went through to the teashop to get a better look. The snow was quite heavy now, large flakes falling in a soft steady patter. That sense of hush, as it layered the ground and the window ledges outside. She was aware of the bridesmaids and Lucy having to travel this afternoon, and began to feel a little uneasy.

She went up to see how Joe and the others were getting on in the hall.

Malcolm came in flustered at the same time. 'I can't get Millie down the driveway.' Millie was his much-loved relic of a car, an old Mercedes. 'I'm meant to be getting some extra tree lights and tinsel from the DIY place, but it's getting lethal out there. I'm not going to get through to Kirkton at this rate.'

'I'll go,' Joe offered. 'I can take the Jeep from the estate, it's a four-wheeled drive, so it should be fine. Anything else anybody needs while I'm out?'

'You could maybe pick up a couple of pizzas and some salad for us,' Ellie asked. 'I've no idea what's for tea, and I can't remember what's in our freezer.'

'Yep, I'll fetch those too, then. Tree lights, tinsel and pizza, your wish is my command.'

'And go steady,' Ellie warned.

'Will do.'

He was a good, confident driver, had managed fine on the snow before.

'Jo-e, I'm getting a bit worried about Lucy and her friends getting here, if the roads are getting bad out there.'

'Yes, when are they due?'

'In about half an hour, I think. Might be longer, if it's been snowing on the way up from Newcastle too.'

'Right, well I'll see how the roads are outside the castle. If it's just our driveway that's bad, we can have a go at clearing it. I'll take my mobile with me and keep you posted.'

'Okay.'

'And, if there's any problems, or if the girls call or anything, tell them to stay put wherever they've got to. Get them to pull over somewhere safe, and I'll go and fetch them.'

Fingers crossed the girls were fine, wherever they had got to en route. The last thing that wedding party needed was any more accidents.

Twenty-five anxious minutes later, Ellie took a call from Joe on her mobile. 'I'm on my way back now. The roads aren't great. But I'm fine in the Jeep. It's settling fast though. See you soon.'

'Okay, Joe.'

'Any news on Lucy's whereabouts?'

'Not yet. I thought about phoning her mobile, but if she's driving I don't want to put her off. She'll need to concentrate. Don't want to ring Daniel about it either, no point worrying him needlessly.'

'No, I agree. We'll just wait a while.'

Ten minutes after that, Ellie's mobile rang again. She saw the caller ID.

'Lucy? You okay? I've been wondering about you all. Where are you?'

'Hi, phew, that was a bit of a tense one. We've got as far as The Swan pub, about five miles away. But that last hill down was certainly hair-raising. Had a bit of a slide. Given me a bit of a fright, to be honest. The roads here aren't gritted or anything.'

'Yeah, Joe said it was settling fast. At least you're all okay, yeah?'

'Yep, we're fine. We're warming up by the fire with a cup of coffee. Blimey, I've just looked out of the window – it's heaving it down.'

'Hmm, right, well don't try and go anywhere. Stay put. I'm waiting for Joe to come back from Kirkton any time. He's got the Jeep. He's already offered to come and fetch you ladies. You can leave your car at the pub car park for now, I'm sure Alan won't mind.'

'Great. If you're sure Joe's okay with that? Blimey,

I'm just thinking, we've got *loads* of stuff in the boot. My wedding dress, four bridesmaids dresses, overnight bags, make-up, the works. Don't ask a bride to travel light.'

'Hah, I'll warn him he's in for several trips then. Are the dresses covered over fine? Don't get them wet or spoilt in the snow . . . Actually go and ask Alan, he's the landlord there, see if he's got spare plastic wrap or anything. He won't mind helping.'

'Okay, will do. Well, this is some start to my wedding. Be careful what you wish for hey. Was it me that asked for snow? I seem to remember . . . It could have waited 'til we all got there. I'm just hoping all my guests can get through all right tomorrow. And Dan, of course.'

'Try not to worry about that now. It could all stop as soon as it started, and the roads will be gritted and fine by the morning.'

'Yeah, you're right.'

'Well, sit tight and look out for Joe. He may be twenty minutes or so yet.'

'Thanks, Ellie.'

'Well ladies, your carriage awaits.' Joe was grinning, and a little snow-dusted as he arrived at the pub.

The girls got themselves organized. Two bridesmaids and the four bridesmaids' dresses were the first to be loaded in to the Jeep. Landlord Alan had found some extra-large bin bags to double wrap the dresses, over the top of their carry sleeves, just in case.

A farmer Joe knew happened to be in, having a quick pint before heading home. He heard the saga of the stranded wedding belles, said he had his old Land Rover outside, and offered to take two more of the girls across to the castle with him. He only had room in the front mind, the back being full of sheep feed. So, Lucy was to stay with her wedding dress and would be the last pickup. Joe said he'd be back as soon as he could.

Ellie had stoked up the fire in the teashop. It would be a nice place for them to gather and warm up before she would take them up to their rooms. She'd got some hot chocolate organized if they wanted, and a plate full of homemade shortbread. She'd checked the central heating was on in the guest rooms, making sure they were warm and toasty, and Ellie had also lit the small fireplace in Lucy's room, the biggest of the rooms, so they could all chill out there comfortably.

They would be fine once they all got here, Ellie told herself. She was a little nervous waiting, with all the buildup and background to this big day tomorrow, she didn't want anything to go wrong now. But, she had confidence in Joe and his driving. He knew the roads well, and would be better than anyone to get them here safely.

Henry appeared. 'Turning into a bit of a snowstorm

this. Most we've seen in years . . . Saw the light on here, thought I'd pop down and see how you're getting on. Busy, no doubt. All organized for the big day tomorrow?'

'Nearly, yes.'

'I know I wasn't too pleased about holding this wedding so near to Christmas. But I can see how you want to make it right for this couple, these friends of yours . . . Where is everybody, anyhow? Where's Joe?'

'Gone to fetch the ladies. The bride and her bridesmaids had some problems getting through. They're stranded at the pub in the village. Roads are getting terrible out there, apparently.'

'Ah, right. Oh, I could have gone and helped. What's Joe gone in? Not that souped-up hatchback I hope, won't be any good in this stuff.'

'No, he's in the Jeep.'

'Good stuff.'

'Should be back any time soon, hopefully. I might go out and have a look.'

'Well, get yourself well wrapped up. It'll be freezing out there. I'm heading back to my rooms for a bit, but if you need anything. Or, if you hear from Joe and he needs a hand. Give me a shout.'

'Thanks, Henry.'

The sky was full of heavy, cold flakes that landed on her eyelashes as she looked up. It was dark out, and yet the falling snow made it appear a cool grey all around her. The snow was already lying a few inches deep in the courtyard, crunching, compacting under her feet. She'd popped a pair of wellies on, as well as a thick coat, gloves, hat, scarf. She walked under the stone arch at the end of the courtyard to the heavy wooden front doors of the main castle entrance, turned the circle handle of the creaky black metal latch, and stood out on the front steps watching the driveway for signs of headlights, the noise of a vehicle. She knew she wouldn't rest until they were all here safe and sound.

Standing there on the castle steps, waiting for loved ones to come home, pulled her back. History never felt far away in this ancient place. A sense of the people who had lived here before you was always near; their lives, their happiness and sorrows. And, would someone else maybe in twenty years, maybe two hundred, stand on these same steps looking out into the snow, waiting, with that same tug of anxiety and love?

There was something . . . lights, yes, at the far end of the driveway, coming closer now. Two sets in fact, one following the other. She felt a lift of relief. The Jeep and an old, rather battered-looking Land Rover pulled up alongside the steps. Joe stepped out and came round to help out two ladies who Ellie didn't recognize. Behind, coming out of the Land Rover were another two; yes, she recognized the long dark hair of Chief Bridesmaid, Caitlin.

Between them, they were trying to carry what looked like a mass of bin bags stuck together with packing tape.

'Our dresses,' Caitlin managed a smile.

'Ah, yes. Come on in, come on in.' Elle ushered them through the arch, heading for to the teashop. 'Here, let me help you.' She took one of the plastic long-length packages, allowing one of the girls to manage her case easier.

They made it into the stone stairwell and headed down the few steps to the teashop, where Ellie helped them hang their dresses, still in their plastic protection, from the teashop door.

'No Lucy?' Ellie asked Joe, over her shoulder, concerned.

'Had to do it in stages. We couldn't fit everyone in, not with all the luggage and dresses. So Lucy's still at The Swan, with her wedding dress . . . Oh, Ellie, this is Jack from Kirkgrange Farm.' He pointed to the chap, who'd been driving the other vehicle, a burly bloke in his fifties. He was carrying two pink overnight cases, and a shoulder bag.

'Oh yes, I know you now, Jack. Of course.' She'd seen him before at local events from time to time. He was a bit of a regular at The Swan. 'Thank you for helping. Can I get you some warm soup or anything?'

'That'd be grand, lass. Then I'll be on my way. Had to do my bit for these damsels in distress. Rather enjoyed it, actually.' He gave a grin, and a wink.

'And girls, hot chocolates or soup?'

'Hot chocolate, please.' 'Yep.' Nods. 'Thanks, Ellie.'

'Right, I need to get back and fetch Lucy,' Joe said. 'Won't be too long.'

'Thank you, Joe,' the girls chanted.

They were glad of the warm fire, and a cosy chair. Ellie soon bringing them warm mugs of hot chocolate loaded with cream and marshmallows. Jack sat sipping his soup, chatting away to the young ladies, in his element. He seemed in no hurry to get home. There was only one more to come (well two, with the driver) then they could all relax properly, and prepare for the big day tomorrow.

Joe seemed to be taking a long time fetching Lucy, much longer than he had when he had gone to get the bridesmaids on the first trip.

Ellie tried not to dwell on it too much, but her eyes kept flicking to her wristwatch, as she chatted to the girls who sat drinking their hot chocolates.

Jack stood up, said his wife would be wondering where he'd got to by now, so he'd better be getting himself home. He thanked Ellie for the soup.

'You're very welcome, Jack, and thanks so much for your help.'

'Thank you, Jack. You're a star,' Caitlin added. 'We'll remember tonight and our snowy antics for a long while.'

He beamed as he ambled across the teashop, heading for the door.

'Take it steady out there, Jack.'

'Will do, I'll be fine. It may look battered but that old thing gets me uphill and down-dale and everywhere, never been stopped by a bit of snow.' He smiled. 'Goodnight, lasses. Have a grand day tomorrow . . . And if you need any more help, Ellie, give us a shout out.'

'Will do, and thanks again, Jack.' Ellie stood up to follow him.

'Stay here, keep yourself warm and dry, lass. I'll see my'sen out.' He tipped his old tweed cap and left.

The girls finished their drinks and the shortbread that Ellie had put out for them. She took them up to their rooms, so they could start settling themselves in.

'Wow, this is so lovely.' Ellie was showing Caitlin into her guest room, she had already shown two of the girls in to their twin suite. 'It's old-fashioned and yet so cute, kind of shabby chic.'

Sue, Joe's mum, had done a fabulous job of sourcing old furniture, some antique, some just house sale stuff, mostly bargains – as they had a tight budget to work with. The great thing was that she had a friend that did restoration and chalk painting work. They'd gone for a soft cream and grey theme, lots of wood-painted furniture and stylish metal bedheads. In the winter months, they used tartan-style throws over the ends of the beds. With each room having a small fireplace and soft lighting, it all looked very welcoming.

Ellie left the girls to get themselves organized and

comfortable. She showed them the little kitchen the four rooms shared, and the bathroom facilities (two rooms sharing, the other two having ensuites).

Back in the tearooms on her own a while later, she felt restless and decided to call Joe's mobile phone, to see how he was getting on. It rang and rang, then clicked across to the impersonal female voice of his answerphone. 'I'm sorry, we're not available right now . . .'

Ellie told herself not to worry. She probably shouldn't have called him in the first place. It was difficult driving conditions, so he'd need to concentrate, not be answering his phone. And the Jeep, unlike his car, wouldn't have hands-free, anyhow. She'd better not hassle him anymore.

She may as well get on and prepare something for tomorrow; there would be plenty to do in the morning so she could make a start now. She took out some broccoli and started cutting it into florets, placing them in cold water for overnight. It was cool in the kitchens now without the ovens on; they'd keep nice and fresh.

Ten minutes later, she stole another glance at her watch. Joe had now been over fifty minutes – for a journey that in normal conditions would take no more than fifteen. She told the scary, irrational voices in her head to pipe down, but she still found herself listening out for footsteps or the teashop door going. She went to have a look out of the teashop windows to the courtyard, tension tightening in her gut. Just snow, falling steadily.

The door then creaked open.

'I can hear the girls are settling in . . . Joe not back yet?'

She turned. 'Oh, Lord Henry.'

He placed a calming hand on her shoulder.

'No, not yet.' She answered his question, trying to sound upbeat.

'He won't be long, I'm sure. I'll stay here a while, if you don't mind. They were drowning out the documentary I was following.'

'Sorry, Henry. It'll just be for tonight and tomorrow.' She felt a little sorry for him. An Englishman's home is his castle and all that, and in this case it kept getting invaded every now and again – no longer by rampaging border reivers, but rampaging wedding guests and tourists.

He gave a small smile. 'It wasn't too bad really. They sounded excited if anything. Been quite a trip up, by the sounds of it. I met one of them on the stairwell. Bit of a dramatic arrival with all the snow. Going to be interesting tomorrow, if it keeps going at this rate.' He nodded to the falling flakes outside the glass.

'Yes, I know. We're waiting on the bride. And then tomorrow, we somehow need to make sure we get the groom and all the other guests here in time for the service. And there I was thinking all I had to worry about was the food and coordinate proceedings on the day.'

'We're always at the mercy of the elements, we just forget it sometimes.'

'Hmm.' Ellie nodded. *Come home safe, Joe, my love. And Lucy, for your Daniel.*

'Here, I'll pop another log on the fire for you.'

'Thanks. Cup of tea, Henry?'

'Don't mind if I do.'

So the pair of them settled on the bench by the fire with some tea, talking here and there, sometimes just sitting watching the orange curls of flame, hearing the fire crackle. Henry struggled with chit-chat, but it was just nice having some company.

At last, there was a glow of blueish light coming through the snowy courtyard. Ellie dashed to look out of the teashop windows. Two figures, the taller one holding up a mobile phone as a torch, between them they carried a large covered item. A powerful rush of relief ran through her.

Ellie was soon at the teashop door holding it open, letting in a rush of chilly winter air. She heard the stamping of feet, shaking the snow off their boots, no doubt. Footsteps coming down.

'Wow, that was an interesting journey.' Joe was grinning, he was fine, though looking rather bedraggled, his hair and jacket looked soaking, with an over-dusting of white flakes.

'Wow, good to see you pair. That took a while. And, how's the bride-to-be? What a trial for you getting here.' Ellie gave Lucy a big welcome hug. 'Here, let me take the dress. I assume it's your dress.' She held out her arms for the large black bin-bag wrapped item. 'I'll hang it up for you, then we can take it to your room in a mo. The girls are up there already, settling in.'

'Thank you. Well, Joe here has saved an old lady stuck in her car,' Lucy announced. 'She couldn't get through bless her, and had slid and blocked the road. She was a bit shaken up apparently. So then he took her home, out in the hills somewhere . . . been a bit of a hero by the sounds of it. As well, of course, as saving five bridal damsels in distress.' She smiled, relaxing now she'd got to the warmth and refuge of the castle.

'You make it sound very dramatic,' Joe added. 'The old lady didn't have much chance in that little hatchback, it was sliding all over the place. She seemed a bit shocked and upset . . . She'd been visiting a friend who was ill, got caught out by the weather heading back. Anyhow, I got her car pulled up safely out of the way, and took her home, that was all. It was only just past Kirkton, up the valley a bit. She said I could have left her at the pub, but then it would only mean someone else would have had to try and come out and fetch her. I knew I'd be fine getting there in the Jeep.'

'So, I thought I might be spending the night in the pub in my own, when he didn't seem to be coming back. It was fine, I was cosy, warm, sat by the fire. Alan was very chatty too . . . Nice to be here, though. I've made it! And the dress! Crikey, I just hope everyone will be able to get through tomorrow.' She frowned.

'We'll find a way,' Lord Henry who was still there chipped in. 'Where there's a will there's a way. I've lived here many years in this castle, and a bit of snow never stopped us, did it, Joe?'

'No, that's true. And, the weather's so changeable, it could all be melting away by morning.'

Ellie was nodding. 'Right then, Lucy, Joe, can I fetch you a warm drink, something to eat?'

'A coffee would be great,' replied Joe.

'Lucy, hot chocolate? The girls enjoyed that when they got here.'

'Sound perfect.'

'Then you can start relaxing and go up and join your bridesmaids. There's one big day ahead for all of you.'

'Yes, exciting. But what a crazy start.'

They ended up sharing a pizza supper with the bridal party – the girls had intended having a pub tea out that evening. But no one was heading back out on those roads tonight. Luckily, Joe had been indecisive about flavours when he'd gone out earlier to fetch the pizzas for himself and Ellie, and ended up buying four, intending to save two in the freezer. Ellie also found two spare quiches in the teashop freezers, as well as making up some salad and a couple of garlic breads. She also remembered there were some chocolate brownies in a tub in the kitchen – she'd had the urge to bake a batch of the salted-caramel ones that were Daniel's favourite a few days ago. They had them after the pizzas, warmed through, as dessert with some ice cream, and they toasted the bride-to-be with a glass of prosecco.

They ate, balancing plates on their knees, in Lucy's room which was the largest, borrowing stools and chairs from the other guest rooms, with Lucy perched on the four-poster bed. Even Joe joined them for his supper, a token 'hen', after all his help in getting them safely there. Henry had had the offer to join them too, but politely declined saying he'd take a slice of quiche and some salad up to his rooms, he'd let them have their fun, and wished them all a good evening.

Fully aware of their very busy day ahead, Joe and Ellie slipped away by eight thirty. Ellie doing a half-hour more preparation in the teashop kitchens, to get a step ahead for the morning, but then joining Joe back in their apartment. It had been a long day and she was tired. A good night's sleep was probably the best idea at that point.

Snuggled up with Joe in their bed, she felt so very grateful to have him in her arms. Lying together, skin against skin. The hush of a cold winter's night around them.

She nestled up against the security of his broad back, reaching up to touch the square line of his shoulder, the curve of his neck, tracing fingertips down the start of his spine. She then placed a kiss on each shoulder blade. So glad that he was near.

He turned to face her, side by side. It was dark. She could just make out the line of his cheek, his messy hair, but no more. There were no streetlights around the castle, just an old Victorian-style lantern within the courtyard, and the snow still falling had snuffled out the moon. She felt his breath on her cheek. Then his need for her, hard and firm against her hip. She smiled. You could never keep a good man down! And my, did she love this man.

Earlier, when he'd been so late out in that snow, just the thought of losing him . . . Sometimes it really happened, just think how close Daniel had come. Life took some curve balls and whoomph, that was it. She shivered.

Neither needed to speak. She felt his lips press against hers, so beautiful and loving, with a promise of now and all his tomorrows. She lifted her hand to ruffle his hair, then pressed firmly against his scalp holding his head to hers, the kiss now intense, passionate.

He was here. That was all she needed. And they danced their dance of love, as he cupped her breasts, traced her body with this hands, and took her to him, loving her back with every fibre in his body.

Afterwards, gently stroking his hair, tracing his cheekbone, then his lips with her fingertip, getting sleepy now. 'My love,' was all she said. And he held her close, as she fell asleep in his arms.

34

The alarm buzzed to life. Six-thirty a.m., and Ellie woke to the thought that she had sixty-plus people to cater for. Then, with the memory of the snows of yesterday, came the added realisation that they also had a disabled groom in a wheelchair to get to the wedding in the first place, plus the vicar, and a convoy of guests.

She gathered her fleece dressing gown around her, found her slippers and made her way to the window. It was still dark out there, hard to tell, but it looked like the snow had finally stopped. She wrapped up in warm layers, and headed down to the teashop. Thank goodness, her delivery of food supplies had come yesterday morning before all this had started. Her first job of the day was to make the slow-cooked casserole of beef and Northumbrian ale ready for the main course mid-afternoon; over several hours it would become melt-in-the-mouth tender and tasty.

Once that was done, and the three huge pots were in the ovens, she noticed it was getting lighter. She headed up the stairwell to take a look out across the front of the castle. The snow had stopped to break on a beautiful blue day. The sunlight glistening off of white layers that covered everything. It looked pretty and magical, but also *deep*. She couldn't make out the driveway at all. The tyre-track ridges from the Jeep and Land Rover last night were totally gone.

Joe would surely be up by now, getting things organized in the Great Hall probably. She phoned his mobile. She was sure he'd have seen how deep it was on the drive, but she ought to alert him just in case.

'Joe.'

'Hi, yeah.'

'Joe, the snow's pretty thick out there. Have you seen?'

'I know, there's no way me, Malcolm and Colin can dig *that* driveway out . . . But don't worry. I'm on to it.'

There would be no wedding without a groom and a vicar, at the very least. And it would be a poor show without the wonderful friends and family that Lucy and Daniel wanted to be there to celebrate with them. So, Joe and Colin set off on Mission Road Clearance. Joe's first port of call was to the estate farmyard. They would definitely be needing something bigger than a shovel.

* * *

Lucy and her bridesmaids were due down at the teashop for a bridal breakfast at 8.30 a.m. Irene and Doris arrived at the castle, looking rather dishevelled, at twenty-five past eight, nearly an hour later than planned. Luckily, they didn't live too far away. Clifford had got them so far in his trusty X-Trail apparently, and they'd trekked the last mile in their wellies, bless them. So, Ellie had her Team Teashop helpers at hand. She had set out a large table by the fire, with a posy vase of white carnations and greenery, and all the cutlery and crockery was set out ready. Ellie was warming croissants and pastries to go with a selection of local jams and honey, then, she was going to make the girls smoked salmon and scrambled eggs served on toasted bagels. Something to keep them all going through the morning, but not too heavy either – they all had their dresses to fit into.

Lucy popped her head around the kitchen door. 'Morning.'

'Hi Lucy, did you sleep well?'

'Not too bad. Was excited and a bit anxious all at once . . . Not anxious about getting married, of course. Just about Dan and the other guests all getting here safely. Every now and again, I'd get up and check out of the window. It didn't stop snowing until about 3 a.m. in the end.'

'We'll get him here, Luce, *and* all your guests . . . Somehow, we will. Joe's on the case with a masterplan

right now. So you just try and relax. Go join your bridesmaids and we'll get you your breakfast. I'll organize some
tea and coffee for you all, right now.'

Irene was soon going through to the teashop with pots
of breakfast tea and fresh coffee. Then Ellie followed with
orange juice and chilled champagne. *Well, Nanna, we're
on the Fuck's Bizz, she said to herself.* Nanna had mixed
up the words many moons ago, at a family party. Ellie
and her brother Jason had creased with laughter, getting
a stern talking-to from their father. Ellie smiled; though
she was sad she was no longer here, the Fuck's Bizz
misnomer remained, along with many happy memories
of her beloved Nanna.

'Champagne anyone? Buck's Fizz?'

'Oh yes, how lovely.'

'The perfect start to the perfect day, I think.' She started
pouring the juice and champagne into flutes. 'And would
you all like smoked salmon and scrambled eggs?'

There was a general consensus of yeses.

'Coming right up, then.' Ellie left them saying cheers,
clinking glasses, and tucking in to the croissants.

'We've managed to clear the driveway, finally.' Joe appeared
in the kitchens a while later, with a dusting of snow
sprinkling off his heavy-duty coat. It was nearly ten thirty.
'We rigged up the quad with a bucket scoop. It's taken a
while.'

'Well done, that's good.'

There was no answer. He didn't look too happy.

'Isn't it?' Ellie continued, hopefully.

'But then . . . when we got to the lane, nothing has been gritted or snow-ploughed. There's five miles from here to the main road in the village. It would take us a week, not a few hours to clear that.' He looked dejected.

Oh God, and Ellie had put such faith in him, but he was only human after all.

'It's too deep for the 4x4s now. Even the Jeep would be no good.'

'Ah, I see, and I wouldn't want you risking anything. Not to the point where it's dangerous . . . Oh shit, how're we going to tell Lucy? She's upstairs, all happy, getting ready with her bridesmaids.'

'I know. I'm not giving up just yet. There must be another way . . . Don't tell Lucy anything, not yet, no point worrying her. Look, we've got a couple of hours on our side, at least.' The service was booked for 1 p.m.

Ellie crossed her fingers behind her back, and gave him a kiss for good luck, as he set off out again.

All she could do was try and keep her mind on the job of preparing the best food possible, hoping that the guests could actually make it there to eat it.

Soon after, Joe took a call from a concerned Daniel. He had travelled up from Newcastle with his best man, and had got as far as the petrol station just off the A1. He and several other guests had parked up there for now, as the roads seemed pretty impassable thereafter. They were just eight miles from the castle. There just had to be a way.

'Right, thanks for letting me know. I'm trying my best. Leave it with me, Daniel. I'll keep you posted. Keep your mobile handy.'

'Will do. We'll just pop in and get ourselves a takeaway coffee. Looks like they've got a machine in there. . . . Rob, get my wheels out of the back, mate.'

They were obviously getting his wheelchair out of the boot.

'Right, thanks, Joe. We'll sit tight till we hear something.'

'Yep. I'll be in touch soon.' Joe was determined to do everything he could to help this guy.

All they needed was a miracle to clear eight miles of lanes.

A miracle, or as it turned out, a friendly farmer, a tractor and a snowplough attachment. And who was ready to step up to the mark? Jack, the farmer from last night.

He trundled down the driveway in his massive green John Deere, stopping as Joe and Colin were coming back out on the quad to do another recce.

'Heard about the roads still being so bad. Can't trust the council to get it done. To be fair, they've got to concentrate on keeping the main roads going. So, here I am, couldn't let those lassies down now, could I?' He was beaming from his tractor cabin. 'My wife's a bit of an old romantic too, said I had to do my bit. Not that I needed much persuading mind, a bonny lot of lasses they were too . . . If I'd been a bit younger . . .' He winked.

'Well, I'm bloody glad to see you.' Joe grinned.

'So, where do you need me to go first?'

'The groom and most of the guests are coming up from the A1. The vicar too. So, if you can clear through to that junction that would be brilliant. We'll sort you out with a few pints put by at the Swan for another time, by way of thanks.'

'Sounds a good deal to me. Right, I'm away then. Let's get Bertha into action.'

'*Bertha?*' Colin and Joe looked at each other.

'Big Bertha, my beloved . . . tractor.' He patted her green metal flank fondly out of the tractor window.

'Thanks, Jack. I really appreciate this. Can you give us a call when you manage to get through, that'd be great?'

'Of course. Got your number still from last night. And you're welcome. It's about time we had a bit of drama round here. Liven things up a bit.' And so Jack and Bertha set off, back to the country lanes, en route for the A1. Mission Road Clearance was back on track.

Joe gave Ellie the good news, phoning her from his mobile.

'Ellie, we've got a solution. But there's still eight miles

of roads to get cleared, so we're not out of the woods quite yet. Just keep Lucy and the bridesmaids occupied.'

'That's no problem, there's plenty going on with hairdos, nail glossing and make-up sessions up there at the moment. I've just looked in on them.'

'Great.'

'Oh, and I've just had the lady vicar on the phone too. Wondering what it's like up here.'

'Right, well can you phone her back and let her know we're getting the roads clear from the A1 side, so tell her to leave it for an hour or so, then she can try and head that way. If there's any problem, I'm sure Colin will go and fetch her in the Jeep, so offer that option too.'

'Will do. Thank you, Joe.'

'Not me to thank. It's all down to Jack and Bertha.'

'What?'

'I'll explain later. Gotta go, loads to do yet. Need to get back to the Great Hall and help Derek and Malcolm finish setting up now.'

Ellie then took a call from Wendy who was having trouble getting through from Kirkton, and had had to turn back. All the bouquets, buttonholes and table decorations were in the back of her little van, but they weren't getting through as yet. Ellie told her to stay put safely at home for now. She'd mention it to Joe, yet another challenge.

Ellie remembered all the mistletoe, ivy, holly and sprigs

of pine that were in a pile in the gardening shed, where Wendy and Colin had placed them, after scouring the grounds and cutting what they needed, ready to entwine with the shop flowers she was going to bring in that morning. They were to dress the balustrades in the court-yard, and the window sills of the Great Hall.

It felt like they were organising an army! Amazing what havoc one heavy fall of snow could do, and also what one lovely community could do to pull together to counter that. She wondered if Bertha was Jack's wife; she'd never met her before.

35

Jack and Bertha had performed miracles. All the guests were now assembled in the Great Hall having a welcome cocktail of sloe gin and bubbly; a warming fizz. Last to come was Daniel, who was still making his way here. His best man had just arrived separately with his wheelchair. It was now already 1 p.m., but the vicar was happy to wait a few more minutes to start the service.

There'd been a convoy of 4x4s from the petrol station just off the A1, to ferry them through. Word had soon spread that there was a wedding party in need of help, and the locals soon stepped up to the mark. Turned out that the chap who owned the garage was a biker himself and had met Dan at a rally at Duncombe Park in Yorkshire two years before. He'd heard of his road accident, and realising who they were helping, quickly spread the word.

Wendy dashed in to the hall discreetly with Lauren,

who helped her set out the table decorations and light all the storm candles at their centrepiece. They looked beautiful, giving a soft glow around the room. As they realized Wendy was going to be late in, Irene and Lauren had earlier done a fabulous job of twining the holly, ivy, pine and mistletoe on the window ledges and along the balustrades outside. Lauren was a keen art student as well as waitressing part-time at the teashop, doing her A levels at the nearby Sixth Form College, and had enjoyed the chance to get creative. Wendy had tidied the displays up just a touch, and applied some twists of floristry wire to keep them steady, threading through some ivory roses and the soft blue Scottish thistles for some extra colour, and to echo the bouquets, but she was very impressed.

'Might have to take you on when I need an extra pair of hands in the shop, Lauren. If you're ever looking for any weekend work, give me a shout. You've done a brilliant job. Thank you. We've just made it in time, by the looks of it.'

There seemed to be a small ripple of excitement through a group of male guests just then, some whispering and a nod or two, a few of them making their way outside. Wendy spotted Joe heading out too, and decided to go take a look. They made their way out across the courtyard, through the stone arch and heavy wooden door, to the main entrance steps.

Coming down the driveway was a huge green tractor, that had a thick white ribbon tied on the front in a V shape up to each the side window. It gave a boom of a toot, and the driver and his passenger started waving. Wendy recognized one of the local farmers, Jack Butler. Perched on a ledge seat next to him was what must have been the groom, smart in a dark grey suit and pale blue satin tie. He was beaming from ear to ear. His best man, Rob, had lined up his wheelchair at the base of the steps ready, where Joe and Derek had placed a portable ramp up to the main doors.

The small group gathered on the steps, which was made up of the ushers, best man and a couple of close friends, cheered as Jack parked up, Bertha having her finest moment yet. The farmer walked around to help Daniel down with a 'Sorry, mate' as he more or less hoisted him in a fireman's lift into his wheelchair.

Dan was still smiling however, as he sat down. Jack passed his crutches from the cab across to Rob. Jack and Daniel then gave each other a firm handshake.

'Cheers, mate.' Dan had the glisten of a tear in his eye. 'We couldn't have done this without you.'

'And I couldn't have done this without *her*.' Again, he patted the flank of his beloved tractor.

'I'd wanted to arrive in style,' grinned Dan. 'I have to admit I was thinking more in terms of a Harley Davidson back in the summer, but hey, things change and that arrival certainly made an impact . . . Will you come back this evening for the reception, yeah?' he asked Jack.

'There's loads of food and drink organized, so I hear. I'd really like that. Bring your wife, your family. Honestly, you deserve a pint or two at least for all this.'

'Well, I might just take you up on that.'

'Mention it to the others too, all the 4x4 drivers, and the minibus man who got all the guests here. They'll all be welcome for a thank you drink and a bit of supper.'

'Right-o. Will do.'

As the tractor revved up again to head off, another cheer went up.

Then Dan put a finger across his lips. 'Right lads, no one mentions I'm here yet, okay.' He scanned the small audience, who nodded. He caught Wendy's eye too.

Joe was next to him, offering to help push the chair up the ramp. 'Come on then, we have a wedding to get to,' Joe grinned.

Malcolm popped in to see Ellie, who was on her final preparations for the prawn and smoked salmon starter, in the teashop kitchens.

'Dan's here. He's made it.'

'Oh, thank goodness. I've been feeling quite tense all morning. Oh, Lucy will be so happy.'

'But you can't say a word . . .'

'Why on earth not? She's been in a right fret, worrying about his journey in the snow and ice. Especially with what's happened.'

'Joe said I have to tell you to keep schtum, Daniel is insisting, and you just need to get her to the chapel for a quarter past one. Well,' he glanced at this watch, 'that's fifteen minutes now. I'm popping back up to manoeuvre the guests in to the chapel ready.'

'Okay, I suppose. But I still think it's mean, if she doesn't know if her groom's there. She's all made-up and ready to go, and she's already had such a nervous morning. And, been kept waiting now too. The least I could do is calm her nerves.'

'It's really important to Dan, that's all I know.'

'Okay, but you men are such meanies.'

'Now don't brand me with that, young lady. I couldn't be mean if I tried. Well, only if I tried *very* hard.'

'No. Sorry, Malc. I just want it all to go perfect for them.'

'I know, pet. But, don't shoot the messenger.' He winked and dashed out.

'Right ladies, how's it going?'

The scent of perfume hit her, as Ellie entered the room. There was chatter and giggling. Brushes, make-up bags, hair tongs and straighteners, lipsticks and eyeshadows were strewn around the surfaces, as well as half-empty champagne flutes lined up on the dressing table. Four of the towelling robes were discarded and replaced by stunning floor-length lavender-shade bridesmaids' dresses, with cosy ivory shrugs to keep their shoulders warm.

Their hair was up, piled into soft topknots, with wispy waves framing their faces. Apparently the original hair-dresser had been unable to rebook, so they decided to do it themselves and help each other out. They'd done an amazing job. The girls really did looked stunning.

'Wow, you lot look fabulous! I love the colour of those dresses.'

Lucy was having her rollers taken out by one of her bridesmaids, who was softening the bouncy dark waves. The bride-to-be turned to Ellie with a nervous smile, her make-up was done, and she looked so pretty. All she had to do next was to step into the dress, which was out of its cover and looking exquisite, all ivory lace and subtle beading, hanging from the wardrobe door.

'Is he here yet?'

Ellie's heart flipped. She hated having to lie; seeing Lucy's face drop. 'Well, I've heard he's on his way, nearly here, actually.' She tried to make it sound positive. 'So I've been asked to get all the bridesmaids into place by the chapel, and to bring your father across now, Lucy. The vicar is here ready, so we're nearly there.'

Lucy's hair was teased out to a stylish finish, and then the bridesmaids started gathering together near the door.

'By the way, the bouquets are all ready to collect as you go in to the castle from the courtyard. The florist's done a marvellous job, but she was slightly delayed. We thought having them there would save carrying them across the snowy courtyard. Malcolm and Derek have tried to dig some pathways out, so it's not too bad. *But,* there is one other issue . . .' She looked down at their feet. Yes, she'd thought so. 'Satin shoes . . . not ideal in the snow, and they'd get ruined, so in the corridor I have lined up a selection of wellington boots.'

'You're kidding.' 'No way.'

'Well, it's either that, or spoiled, wet shoes all day. I know which I'd rather. You can swap them as soon as you get in from the stone steps outside, at the passageway to the chapel and Great Hall.'

'Hmn.' 'Well yeah, that makes sense.'

'Chief Bridesmaid says yes,' Catlin announced, and they all laughed.

'Do I have to wear them, too?' Lucy looked aghast.

'Well, if you don't want to trash your wedding shoes, yes hun,' Ellie conceded.

'Bloody hell, some glamorous bride I'm going to be. Thank heavens, we haven't got *Hello* Magazine here. Not that there was ever a chance in hell of that, but you know. Hey, has the photographer made it yet?'

'Yep. He's here, and ready to go.'

'Well, that image'll be in the album for sure, then. Bride wears Stella McCartney and green wellies.'

'Might set a new trend. Could get you into *Country Life*!' Caitlin grinned.

'Hah, and who the hell was stupid enough to wish for

snow for her big day?' She already knew the answer, of course.

'Yep, you.'

'Right, I'll see these lovely ladies across to the chapel . . . be back very soon.' Ellie smiled.

'Let me know if he's there yet then, yeah.' Lucy looked a bit emotional.

'Of course.' Ellie hoped to God, Dan *really* was there, and Joe hadn't been asking Malcolm to spin some yarn to appease her. What if he was stranded somewhere, or had had some other accident on the way? She put that thought to the back of her mind. 'I won't be long.'

'Yes, okay. See you all soon, guys.' Lucy smiled. 'I think it's time to step into the dress then, before my dad gets here.' She took a deep breath.

'Need a hand?' Ellie offered.

'No, I'll be fine. You lot go, get on.' Her eyes looked a little misty, bless.

'See you in a minute, petal. We'll all be waiting ready for you,' Caitlin added. 'And no getting emotional and crying now, or you'll ruin your make-up.'

They all gave Lucy a hug in turn. Ellie didn't know about them, but she felt she could burst into tears any second. She held it in.

There was much giggling in the corridor, as the brides-maids mixed and matched wellies to get the best fit. One was in a navy pair, one in spotty, and two in traditional green Hunters. Ellie had had a root about in her wardrobe, borrowed Doris's that she'd come in with, and found a couple of pairs in Deana's office.

Ellie took the four pairs of satin shoes and popped them in to a cardboard box to carry across for them. As they got to the bottom of the stairwell, ready to step outside, they could see that the snow was about a foot deep, aside from the paths that Malcolm and Derek had dug out earlier.

'Right girls, I suggest a hitch up of skirts,' Ellie warned.

'Tuck them in your knickers, if need be,' Caitlin announced.

So up went the skirts revealing the wellie boots in all their glory. And click, at the top of the stone steps, to greet them with a camera flash, was the official photographer. Hilarious . . . But those quirky photographs were often the best.

There was no sign of Daniel when Ellie delivered the bridesmaids plus shoes to the entrance of the chapel within the castle. She mouthed to Malcolm, 'Is he here, yet?' All he did was shrug, with an odd smile. Ellie met with Lucy's father, who also looked slightly disconcerted. As they walked back over to Lucy's room, her curiosity got the better of her, she had to mention the apparent lack of groom.

'Have you seen Daniel, yet, Mr Coates? I've heard he's here.'

'No, he's not where I'd expect him to be by now which is down by the altar with his best man. But, Joe has assured us all is well. I'm just to take Lucy across, and walk her down the aisle. That's all I know.'

'Okay. Well let's just stick with the plan. And maybe it'll be best not to alarm Lucy with any detail.'

Ellie knocked, and entered. Lucy was stood in the middle of the room ready in her gown. Wow. Lucy looked just beautiful, radiant. Ellie was filling up, yet again. Ah, it was going to be one of those days when she needed a tissue, she could tell.

'You look amazing, Lucy. Wow. Dan is going to be so happy.'

'Here's there then?' She smiled.

'Ah yes, so I've heard.' Not exactly a lie. How could she possibly say anything else?

'Ready, love?' Mr Coates crooked his arm, ready for his daughter to take.

'I've been ready for a long time, Dad.'

'I know, pet. I know. It's been a tough few months.'

Bloody hell, Ellie wished she'd thought to put on the waterproof mascara this morning. 'Right folks, I'll see you across to the chapel . . . Oh, your shoes, Lucy.'

'Oh, yes. Can't wait for this bit.' She handed across her beautiful ivory-satin slippers.

'There's a pair of wellies out in the corridor for you.'

They headed out through the door, where Lucy paused

to slip on the green wellington boots, with a wry smile. 'Don't exactly feel like Cinderella in these. But mind, they're a good fit.'

'I'll have to help with your skirt and the train too, as we cross the courtyard. I'll keep it up off the snow.'

'Right-o, well here goes.'

They started the descent down the stairwell.

Ellie hoped to God, Daniel was there and waiting when she got them to the chapel.

Lucy swapped her wellies for the satin shoes at the top of the steps, noting how pretty the balustrades looked with their floral decorations. She collected her wedding bouquet from a proud Wendy, exclaiming how stunning they were. The photographer was snapping away merrily.

Lucy and her father walked along the short corridor to the chapel, where her bridesmaids were waiting expectantly. Caitlin exclaiming, 'Oh Luce, you look absolutely beautiful.' She gave Ellie a little dart of her eyes, but Ellie wasn't quite sure what to make of the gesture.

The bride squeezed her father's hand, 'Here goes.' And, they walked towards the open chapel door.

Derek was sat ready at the organ and began bashing out 'Here Comes the Bride' in a slightly wonky manner. The guests all turned, there were oohs and aahs, yet Ellie picked up on a slight unsettled murmur amongst them.

Smiles were soon plastered on as Lucy slipped her arm through her father's and made her first few steps down the aisle. The bridesmaids filed in behind, being careful not to step on the beautiful ivory lace train. It all seemed to be going to plan, until Lucy paused, turning to look at Ellie over her shoulder, with a frown, and mouthed, 'Where's Dan?'

The vicar was beaming beatifically from the altar. Malcolm was stood, where in theory Dan should have been, which was a worry, though his orchestrated hand gestures were seeming to indicate for the congregation to stay calm and that all was well. 'It's all okay,' he mouthed back to Ellie.

Lucy was whispering to her dad, whose shoulders just shrugged.

The wedding music kept playing, so Lucy kept walking forwards, until rather bemused, she reached the end of the aisle.

As Ellie watched the scene unfold, her heart was racing. It was all going horribly wrong. What on earth was Joe . . . yes, where exactly was Joe? And Dan, and his best man, Rob, bloody well playing at. Whatever it was they'd spoilt the occasion now, with the bride at the altar groomless and looking panicked.

Ellie felt a tap on her shoulder. Turned to see Joe, who beamed at her, and gave her a wink. 'Ah-hem, excuse us.'

And there beside him was Rob, pushing Daniel in his wheelchair to the central aisle.

Oh, thank heavens. Just a few minutes late then. Perhaps it was the snow and the difficult roads that had held him up, after all. Shame no one had stopped poor old Lucy heading off down the aisle first.

Joe gave a nod to Malcolm, who in turn gave a nod to Derek. The keyboard struck up again with a lovely Chopin piece that Ellie recognized from her own wedding day.

Rob positioned the wheelchair at the far end of the aisle, put the brake on, passed Daniel his crutches and stood back. Daniel began positioning them under his armpits and managed to stand up. He took a long, steadying breath, then began to walk slowly, but steadily, down the aisle, supported by the crutches. There were smiles all round, none bigger than Lucy's from the front. Halfway down the pews, Daniel paused. It was no doubt getting difficult for him, painful for sure. It felt like the room was holding its breath.

He leant one of the crutches against the pew side, and steadied himself by holding on to the wooden pew top. He removed the other crutch from under his arm. Looking straight at Lucy, he took one step out into the centre of the aisle. Let go of the pew, and took another step. Slowly, determinedly, he took another step forward. His legs shaking with effort beneath the smart grey trousers of his wedding suit. Ellie felt her heart in her mouth, willing him on.

Lucy's father took a step back, leaving Lucy with arms outstretched towards her fiancé. Twelve slow unsteady steps Daniel made to his bride, but he did it. As their fingertips reached there was a roar of cheering, and clapping from the congregation. And a loud 'Yes!' from his best man. Dan turned to see their reaction, gave a broad smile and turned back to his bride, who was now crying.

Malcolm had a chair placed ready for Dan, which he now took, the effort taking its toll. Ellie realized she was crying too, along with most of the congregation by the looks of it. Joe placed his hand on her shoulder.

And so, the groom had walked down the aisle to his bride.

The service was truly lovely, the determination of its leading man setting the tone. The vicar spoke about love, of striving in the face of adversity, of the importance of caring for each other both in sickness and in health. The words of the service so much more powerful and meaningful after what they had just witnessed. The sense of love and support within that small chapel room was immense.

Daniel stood up once more when it was time to place the ring on Lucy's hand, and managed to stay upstanding to kiss the bride. And again to more whoops and cheers from the congregation, who were all definitely in party mood now, ready to celebrate this wonderful occasion.

36

After congratulating the bride and groom, and handing over to Deana's capable hands for a while (as well as the team of Joe, Malcolm, and Derek), Ellie dashed back to the kitchens to see how Irene and Doris were getting on with the last-minute preparations for the meal.

All was going well, there was a production line of salmon and prawn parcels all plated up. Irene was dotting sprigs of dill on the side of each. Lauren, who as well as turning into a florist's assistant, was also helping to wait-ress today, was armed with a basket of fresh-baked honey and sunflower seed bread rolls ready to take up for the side plates.

'Well, have they tied the knot?' Doris piped up.

'Yes, it was really lovely. So poignant. I bet I've got panda eyes. Daniel managed to walk down the aisle to his Lucy. Not a dry eye in the chapel.'

'Aw, how wonderful. So, he can walk again. Marvellous.'

'Just a short way . . . You should have seen the determination in his face, very much mind over matter at some points.'

'Bless.'

Lauren said, 'That's *sooo* romantic, and fab for him.'

'Looks like you've been working hard, and it's all going well down here, ladies. Thank you so much.'

'The two lads from the village who are helping to wait on are ready to go out too. They're just in the teashop. Too many cooks in the kitchen as it was. So we're ready to serve, when you are,' Doris announced.

'Okay. Well, I'll give all the guests five more minutes to chat and settle themselves again after the excitement of the ceremony. Then, I'll get Malcolm to announce the meal, and get them all seated in the Great Hall. That'll be perfect.' She gave a thumbs up to her catering team, and headed back up.

As she walked back in to the Great Hall, it struck her how different and beautiful it looked, like some kind of back-in-time castle winter wonderland, with a touch of C. S. Lewis's Narnia. Wendy and Lauren had done a brilliant job of the floral arrangements, with swathes of ivy, holly, ivory roses and mistletoe in the window ledges, table decorations that echoed the bridal bouquets, with more roses, greenery and the blue of the Scottish thistle. There were tall storm candles within each centrepiece that gave a warm, glow and a gorgeous vanilla scent that mingled with the perfumed scent of the roses.

Doris and Irene had taken great care with setting the tables out, and with Lucy's thoughtful wedding favours (mini kilner jars filled with hot chocolate mix and marshmallows for the ladies, decorated with snowflake patterned ribbons, and a matchbox toy Harley Davidson motorbike and a warming miniature of whiskey for the men) and her hand-painted name places on ivory and silver-edged card, it all looked beautiful. Lucy had the guest table plans strung up with grey wooden pegs within a huge frame, so they looked like bunting. Malcolm, Derek and Colin had decorated the impressive Christmas tree with white fairy lights, silver tinsel, and silver and pearlized white baubles. On closer inspection, Ellie could see that Lauren had carried on the ivy and mistletoe floral touches throughout the tree too.

'Ellie, the hall looks so amazing.' Lucy dashed over to her. 'It's like it's transformed into a winter palace. Thank you so much.'

'Well, there's a whole team behind it, not just me, but I will pass on your thanks.'

'Aw, I've been so excited about my big day I've forgotten all the hard work that everybody has to put in to make it work, sorry.'

'Don't be so daft. That's what we're here for. And it's been a pleasure to make your day special for you and

Dan, honestly. Now don't worry about us, you just get on with having the most fabulous time.'

'Will do, hun. Thank you.' She gave Ellie a big hug, and skipped off back to her groom and the family and friends who were about to come through to the hall. Something caught her eye as she neared the big oak doors. She stopped in her tracks, and headed over to the corner table. Ellie realized what she had just seen.

Lucy turned with her mouth open, followed by a big smile. 'Oh my. Wow, Ellie, I've just spotted the cake. Did you make it yourself? Look at all those flowers decorating it, they look so real, are they actually icing? Each rose petal is so detailed. And the soft blue of the thistles . . . just like the ones in the bouquets. And the icing all over seems to have a touch of sparkle. I love it, love it, love it.' She was literally bouncing.

'Glad you like it! That's fab.'

'It must have taken you absolutely ages.'

'Just a bit, yeah. I tweaked the original design we had in mind from the summer to match the winter-flower colours of your bouquets, and I couldn't resist putting you two in icing figures on the top.'

'Hah, yes. Look at that. I get it, it's us, the hair colours and everything. Just brill.'

Ellie had put the pair of them in cartoon-style icing figures, sitting down on a bench seat under an arch of more tiny flowers and icing greenery.

'Oh, I can't wait to show Dan. It just seems too good to cut though.'

'Ah, you'll have to, it's tradition. And it's got to be tasted. It's not just for show, you know.'

'I bet it'll be gorgeous. Right, are you ready for everyone to come through yet?'

'Yes, I think Malcolm will be gathering the clans as we speak.'

'Perfect. My tummy's rumbling. I'm getting hungry now all the nerves have gone. It's really happened, Ellie. I'm married. Yay!'

'I'm so, so happy for you both. I'll have to get going too, and go and help my staff out. Catch you later, Lucy.'

'Yep, thank you, Ellie. Just loving it all so far . . . And you and Joe must come and have a glass of champagne with us later, when you get a chance. Have a whole bloody bottle in fact. You deserve it. Promise you will.'

'Yes, I promise. I'll look forward to it.'

The meal went well. Service was smooth, the guests happy, with murmurings about how delicious the salmon and then the beef dishes were, which made Ellie glow with pride. She'd come a long way from the young girl who had a dream of running her own teashop, not only did she now have a successful teashop and a lovely hard-working team of staff, she'd become a wedding coordinator and event caterer. Sometimes taking your chance on your dream, and working hard towards that really paid off, and took you places you could hardly have imagined. And, the best part was, the people she had met along the way, worked with and helped, and one in particular whom she had fallen in love with. She caught Joe's eye across the room, and gave him a smile that, hopefully, said it all.

With the hot food now served, Ellie and her waitresses set about displaying the array of desserts they had created. With sweet things being her forte, she'd had great fun baking over the past few of days. They were set out buffet-style, so the guests were able to help themselves, a little of everything was quite possibly the way to go! After all, who'd want to miss out on passion fruit cheesecake, profiteroles stacked like a French wedding cake, warm salted-caramel chocolate brownies, chocolate fudge cake, or the bride's favourite chewy-in-the-middle meringues with clotted cream and fresh raspberries?

Ellie had also made mini shortbreads and chocolate truffles to go with the coffee and tea that was to be served later. She was keeping back her 'cake' of local cheeses, as a surprise for the bride and groom during the evening event – when the band and dancing would liven things up again.

37

Dan got slowly up to his feet, steadying himself against the table. His efforts in the chapel earlier had evidently having taken their toll.

They had already had the father-of-the-bride and best man speeches; warm and humorous, with several anecdotes, words of inspiration, support and love. But Dan had words of his own to share. He rapped a spoon against the table top, and the Great Hall hushed.

'This won't take long, as I have precisely two minutes before my legs buckle.'

A warm chuckle of support filtered around the room.

'I just wanted to thank you all for coming today, and to Joe and Ellie for making this such a special event with everything you've done here at the castle. Amazing.'

A round of applause ensued, bringing a tear to Ellie's eye. Joe beamed across at her.

'And, more than that, for all *your* support, that's every-body in this room honestly, my family, my friends, every step of the way since my accident. We appreciate it so much.' He looked across at Lucy, with such feeling, 'And for Lucy, my gorgeous wife. Yes, my wife now . . . at last, and I couldn't be happier. Through thick and thin, sick-ness and in health, and already you have proven that so much. Thank you for waiting, thank you for keeping me going when things got tough. Thank you for loving me, and inspiring me to fight for every single step I made today. The future's looking good, honey. And when I'm fit and well, I can't wait to get back on my Harley and have you pillion.' There were some raucous jeers from the ushers at that. 'I can't take you lot anywhere, can I? Pipe down lads.' But he was laughing. 'Right, that's my lot. My legs are swaying. Thank you and cheers everyone!'

'A toast to the bride and groom. To Lucy and Daniel.' His best man, Rob, stood and raised his glass.

'The bride and groom!'

Lucy then stood up, looking at Daniel.

'I know it's not traditional for the bride to make a speech. And you probably all want to get to the bar and get dancing. But . . . just a few words.' She took a slow breath. 'It's been a difficult few months. But more than ever, I love you, Dan, and I'm so looking forward to our future together. Your courage and determination are such an inspiration to everyone, and I'm so proud to be Mrs Edwards.'

Ellie was full of admiration for them both. Their relationship was built on solid ground; love in the face of adversity. A round of applause broke out around the room.

'Right, time to drink champagne and dance on the tables, folks!' Lucy grinned.

The guests had mostly emptied from the hall, many heading for the bar that had been set up in the drawing room next door. Some had gone for some fresh air or a sneaky cigarette outside, others back to their rooms for a lie down and a bit of a break, some were chatting in the corridors, and some were outside taking photos of the wonderful snowy castle and grounds . . . A snowball fight had broken out amongst the ushers, a couple of the bridesmaids, and the groom's dad and uncle. Suits and gowns became plastered with white pads of snow, hairdos became frizzled, but there was laughter all round. On hearing a boomph of a snowball against the drawing room window, Dan even got himself out there, launching an attack on Rob and his ushers from the relative safety of his wheelchair tucked behind a low wall – though he then became a sitting duck once they realized where the new icy ammunition was firing from. The bridesmaids had forgotten about saving their dresses, and having discarded their shoes at the exit, were running about barefoot, the mad things.

Lucy caught up with Dan, and not fancying a snow-ball-wrecked hairdo quite yet, quickly shifted him back out of the firing line and to safety inside. He was grinning from ear to ear. 'Got some great shots in there, low level missiles from behind the wall. No one figured where I was for a while.'

'Look at you, Dan. You're covered. Think I'll need to towel dry you.'

'Ah, it's fine, the suit will dry clean. Come here you.' And with that, he pulled her into his arms and onto his still snowy lap.

'Ooh, your hands are freezing.'

'All the better to tickle you with, Mrs Edwards.' And he found the bare, warm skin of her back above her dress, and beneath her furry cape.

'You absolute devil.'

But her crossness soon melted, like the snow in his lap, and they kissed tenderly, passionately. They stayed there a while like that, in the outer doorway of the Great Hall looking out to the gardens, she sat on his lap with his arms wrapped around her, both in the wheelchair, watching the others lark about in the snow.

'It's been a fabulous day,' he said.

'The best.'

* * *

'Testing. Testing. And a one, two, three, four.'

As the band were doing their last checks, Ellie set up her final catering of the day. A buffet of sandwiches, rolls, an urn of winter vegetable soup, and the cheese 'cake' extravaganza that even she had to admit looked fabulous. She'd stacked up a large Stilton cheese circle, with a strong cheddar, a Northumbrian nettle and herb, a soft wheel of goat's cheese. One on top of the other, in decreasing sizes upwards, with a whirl of ivy and fruits, grapes, apples, plums and a weave of ivory-coloured roses. It looked like some wonderful old masters painting of cheese and fruit, but it was real and ready to eat. A wicker basket of savoury biscuits, bread rolls, and a selection of local chutneys, stood beside it.

The desserts from the wedding dinner were still plentiful, so they were on display too. Some of the 4x4 drivers and their wives had turned up as invited by the very grateful Daniel for the evening event too, laden with extra goodies, pies and sandwiches. The Northumbrians were well-known for their hospitality, and were never likely to turn up empty-handed. There was plenty to keep everybody going should they get the munchies through the evening. Ellie put her final touches to the buffet, as Doris and Lauren brought up plates and cutlery wrapped in cream-coloured napkins.

'Right, time for that glass of champagne, Ellie . . . that's it. You've worked long and hard enough. Come on.' Lucy grabbed her hand and whisked her away, smiling at Doris and Lauren who were nodding in agreement.

'Go, have some fun,' Doris said. 'It's all just about ready here now, anyhow. We'll keep an eye on the buffet and top it up, if need be.'

Lucy poured Ellie out a flute of chilled bubbly. The first sip was delicious. The bubbles popping on Ellie's tongue, and that wonderful fragrant fizz as it went down.

'Cheers, gorgeous Ellie. Thank you so much for making our wedding day so wonderful. I'll never forget this day as long as I live.'

The band were starting up, and there were calls for Lucy to join Daniel who had wheeled himself in his chair to centre stage of the dance floor area. Ellie recognized the first bars leading in to Aerosmith's 'I Don't Want to Miss a Thing', Dan's favourite band.

'Looks like you're needed for the first dance.' Ellie smiled.

Lucy joined her husband on the dance floor. She held his hand and twirled around his wheelchair. Dan was looking tired, but oh-so-happy. The sparkle in his eyes glinting as he watched his wife, with the biggest smile on his face. Dancing was beyond him for now; the steps he'd taken today a challenge in themselves. He held out his arms and she took her place on his lap, looking cosy and joyous, just so full of love, the pair of them.

Ellie felt a warm hand in the small of her back, Joe nestling up beside her.

'Don't they look so happy,' Ellie said.

'Yeah, they do.'

'To think, it might have been so different.'

'I know . . . but hey, they've made it through. They've had their special day.'

Life would take you on its journey through love, hurt, joy, pain, and all the shades of emotion in between. But you had to hold on to the happy, find a way through, and reach for the stars.

Lucy and Dan were beckoning for the guests to come and join them.

Joe led Ellie to the dance floor, holding her close. They chose a spot near the Christmas tree with its glow of fairy lights, and tinsel. The gentle sway of movement between them was soothing. She cherished the feel of him in her arms, the warmth of his hand against her back, his other hand on her shoulder. They shared a tender smile and she couldn't resist planting a short, sweet kiss on his lips.

'I love you, Joe.' The words spilled out before she'd even had time to think about it, or consider that they were in a public place.

'Love you, too.'

She snuggled a little closer. They weren't usually into public displays of affection, but tonight it just seemed right, like it had to be said. All too often those words, what they meant, was assumed but left unsaid – they were both so busy, working, and just trying their best to keep up with everyday life, most of the time.

But yes, why shouldn't you tell someone you loved them when they were the best thing that had ever happened in your life? Good times, bad times, boring times (actually Joe had never got boring, yet!). Why was it that sometimes life just seemed to take over, and you didn't tell that person, even though you felt it in your bones every day?

What if there was a lorry, or a bus, or a patch of ice, and boomph it all got taken away? Ellie felt a little queasy just thinking about it. Thank God, Dan had made it through for Lucy. She glanced across at the bride and groom, still centre stage, Lucy now sat on Dan's lap, sharing his wheelchair. They were chatting and laughing, looking so relaxed and happy. What if their dream had had to break? It didn't bear thinking about. Ellie felt a tear form in her eye.

'You okay, Els?' Joe's voice was tender, loving.

'Yeah, just feeling a bit emotional, and probably a bit tired. I was just thinking about Lucy and Dan for a moment there, how close they came so close to losing it all . . . It's okay, I'm fine, really.'

Joe held her to him as they took up the slightly faster rhythm of the next song.

Peeking over Joe's shoulder a few seconds later, Ellie caught sight of another couple dancing. Lord Henry had his arm politely placed around Sue's waist, Joe's mum. She was smiling and talking to him as they twirled around the floor. He was actually a surprisingly good dancer. As they waltzed their way around the outer area of the slower dancers, he looked like he'd bounced right out of a black-and-white film, tall and smart in his black dinner jacket and trousers, crisp white shirt and bow tie. And he looked happy, and more relaxed than Ellie had ever seen him.

She nodded at Joe, and then across at the pair of them, pointing with her gaze.

Joe raised his eyebrows, and smiled in surprise.

Then, Joe and Ellie fell back to the steady rhythm of their dance, concentrating on each other once more. The room seemed to fade around them. Her head resting against the dip of his shoulder. He held her so very close, and she heard the soft murmur of his words. 'I love you so much, Ellie.'

They would have their own curve balls to face, they had already, but they would hold on to their dreams of a family. Happy times and sad times lay ahead, but they knew they would face them together.

Christmas Eve, one year later

'I can't believe we're so late putting the tree up this year.'
  'Well, we have had a lot on our plate.'
  'Yes.'
  They both looked across at the Moses basket that stood
on the wooden table, where little Jack Henry lay, thankfully
now settled and asleep. He was one month old, had beautiful dusky-blue eyes, soft fuzzy dark hair, and was adorable.
  Henry would be over soon for some supper, and no doubt
a Grandpa cuddle. Her parents, Jay and his now fiancée
Carmel, as well as Joe's mam Sue were driving up to join
them tomorrow, Christmas morning. Ellie had insisted she
still wanted to do Christmas lunch for everyone this year.
After all, it was baby Jack's first Christmas, and she couldn't
imagine them not being all together at the castle. She had

offers of help with peeling the veggies, her mum was bringing a roasted ham and a trifle up, and Sue had made the stuffing. Just yesterday, Irene had brought round a huge Christmas pudding and some homemade rum sauce for them all too.

Ellie took the last decoration out of the box; the wooden teddy bear from the Christmas market in Berwick-upon-Tweed. She placed it carefully on a branch of scented pine. 'There.'

'Perfect' said Joe as he stood beside her, placing his hand gently on her shoulder.

'Just perfect.'

Acknowledgements

Thank you to my lovely family: Richard, Amie, Harry. Writing a book from scratch in four months has been challenging to say the least, so thanks for putting up with the fallout.

Once again thank you to teashop queen and friend, Julie Lee, for baking the most gorgeous cakes, creating the Choffee Cake, and inspiring me to write about a teashop in a castle in the first place. And to all my fab friends for keeping me going with chats, walks in the rain, prosecco and the newly discovered Northumbrian Mojitos.

Thanks to all the team at HarperImpulse, HarperCollins, and especially to my lovely editors Charlotte Brabbin and Charlotte Ledger who have steered this book into shape. To Hannah Ferguson, my agent, thanks for all your advice so far, and I'm looking forward to my writing journey with you.

Caroline Roberts

To the Romantic Novelists' Association with their fabulous New Writers' Scheme, and the lovely friends I have made within that organisation, thanks for being my support network all the way.

My sister, Debbie, keep going, you are *so* close to getting published with your young adult novels. All the hard work will pay off soon, I'm sure, and then we'll be celebrating big time!

To my readers, without you, my books wouldn't have a home to go to. I've loved hearing from you, and thanks so much for all the comments and feedback I've had on *The Cosy Teashop in the Castle* so far. I hope you enjoy this sequel. *Happy reading!*